SCONES and SLAYERS

BLUE MOON BAY WITCHES
2

SIERRA CROSS

Copyright © 2023 by Sierra Cross and Enigmatic Books
All rights reserved.
Cover Design by Arcane Covers
Interior Formatting by Qamber Designs

To all my mentors, with gratitude

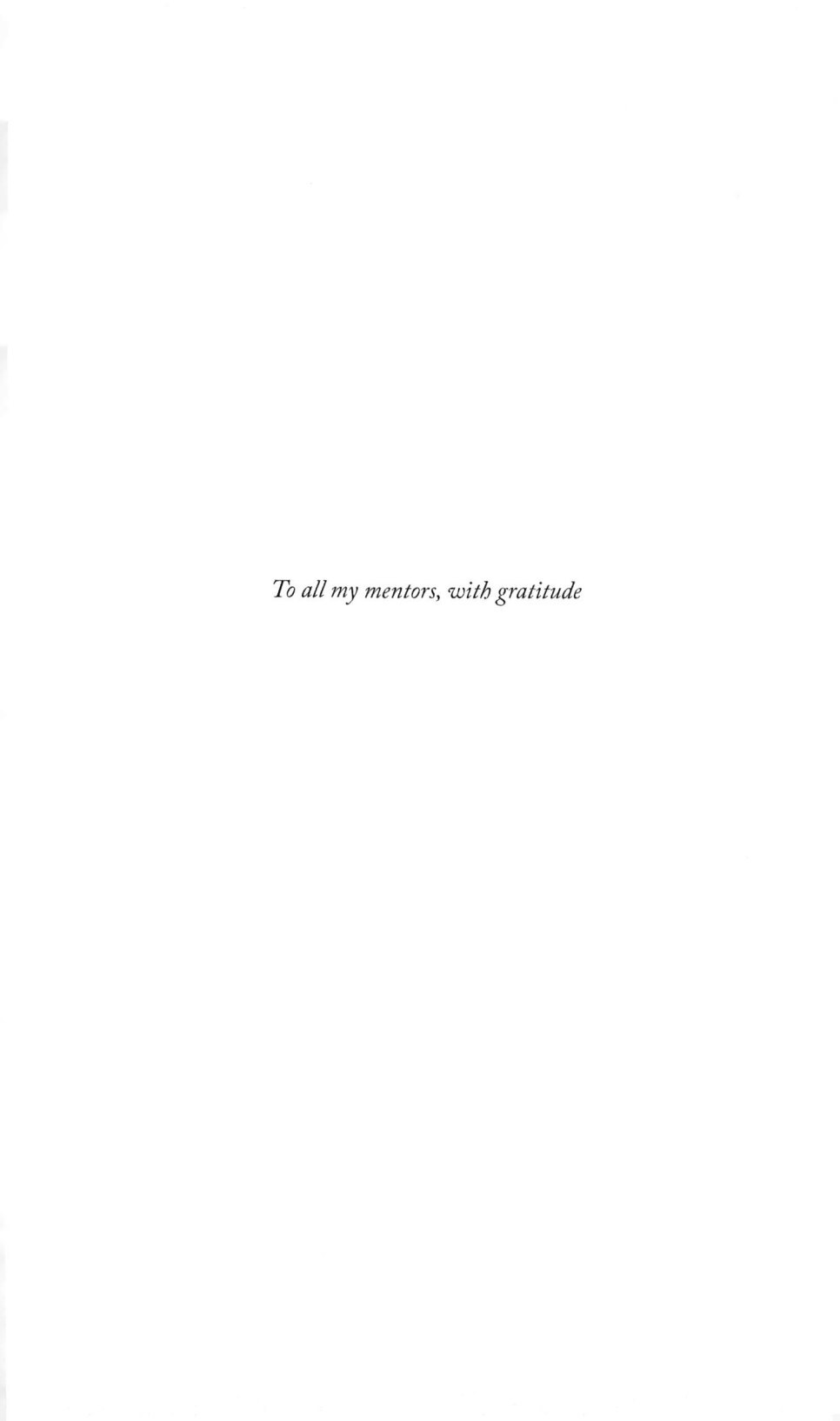

SCONES and SLAYERS

CHAPTER ONE

TO THE HANDFUL of slow-season tourists lingering over their lingonberry crêpes, the air inside Purrfect Pancakes smelled as sweet as sugar.

Only we witches could sense the powerful Green Magic buzzing through the diner, as it always did at noon on the month's first Tuesday when we collectively took over the back room.

Through the pink-gingham dressed windows, December sleet pelted the beach boardwalk outside. Yet to us in here, talking shop and sharing spells, the world smelled like spring.

Fresh. New. Alive.

Green.

A baker's dozen of us crowding the giant farmhouse table generated boisterous conversations, flowing as fast as the coffee our waitress was attentively refilling. Ethereal, glowing grass and dandelions shimmered into bloom on the checkered tile, but they were undetectable to Ordinals, just like the grassy scent of our magic.

And if anyone got too close, our clever sign reading "Postmodern Feminist Book Club, All Are Welcome" assured that they paid no attention to what we were saying.

I used to look forward to the Green Witch Association breakfast all month.

Now? I'd only showed up so I wouldn't let down my mentor, Granny Sage.

Between keeping the bakery's lights on and solving murders—my new side hustle, which paid nothing—my spell skills were in a rut.

I still couldn't even teleport, which was embarrassing since my car died last week.

Gran's magical health was slipping more each day, and I was far from ready to take over Sage's Bakery.

As if that background hum of stress wasn't enough, I had something scarier on my brain today: vampire hunters.

A secret cabal of vampire hunters had threatened to stake my friend Britt. If I was taking a morning off work, I should be investigating her sire's suspicious death. Not here, geeking out with other kitchen witches over pancakes.

It didn't help that our chapter president, Jacinta Hyacinth, was obsessively organized and perky, like a cruise director from hell. She'd just forced us all to watch a PowerPoint going over the rules of this year's Secret Santa, which were identical to last year's rules and the year before.

"Don't worry if you're lost, ladies." Jacinta flipped to a slide with a clip art drawing of a confused-looking witch, pointy hat askew. Did she think we were all morons?

Yes, yes she did.

"I'm throwing a lot at you all at once," she went on with an encouraging smile. "But FYI, I've cross-posted these guidelines to our GWA chapter's site, in the Secret Santa FAQ…"

I gritted my teeth, stirred more sugar into my coffee, and ignored Jacinta's alphabet soup droning till it was mercifully over.

On the opposite end of the table from me, Gran was holding court, as extroverts do. Keeping her seatmates spellbound, letting her pumpkin waffles grow cold, as she gave tips on casting the perfect memory spell. Her magical expertise was legend, and I was grateful she still had the ability to teach. Unfortunately, the spell talk was over my head.

Stupid magic skills rut.

Luckily, to my left, our two youngest member witches were commiserating about how early their a.m. college lectures were this semester. Now that was more my speed, and for once I even had a spell tip.

Gold star bait from Jacinta.

"Try lark's brew," I said to the yawning girls. "It's an elixir to help you wake up early and refreshed."

The young women glanced at me with bleary curiosity.

"Isn't that one of those new biologic spells?" said Yolanda, a petite teenager so cute she could turn her mom's knitting projects into a fashion statement. Her boxy cardigan and knitted pom-pom hat looked brand new.

"You got it, Yo." I couldn't help but feel a cozy warmth at being the helpful, young witch that newbies looked up to. "It's cutting-edge magic, really fascin—"

"Save it for some spell nerd who cares." Amethyst scowled and knitted her pierced eyebrows, which only made her look like a concerned owlet.

She was a first-gen witch, born to Ordinal parents, and was currently going a bit overboard with the edgy Goth girl phase most first gens went through. But it was hard to take her prickly words to heart when I just wanted to boop her nose.

"We don't have time to sit around mixing brew like a couple of crones," Amethyst said. "Our new film professor assigns way too much homework. We're both working four shifts a week here after school, and we also have…other stuff."

Other stuff? I was suspicious of her vague phrasing. What did I want to bet that "stuff" amounted to dating inappropriate boys?

Not like I had room to judge. My last boyfriend was an energy-leeching demon.

"Lark is a game changer," I assured Amethyst. "Trust me, when Gran had me taking all those college business courses a couple years ago…" I trailed off. Was that ten whole years ago? "Anyway, I used to make a nice big pot of this elixir at night before class."

Yolanda's big brown eyes widened. "*Every* night?"

"Sounds like a ton of pointless work." Amethyst twisted her black-cherry painted mouth, like she'd found a newt's tail in her latte. "Can't we just order it online from Wizard's Warehouse?"

"Sure, and I *could* serve pre-packaged cookies made by factory robots instead of hand-rolling my own magical dough." Augh, was this how journeyman witches thought these days?

"Yes, girl, Wizard's does carries lark's brew in tincture form nowadays!" a cheery female voice piped up behind me. "Or my night-owl butt I wouldn't have gotten through design school."

We all glanced up to see a witch who looked as if she'd leapt from the pages of a magazine. Sleek black hair bounced around her tan shoulders. Her yellow bodycon minidress was paired with ice-grey cowboy boots, a bold departure from the pointy-toed, black granny boots most of us wore. As she slid into the empty chair beside mine, I caught a whiff of some vanilla-bomb perfume.

"Killer boots." Amethyst's voice was insta girl-crush shy. "You must be Leia, the new Beige Witch in town."

I froze. Beige? That explained the heady scent. Beige Magic smelled like perfume. I should know: my elegant Beige Witch mother always smelled like Chanel No. 5, my older sister Bea like Glossier You, and my younger sister Cindra like Black Opium. But what was a Beige Witch doing at our meeting?

"Enchanté, y'all, I'm Leia Lin." The witch gave a graceful wave, and I nearly strained my eye-rolling muscles. "I'm visiting from Los Angeles, got a six-month contract with Kensington Industries. They're redecorating their properties away from that cringe eighties stuff and wanted a magical touch."

Amethyst squealed. "You're a designer? From L.A.?" Gone was the perma-scowl. She was gushing as if her favorite influencer had come to town. "It's only the most glam magical city in America."

"Are you friends with any mermaids, or gargoyles?" Yolanda added shyly. "I bet in California, magical society's more open-minded."

"Hopefully," Amethyst added with a sigh. "We have a vampire friend who wants to move there…well, really anywhere but here."

Leia chuckled. "Didn't want to say it, but yeah. Some interesting small-town vibes here."

Uh, what was *that* supposed to mean?

I poured more syrup onto my pancakes and tried to hide how irked I was at the implication that Blue Moon Bay was some benighted backwater. Sure, the vampire hunters didn't cast us in the best light. But they were an aberration.

"We have gloomy winters here, too," I piped up. "I've seen a lot of Cali folks give up and go home … and there's no shame in it."

"You're sweet to worry about me." Leia dazzled me with another smile. "But my hair and make-up glamours can stand up to your rainiest weather."

"Make-up glamours?" Amethyst stared at her. "I thought we weren't allowed?"

I sighed. "*She's* allowed."

Not gonna lie, it was the one thing I envied Beige Witches. Our oath of magic forbade spells to improve our looks.

"I can teach you the basics if you want, it's easy," Leia said, seemingly unaware she'd just offered a major Green Magic taboo. She scanned the menu nonchalantly as we goggled at her. "Hey, can one of you fab witches point me to Jacinta, pretty please? She said she'd introduce me around so I can maybe pick up some side gigs."

"Sure thing." Yolanda leaned back in her chair and performed a complex maneuver of poke-nudging Jacinta, who was two chairs away still listening to Gran. "Hey, Mama?"

Yes, the chapter president was Yolanda's mother.

You'd think she'd drive any kid to rebel, but Yolanda Hyacinth was as dutiful as they came. Each afternoon, she cheerfully worked side-by-side with her mom at the diner. She'd been pouring coffee and working the register since she was a little kid. Jacinta bragged to anyone who'd listen that Yolanda was majoring in marketing to become her official business partner.

The crones at the table glowered when Leia was introduced, and it made my petty heart smile. What can I say? Growing up, being constantly compared to my elegant mom and sisters—by the same elegant mom and sisters—had left scars.

I was glad when Leia delivered her spiel in a bubbly voice and was reaching for her purse to go. But then Jacinta fork-tapped a glass of ice water to get our attention again.

"Listen up, ladies." The table quieted, and Leia remained in her seat. Drat. "Another meeting has flown by in joyous *community building*. Now it's time for me to unveil one of my signature surprises that'll set you all abuzz for the next month."

Amethyst mimed sticking her finger down her throat. Yolanda didn't seem to notice; she was too busy gazing in admiration at her mom, the leader.

"I'm proud to announce a bold new initiative. The Blue Moon Bay Area Green Witch Association Mentorship Project. It's the brainchild of our leadership, me." Jacinta gave a modest shrug, then began passing out a stapled handout. "It's only a thirteen-hour-a-week volunteer commitment."

The older witches in the room were all impersonating deer caught in the headlights of a double decker bus. But all I could think was, *this was my big break*. Gran had been an amazing mentor, but now, sadly, with her magic waning, I needed another one. Painful as it was to think about.

Jacinta had done me a solid. For once.

Lorelei Verdell, the tiny, forty-something witch who owned the garden store, was the first to recover from the shock. "I don't see how any of us have time for such a major commitment."

"That's why I didn't want to trouble you busy bees," Jacinta cut in smoothly, "with a cumbersome email thread. Who did all the planning work for you? You're welcome."

Lorelei blinked. "You do understand what volunteer means, don't you? You can't volunteer others—"

"This. Is. My. *Gift* to our community." Jacinta ran her fingers through her cinnamon-red, bobbed hair, fervent emotion painting her cheeks. "Mentors listed on the left side of page one, mentees on the right."

"Here we go," Lorelei muttered.

The rest of the town's elder witches joined her in a sigh of resignation. This was simply how Jacinta led. She was born to organize other people in a fundamentally annoying way, like a border collie nudging wayward sheep with a well-timed butt nip. We were all used to it by now, and no one had ever attempted a coup.

Because when push came to shove, no one wanted that job.

With eager butterflies in my stomach, I scanned the page for my new mentor.

But weirdly, I couldn't see my own name listed anywhere.

"Hey, Jacinta?" I raised my hand. "You forgot to … oh, oops."

I frowned at the projector. *Hazel,* there I was. "You accidentally put me on the mentor side."

"Yes, honey, isn't it amazing how time flies?" Jacinta quipped, and a few other witches cackled.

I blushed. "I'm still in my twenties."

"Your late twenties. Verrrry late."

"Still counts," I growled. "And I'm—oh my gosh. Says here that *I'm* supposed be mentoring your daughter, Yolanda? Surely that's a mistake."

It would be bananas for me to mentor anyone.

"Oh, no, I don't make mistakes," Jacinta said. "Hazel, you came late to Green Magic. You faced serious obstacles." True: my mom, dad, and two sisters. "But in just a few years, you've forged a place for yourself among us. My Yolanda will benefit from your example of hard work and determination."

I shook my head, unable to believe what I was hearing. Her praise was undeserved. I wasn't some dynamo star witch. If I worked hard, it was only so I wouldn't let Gran down.

Gran.

She could be my out, proof I wasn't ready.

"You know, technically I still *have* a mentor myself." I gestured to Gran, whose clicking knitting needles now moved like tiny hummingbirds. "So, wouldn't it be weird if I—"

"Nah, you go for it, Hazel dear." Gran waved me off, as I should have predicted. "A-okay with me. You'll be doing good for this community that's done so much for you."

"Hear, hear. And also…" Jacinta gave me her brightest marketing smile, and I sensed she felt she was about to play a trump card. Little did she know she had no leverage over me. "Yolanda thinks you'll be a cool mentor."

Me, cool? A teenager spoke those words? I turned to Yolanda, who smiled sweetly and nodded. My heart felt all warm and fuzzy, then sank like a boulder as I realized what this meant. "I'll have to think about it."

"What's there to think about?" piped up my traitor of a Gran. Jacinta chirped, "I'll put her down as 'warming to the idea.'"

Helplessly I searched the table for allies, but all I saw were looks of mild amusement. So, that's how it was. Every witch for herself.

"It's just, I'm really busy these days," I stammered. "And, um, not sure I have quite the right skillset…?" My weaselly speech trailed off. Yolanda's posture suddenly slumping made me feel crushed by guilt.

But how was I supposed to be a mentor when I was a mess?

"Miss Hyacinth?" Amethyst didn't raise her hand. "Sorry, but I'm not feeling Lorelei as my mentor."

"Mind your elders, child," Gran admonished her. "Be grateful that a sterling witch of her caliber is willing—"

"Woot woot! Y'all heard the kid, I'm off the hoo-ook." The gardening witch banged the table and did an improvised victory dance, as several others squinted with bald-faced envy.

"I feel like I want a different kind of mentor," Amethyst went on, and turned to the beautiful newcomer. "I'm vibing with Leia here."

Gasps filled the room. Green Witches weren't easily shocked, but asking a Beige Witch to mentor you was over the line. Even for a clueless, first-gen witch like Amethyst.

An odd look contorted Leia's face. Was she stalling? Kicking herself for not having snuck out earlier? Beige Witches loved to heap contempt on us "kitchen witches," so I knew there was no chance she'd say yes. Even so, as the silence grew, I wanted to scream.

Then, Leia flashed her pearly, probably glamoured teeth. "Girl,

I'm floored! What an honor. Of course, since your magic is Green, I can't be your mentor."

Called it. *Sorry, kid, but it's for the best.*

"…At least not in a traditional sense. However, I'd be happy to take you thrifting. Mix up kale smoothies with you. Teach you the basics of Beige." She winked. "See what I did there? Yeah, I know y'all call us basic."

The elders goggled as she and Amethyst fist bumped across the table, and I felt a grudging respect for how gracefully the Beige Witch handled that curveball. Sure, she'd be a toxic influence and stuff her charge full of nonsense and kale, instead of knowledge. Still, she'd come here to network, been adopted by a sullen teenager, and rolled with it.

Meanwhile I ended up making a huge fool of myself, wriggling like a worm on a hook, and disappointing a sweet kid like Yolanda.

In Blue Moon Bay, your fortune could turn on a pancake.

CHAPTER TWO

"WHO DOES THAT Jacinta think she is, the queen of town?" I fumed to Gran as we strolled down Ocean Street past the icy pier, where an adorable grey-haired couple posed for selfies, each nearly swallowed by their respective puffer coats. "Assigning volunteer work? It's like having an extra boss."

"That witch has always been a striver and a try hard." Gran dismissed our leader with two of her choice insults. "But would it kill you to mentor the kid?"

I gaped at her. "Really?"

So, this was why Gran offered to walk me in to work, instead of *poofing* home with a snap of her fingers? She wanted to put the pressure on about Yolanda? Too bad, I was already under pressures of a different kind.

"I start baking five a.m. every single day," I reminded her. "With you semi-retired, I've got to hustle to ramp up. Next time some corporate café muscles in, we could lose the bakery. It's all up to me now, and I'm not ready."

The look of sadness in Gran's hooded eyes gave me a twinge of guilt for my tirade. I didn't mean to sound like I blamed *her* for losing her magical ability.

I didn't want to think about the fact that she was losing it at all.

"Sorry," I said quietly. "It's not just work. I'm also worried about Britt and the vampire hunters."

I regretted the words as soon as they'd left my lips. Gran no longer looked sad but bewildered. She gazed out the whale-gray horizon, as if the sea held the answer to some riddle.

"'Fraid I don't quite understand this vampire business, Hazel dear," she said. "Time was, you could count on a Green Witch to take care of her own."

"*Her own?*" I cringed. Sometimes Gran could be downright old fashioned. "I barely know Yolanda, and these hunters are threatening to stake innocent vampires."

Gran chortled. "Please, how many of *those* could there be?"

"Uh, Gran, that sounds a little bigoted." I scanned the empty block and prayed no vampires was listening in. Or, heaven forbid, Leia from L.A. "And how about Britt, for one? You love her."

Nearly everyone liked Brittany Salazar, the five-foot-tall ex-high-school cheerleader and mean girl who'd unexpectedly become my friend this fall. Though magic powers only enhanced her natural pixie-queen-bee vibe, getting turned at eighteen had also given Britt empathy for those who faced challenges in life.

Ever since the vampire hunters hit her with that death threat, Britt had been crashing on my futon. Storing her yucky blood vials in my fridge. Whimsically rearranging my furniture with her super strength. Direct sunlight gave her migraines, so she streamed comedies all day and lived in satin PJs, washing down pizza and candy bars with my best wine till her waitress shift started at the Drunken Barrel. Calories magically fled her undead body, leaving her svelte for eternity.

After three days, I was low-key starting to see the hunters' point of view.

Gran and I reached the slippery crosswalk, and I took her elbow as usual. She shook me off.

"Fine, Britt's as cute as a button. But your priorities are cattywampus." Gran folded her arms, stubbornly staying put.

My patience wilted, like a houseplant at Mother's. "I'd love to stand here in the freezing cold arguing," I said. "But I gotta get back to running your bakery."

"Our barista's hands can serve a muffin as well as yours can." Gran tutted and a rare smirk crossed her features. "Them older gals would rather flirt with him anyhow."

At the mention of our hot, new, shifter barista, I glanced at my watch and my neck muscles tightened. "Oh wow, Kade's been working solo for three hours."

Gran narrowed her gaze. "You say that as if you don't trust a grown man to run a cash register. What, are you worried he'll rob the till?"

"That's ridiculous." I inspected my chipped apple-green manicure. Okay, part of me didn't entirely trust Kade de Klaw, who had a sketchy past.

"While we're on the subject." Gran peered down her thick, black glasses at me in that way only older people can do to see your entire soul. "Has it ever occurred to you why that boy had such a troubled youth?"

I stifled a groan. "Don't say because he had no mentor.'"

"No. Mentor."

Lifting her posture, Gran finally took a careful step onto the slippery crosswalk, braving it without help as I hovered along beside her, itching to take her elbow but knowing she was too proud to accept help from me in the middle of an argument.

"A magical child *will* find trouble," she huffed. "Why'd you think I hired you at seventeen?"

"You needed a pie slave?" I muttered under my breath.

Gran looked taken aback for once. "I say this with love, but your first pies were not Sage's quality."

I laughed despite myself, remembering that shrinking, mousy girl who'd first shuffled into Gran's bakery kitchen for a pie-making lesson. Gran was right. I'd grown as a baker and as a witch, thanks to her. The wave of gratitude washed away some of my annoyance.

But only some.

"I say this with love, too, Gran. Your ideas are out of date."

"Well, that's appropriate, I'm eighty-six," she said reasonably, and took my elbow at last. We headed down the block side by side. "Yolanda's magic is brand new, shining with potential. It must be tended with care, or it could grow destructive, and—oh, my word!"

On the corner, Sage's Bakery jumped into view. A blue squad car was parked in front, its lights flashing. Elliot James, our town's hot deputy and my forever crush, was wrestling a large, pale-skinned man to the sidewalk.

A ski mask hid the man's features, but his broad, muscular build suggested he was young.

"Gran!" My heart pounded as I took in the full picture. "That guy just tried to rob the bakery."

"No—it can't be." Gran shook her grey head weakly. "Who would do such a thing?"

"No idea." But even as I said it, my brain was noting that this robber looked an awful lot like our new barista, Kade de Klaw.

I took off running.

CHAPTER THREE

THANKFULLY, I DIDN'T have to get much closer before I could tell the robber wasn't Kade. This dude's shoulders were truly massive, and when Elliot tore off his mask, a mop of nut-brown curls spilled out. His diamond-like stare framed a teenage face that was all hard angles, blank neutrality.

Whereas Kade had open, boyish features seemingly at odds with his jacked body. And auburn hair that fell over his eyes, making me want to smooth it back.

I felt a stab of guilt that my brain had gone right to suspecting Kade. In the shameless tradition of brains, though, mine pivoted to worry. What if Kade had gotten hurt in the robbery? The cashier was a prime target, at least on TV shows.

"Hazel. Don't even think about going in." Elliot had spotted me just as he was folding the reasonably compliant suspect into the backseat. "Let me handle this."

"You did handle it," I shot back. "Thanks, by the way. Now I'm going to check on my bakery."

"It's not your bakery," he called after me, "it's my crime scene!"

I stormed in, figuring he had his hands full and wouldn't follow.

Breathless, I stepped into the front room. No Kade. No customers. The floor I'd mopped to a high shine last night was littered with half-eaten biscuits and scones, and muffins whose tops had been nibbled off.

Queasiness squirreled through my guts. Did the thief raid my display case for snacks? The idea of him mouth-mauling my lovingly baked, magical treats shook me even more than the sight of the open cash register.

"Miss Greenwood, what are you doing back here?" a crabby voice demanded. Sheriff Gantry lumbered out of our kitchen, leading a second man in cuffs.

This one looked to be in his early twenties, rockstar skinny with a fade haircut dyed avocado. Whereas his younger partner had looked every inch the professional, this guy resembled a deranged cartoon imp. But he carried himself with a CEO's confidence.

"Go on." Sheriff Gantry shooed me again. "Back to your..." He tended to trail off midsentence, as if his own words bored him. "Go stand with the others in the civilian holding area till we're done with..."

"With this episode of justice theater?" The green-haired perp grinned, flashing sharp canines. It was eerie how he betrayed no hint of shame while being arrested for stealing from my family. He looked smug. Triumphant. Like he'd just nailed a performance art piece about robbing a bakery.

With a shiver, I turned back to the sheriff. "The civilian holding area?"

"I was trying to make it sound more official." Gantry blew out an irritated groan. "Back packing lot."

"Got it."

A belch from the green-haired robber made us both jump.

"Hey, Sugar Mama, thanks for the free muffins." The guy waggled his eyebrows at me. "They were *magically* delicious."

I averted my eyes from his leer, a chill running down my back. Did he know I was a witch?

"They're not free." I willed my voice not to tremble. "You're going to pay for stealing from my Gran."

His smirk was full of menace, at odds with his cheery, green-smoothie hair. "You're the one who's gonna pay, kitchen witch." he murmured just loud enough for me to hear. "You're a traitor to both our kinds."

I froze, my heart drumming so loud he could probably hear it. What the unholy hex was he talking about? Why would an Ordinal call me out? Most didn't even know magic existed. And why would he call me a traitor?

"Let's go, Torrin, you ill-mannered lout," Gantry barked, but the green-haired robber held my gaze with pure hatred as Gantry muscled him out the door.

I was still struggling to shake off his glare and his scary parting words as I trudged to the back parking lot.

Half a dozen of our regulars, mostly older women, stood flanking Gran, whose lips were drawn tight in a stoical line.

Margaret from the senior center was there too, for once not bickering with her lifetime frenemy, Helen. Though they did seem to be competing for who would get to stand next to Kade to fuss over him with an ice pack.

Ice pack?

Whoa, Kade was sporting a blackened eye. And a swollen lip.

I made my way to him and his ardent fan club. "You did *not* try to fight them both off."

Kade shrugged, which made his hair fall into his black eye. "You left me in charge."

"This man is no ordinary barista," Margaret crowed. "He's a hero-ista."

For once, Helen didn't quibble. "I'm calling up my grand-niece over at the Gazette." She proudly she held up a red Nokia phone from the Y2K era. "They ought to do a story on how you held off the bad guys till the cavalry came."

"You know, I think it's better if we keep the story to ourselves," Kade cut in. "Don't want my ego getting out of control." He winked, melting both the old ladies into puddles, but I wasn't buying it.

What was the real reason he didn't want any press coverage?

Maybe he doesn't want his black eye in the paper. Gran's voice in my head chided me for casting aspersions about Kade when he'd just taken a punch defending our bakery.

"Um, are you okay?" I hoped my voice didn't betray my guilt for having assumed the worst. Twice.

"I'll be fine," Kade assured me. "I heal fast."

Course he did. Shifter immune systems were superpowered. They weren't as disaster-proof as vampires but were still primed for battle. Elliot was a shifter, too, and no doubt fast healing helped in his line of work.

"Kade and Elliot both acted heroically," Gran spoke up, and all the Kade-admirers turned to look at her somber face. "Nevertheless, it's a sad day for this town. No one's ever tried to rob our bakery. Not in our seventy-five years of service to the community. Something is *deeply* wrong."

"You're right, ma'am." Elliot's deep voice piped up behind me. "Tensions are running high in Blue Moon Bay. I intend to find out why."

Great. Now I really had no choice but to report what the robber had said to Elliot. I'd kinda been hoping to move on from the whole "traitor to both our kinds" thing, but that was apparently unrealistic.

"In the meantime," Elliot went on, addressing the crowd, "we must stand together as a community against these bold criminal attacks." As a murmur of anxiety went up among the group, Elliot nodded to me. "Got all the prints I needed. Floor's swept and mopped."

"You mopped my floor." I tried not to let on that he'd just done something for me no other man had. "So, I can have my bakery back?"

The crow shifter narrowed his dark, hooded eyes. "For now."

My first order of business was serving coffee and snickerdoodles on the house to every customer who'd gone through *that* this morning. Far as I was concerned, they each deserved a loyalty reward for walking through our doors again. Even Gran, who generally disapproved of freebies, gave me the thumbs up before *poofing* home to watch afternoon soaps.

The post-lunch rush kicked off and time went all hazy like it always does. I served red velvet brownies, whiskey chocolate bread, and holiday gingerbread witches. I made small talk with a new moms coffee klatch, then frosted three dozen Earl Grey cupcakes for a special order. The bakery's familiar rhythms soothed me, making me feel normal again, almost.

Kade was mobbed by his female fans all day. The sight of his tip jar at five p.m., stuffed to overflowing with bills, made me smile.

But as I swept the dining room floor after close, I saw it again in my mind's eye defiled by the robbers' crumbs. Their threats echoed in my head, sending a shiver down my spine.

Traitor.

You're gonna pay, witch.

Who the hell were those guys? Did they really target Gran's bakery because of me? What'd I ever do to them, anyway?

And if this robbery was their opening salvo, how much worse would the next hit be?

CHAPTER FOUR

THE SUN WAS already low, and a crescent moon was rising over the waterfront when I locked the bakery door behind me at 5:15 p.m. That was winter in the Pacific Northwest for you. I wasn't just being passive aggressive when I warned Leia.

Though definitely that, too.

I merged into the happy hour sidewalk traffic heading toward the south end of Ocean Street, where Max, Britt, and I were meeting up at the Drunken Barrel.

The Barrel was, as you might guess, a huge dive. But every day at happy hour, it pretended to be an upscale bistro, serving decent tapas and bespoke cocktails to our better-heeled locals and a few savvy tourists. I swung through its familiar scuffed saloon doors and was amused to see that business casual crowded out the usual coastie flannel. Instead of a local fiddler playing reels live on the corner stage, chillout lounge music was being piped in at strategic decibel levels, so that it cozily blurred the roar of conversation.

Which was good, because when I joined their table in the corner, Max and Britt were already arguing.

Well, Britt was, vociferously. Max was stuffing her face with pulled pork sliders and beet, arugula, and goat cheese salad rolls.

"And I don't need some stinkin' shifter bodyguard." Britt

slammed down her empty rocks glass just as I sat down. "No joke. To a vampire's nose, you shifters have—let's just say, a unique aroma."

"Newsflash, you all don't smell like a Lush bath bomb to us, either." Max had finally come up for air from her sandwich. "How do you think I knew you were a vampire before you told us? You've got a subtle Eau de Rot."

"At least my thing's subtle," Britt lobbed back.

They both paused their ancient feud to say hi to me, and Max recommended the sliders.

I flagged the waiter and ordered my usual gourmet mac and cheese app and glass of rosé. Britt asked for another old fashioned.

"What's this about a shifter bodyguard?" I asked.

"She needs protection until we catch these vampire hunters," Max said with finality. "No offense to your futon, but it's not exactly a secure location."

"Oh, you don't have to tell me my security sucks." I sighed and caught them up on the bakery heist. Every detail, from Kade's black eye to Torrin the robber's neon-green hair. And his creepy remarks about being a traitor to my own kind and his.

"Whatever that means," I finished.

Max swore and turned to Britt. "It means you're gonna need *two* bodyguards."

"*Two* stinky shifters?" Britt laughed uneasily into her seared ahi salad. Though she needed blood and only blood to survive, eating food was her hobby. "Let's not go jumping to conclusions. What if Hazel's robbers are just Ordinals high on weed? The munchies, weird laughter, paranoia." She checked off the signs on her fingers. "Why should I be scared of a stoned muffin thief?"

"Because that's not who these people are." Max still looked stricken. "They're scary. They're organized crime—well, organized for shifters."

My heart had been flip-flopping ever since *scary*. "A shifter gang?"

Max nodded, her face grim. "Carnivora. They're dangerous and they can be brutal."

"I don't get it. Why would these shifters have it in for Hazel?" Britt said, patting my arm. "She's like the nicest person in town."

"Aw, thanks."

"More importantly," Max said, "she's a Green Witch."

Her comment didn't make me feel as special as Britt's had, but I knew what she meant. Gran had always taught me that Green Witches were held in high regard by other magical beings. That we were neutral in their war was the only thing shifters and vampires agreed on. They hated each other *so much*—

"Crud." The realization hit me. "They must know I'm protecting Britt."

"How?" Britt's eyes widened. "Are they spying on me too, like the hunters?"

We all gasped at once.

"What if this Carnivora gang *are* the vampire hunters?" I stared at my friends. "Shifters hunting vampires. It makes sense."

Now Britt looked nervous for once. "I was really hoping it was just dumb Ordinals."

"We need more data," Max said, which I think was her way of trying to reassure Britt. "But I think we have our first suspects. That crew would stake a newblood if they thought they could get away with it. Ugh, I'm going to kill Kade and Elliot for not mentioning that your robbers today were Carnivora."

"Yeah, seriously," I said. Elliot worked in law enforcement; he would have recognized two local gangsters. It was irritatingly on-brand that he'd told us nothing. "Wait ... why Kade?"

"My brother used to run with Carnivora back in high school." Max played with her food, obviously uncomfortable with the memory. "Till he got arrested the first time. Thankfully before they could make him a full member."

"Wait a minute, Kade was friends with those guys?" I knew a little bit about switching sides, from growing up thinking I was a Beige Witch.

No wonder Kade didn't want the local paper doing a story. To him it was personal.

"Well, I'm definitely on team 'Get a Bodyguard'," I said, shivering.

Britt glared. "Thanks, *traitor*."

"Too soon!" I protested.

"Two against one, it's settled." Max pulled out her phone and began typing a text. "It's kinda perfect timing, too. I just broke up with this big grizzly shifter, so he needs something to take his mind off things."

I blinked. "You had a whole relationship and didn't tell us?"

"Smelly bear fur?" Britt made a lemon face, then an angry one as the penny dropped. "Hang on, we're hiring your very recent ex to protect me?"

Max looked up from her phone, confused. "What's the problem?"

"What if he hates you for breaking his heart?" Britt sputtered. "What if he wants revenge?"

"Not everything's a gothic soap opera, Ms. Vampire." Max casually reached over to bogart one of Britt's fries. "We just weren't compatible … turns out I might not be as bi as I thought I was."

"I've been telling you that you since high school!"

Max ignored me. "But Graham's a solid dude. And you need muscle in your corner."

"Still stuck on the fact that you kept us in the dark," I said.

"What are you stuck on? It's me." Max poured half the sugar

pitcher into her Long Island Iced Tea and stirred methodically. "I'm cryptic and don't say much, except about stuff you don't care about. Then I go on and on."

She picked the weirdest moments to be self-aware.

"Miss, I'm so very sorry, but we're out of that mac and cheese you like. And also out of rosé."

I looked up to see the thin, boyish waiter with his usual stoical expression. I didn't know his name because everyone called him Scruffy, presumably because of the three hair mustache he seemed so proud of. Britt had told me he was a domestic dog shifter and actually older than he looked. Which was good because he looked thirteen.

"You're out of rosé?" I echoed dumbly. *Every bottle?*

"This is all that's left from the Happy Hour menu." He was holding a plate piled high with greens. Something my mother would eat. "Kale Delight. On the house." He set down the salad with a slight bow and walked off.

"Today is *fired*," I whined. Then I remembered Scruffy was a dog shifter. "Crap. What do you want to bet that waiter's a member of Carnivora too?"

"That little dude? Nah, you're being paranoid." Max peered at my plate. "Ooh, cranberries and feta, that *is* delightful. Cool if I eat your salad?"

I was about to dump the bowl in her lap when Britt blurted out, "I need you two to help me with something tomorrow afternoon."

We both looked up at her.

"I have to run a … painful errand," she said.

"Painful?" Max echoed. "Are we going to the dentist with you?"

"Waxing appointment?" I guessed.

"Oh, you two are so cute!" Britt laughed us off. "Vampires don't have body hair. Or cavities. Or cramps."

"Or friends, if you don't shut up," I said.

"Anyway, it's worse than any of that stuff." Worry shadowed her sweet, heart-shaped face. "We need to pay a home visit to my sire's surviving family."

A shiver ran through me. The hunters were likely responsible for her sire's death; it was important to interview his family. But visiting a vampire den was above my pay grade.

Especially since I wasn't getting paid.

Even Max seemed less than eager. "So how many vampires are we talking about in one house?"

"Hard to say at any given time." While she spoke, Britt began shredding a cocktail napkin. Even more unlike her, she was looking down at the peanut-littered cork floor instead of at us. "Let's just say I've been estranged from that household for long enough the family dynamics could be awkward."

I saw an opening. "Um, if you need emotional support, I'm happy to process with you *after* the visit? Which you go to without me."

"Who said anything about emotions?" Britt gave me a frustrated look. "I need Max's quick wits and agility and your magic. In case one of those undead monsters tries to kill me."

Max didn't miss a beat. "We got your back, B."

Reluctantly, I nodded.

Britt stopped shredding her napkin. She let out a long breath and dropped her shoulders five inches. "Oh good. Thank you both."

My phone buzzed with a text from Jacinta, who normally only group texted at me. What time works best for u to come by tmrw aft to talk w Yolanda abt being her mentor?

I stifled a groan. Could she be any more pushy?

Busy tomorrow, I typed back furiously. *Helping a friend.*

I shoved my phone back into my purse, snatched up my fork, and stabbed a hateful mountain of kale.

CHAPTER FIVE

THE SMALL, CHIC neighborhood of Sunset had always felt separate from the rest of Blue Moon Bay. Tucked into the foothills one steep and winding mile of road from the glitter of Blue Moon Heights, Sunset was known for its quirky custom homes on sprawling lots with backyard chicken coops, tropical greenhouses, mini-goat pens, or *avant garde* yard art. It was where the Bay's creative class dwelled—and until three weeks ago, Britt's sire had lived there, too.

I should have been scared, yet mostly I felt concern for Britt, who was chewing her cushiony lip beside me as she shifted the car into lower gear. Her aviator sunglasses couldn't hide her anxiety, even if they hid the glare from the setting sun that gave this neighborhood its famous million-dollar views.

What did these people mean to Britt? She'd called them monsters, but they'd once been her family. Her only instructions were that Max should be prepared to assume her fly form and observe while I, Hazel, was to smile and not speak unless spoken to. Hatred toward shifters and disrespect for humans, check and check. We were walking into a literal vampire den.

Between Britt's discomfort, my unease, and Max methodically working her way through an entire bag of Macintosh apples, we made the drive in crunchy near-silence until Britt drove past the neo-Victorian mansion of Yalis Meltakis, the flamboyant glass artist whose airy, translucent bowls sold at auction for thousands.

Decorating his property was a breathtaking cornucopia of larger-than-life glass-blown animals and fairy creatures that seemed like they might come to life at any minute. We all oohed and aahed.

"An amazing display," Max mused, her gaze growing thoughtful in the rearview mirror.

"It's beautiful," I agreed.

"Beautiful?" Max spat back, shuddering. "More like a crass and trite Disneyfication of nature, magical beings, and all that I hold sacred. But hey, to each her own."

"Oh my gosh, why'd you call it 'amazing'?" I snapped, feeling tricked.

Britt spoke up for the first time since we entered Sunset. "Because it's a stunning display of wealth. A cool million, just sitting in a guy's yard? Man, must make the two of you feel like a pair of broke losers!"

"The two of *us*?" I was about to point out that Britt was projecting wildly, when Max spoke up, her mouth once again full of apple.

"She's not totally wrong, I *was* thinking about how all that loot's just sitting in his yard. No fences. No gate. No moat filled with glass alligators, which would be cool, but I digress. So why hasn't some punk like my brother lifted all this junk and sold it on the black market?"

"It's obviously warded," I said.

Max perked up. "That's a real thing?"

"Sure, magical security systems are all the rage. For those who can afford them."

What I didn't add is that warding was a touchy subject among witches. The gig was taboo, for reasons that had never been made entirely clear to me by Gran, who simply said no witch with an ounce of dignity would volunteer, and she pitied those who had no choice. Even my mother, who disagreed with Gran on nearly everything, said warding was too depressing and negative to talk about.

I narrowed my eyes in the rearview mirror at the frolicking glass sprites, feeling a twinge for whichever member of my community had been desperate enough to take that job.

On the next block, we passed the famous Onyx Pact compound, four modern eco-homes connected to a giant central yard, all of it jointly owned by the former members of Blue Moon Bay's most successful grunge act. Back in the 90s, Onyx Pact sung about lust, rage, and hopelessness. Now, they were all happily married dads who, from the looks of it, lusted mainly after permaculture guilds, wind-powered tilapia ponds, fresh duck eggs, and broccolini.

Max ripped off another chunk of apple with her teeth and kicked the back of Britt's seat. "Hey, Brittany, was your sire a musician, too? Did he serenade you at school?"

Britt got that uncomfortable, strained-jaw look again, and I tried to shoot Max a clue-up look in the mirror. Apparently, she hadn't gotten the memo about *sensitive subject.*

"No, wait, I bet he was one of those performance art morons," Max went on, clearly trying to annoy Britt into answering. "Like a mime, the deadly serious kind. Black turtleneck, pancake make-up. Did you meet in draaaama class?"

"You can shut up any time." Britt sighed. "Gerard fancied himself an *auteur*, if you must know."

"Do you mean an otter?" I asked, confused at her pronunciation.

"Why would I mean otter?" Britt snapped. "An *auteur* is a filmmaker. As in, screenwriter and director."

"Was he any good?" Max asked, forgetting the taunting for once.

Britt hung a left turn, taking us up Sunset Hill Drive to the very wealthiest part of the neighborhood. "Hard to know," she said, "he never actually wrote anything, unless you count really long texts. But he was passionate about film. Taught Film Lit and Camera Techniques classes at the Blue Moon College for over a decade."

Max nearly choked on her fruit. When she was done coughing, she said, "Hang on, I've met this skeevester! He had a passion all right. For college girls."

Britt's face froze. "Only the prettiest, most special girls," she corrected, her voice sounding oddly younger.

She shook her head and gripped the steering wheel, as if to snap out of a trance.

When she spoke again it was in her usual crisp, confident tone. "He called himself a 'collector of beauty.' Cheesy, but I fell for it. You would have too, don't kid yourself."

"Yikes." I blinked as it all became clear to me. "I didn't realize the old vampire who turned you at eighteen was some kind of gross predator type … never mind, now that I've said it aloud…"

Eighteen was not mature. Eighteen was those witchlings, Yolanda and Amethyst. Who, come to think of it, had mentioned having a *new* film professor. Of course, they were too sheltered to have any idea that the old one had been staked, or that he'd been a vampire at all.

What were the chances he'd have preyed on one of them?

A wave of sadness washed over me. Britt had been just like them when she was turned.

"He didn't seem gross at the time." Britt's normally mischievous brown eyes looked lost again. "More like worldly and sophisticated. I thought he was drop dead hot, even though he looked middle aged. He'd been turned at twenty-eight but he was a turnip farmer in the actual Middle Ages, so he looked fifty. But he could make you feel like you were the only girl in the world."

"Except you very much weren't," Max said with a laugh. "Your dude was scoping out two to three freshmen per class he taught. Heard it through the girl-grapevine after I dropped his class like a hot potato, cause I didn't like the way he was looking at me."

"*You?* Oh, honey, please." Despite her self-assured tone, Britt appeared to have been thrown even further off balance. "I doubt Gerard was into you, Maxy. If he had been, you'd be…" She seemed to be musing to herself. "Of course. His compelling gaze wouldn't work on a shifter. Which means to lure to you in, he'd have to come right out and offer you eternal life. And no offense, that was a perk he reserved for nines and up."

"Also I'd rather die, literally." Max tossed her final apple core out of the window, where it landed on some affluent homeowner's salal and radicchio lawn. "It's a no-brainer. Dodging Prof McSketchy is the only smart thing I did that whole year."

Oof. I winced and waited helplessly as the silence after that unfortunate line grew more awkward.

Even socially-challenged Max seemed to have realized she'd stepped in it. I knew her well enough to trust that she'd been aiming for self-deprecating humor.

Not victim blaming.

Britt's posture was suddenly stiff. Her road focus all-encompassing.

"Hey," Max began uncertainly. "I didn't mean to imply … it wasn't your fault—"

"Here we are." Britt's voice matched her posture, formal and stiff. "This is the house. Where I made bad choices, like not being immune to compulsion."

"That was a well-done snark," Max said. "Hello, nine-one-one? I've been sick burned by a sarcastic vampire."

"Game faces, everybody," I reminded them as Britt turned into the driveway of a colonial-style mansion with an elegant Art Deco fountain in the front yard.

It was on the tip of my tongue to ask how a college instructor afforded to live on this street when I remembered: vampire. *Old* vampire. Those tended to be loaded, compound interest being even more miraculous when your body had no expiry date.

On second thought, if he was born in the Middle Ages and only lived here, Gerard must be a spectacular screwup.

Unlike the home of Yalis Meltakis, this property clearly had a (non-magical) security system, complete with cameras and fencing and a gate. A black metal one with a code and a fancy intercom.

Britt pushed the call button. "Max, buzz off," she commanded in a growl.

"Look, I know she made some insensitive comments, but surely you two can talk it out—oh, gotcha."

A fly had begun to buzz above my head, making a nuisance of itself. I checked the rear-view mirror to confirm that Max had vanished.

"Cameras," Britt hissed at me, just as a video display lit up on the intercom.

A pale-skinned young blond woman fixed us with a guarded stare. "What business?"

That was it. No greeting. Just a two-word demand, delivered in lightly accented English.

"Marie Pierre, it's me, Britt."

At the woman's blank look, she tried again.

"Britt Hansen. I know it's been a while. You, uh, used to refer to me as Beer Hall Chick?"

"Ah, my dear Britt-any! You have returned to us at last." Marie Pierre's delicate young face broke into a smile that was equal parts sad and fond. She disappeared from the screen and the gate opened.

"I'm a little surprised you remember me," Britt said once Marie Pierre had ushered us into the sitting room and Earl Grey tea had been served by a non-uniformed housekeeper, along with delicate almond cookies and a single vial of blood set before Britt. "Given … how many newbloods there must have been, over the years."

"But none like you!" Marie's gaze met Britt's warmly; evidently the woman had no fear of vampire compulsion. "So vivacious, a petite diamond in the rough, serving your swill in that hideous dive before he gave you the One True Life. But then, all of Gerard's creations had humble beginnings, me more than most." She ducked her head modestly.

Gerard's creations? One True Life? The words were creepy enough, but what made it worse was her obsequious awe toward the dead vampire. It's like she was in a cult.

"Yes, well, we've all moved on to bigger and better things," breezed Brit, who still very much waitressed at the Drunken Barrel. "Anyhoo, I came by to—"

"Pay your respects to the vampire who made you what you are?" There was that beatific smile again. This woman seemed to be under Gerard's spell, even now.

"Erm, sure?" Britt gritted her teeth. "But really also to see you, and offer any help I can to the newbloods, assuming he left any newbloods?"

"Correct assumption, my dear." Marie Pierre's smile stayed on, but did it seem a bit forced now? "His appetite for beauty could not be quenched."

I shivered with revulsion at the thought of the old turnip farmer literally quenching his thirst with the blood of young women. Marie Pierre would probably need years of deprogramming.

My shivering unfortunately caused Marie Pierre to finally notice my existence.

"Dear Brittany, what a kind gesture to bring us a dolly." She smiled warmly. "Blood is always a welcome gift."

Cold terror pulsed through me, and housefly Max buzzed in my ear as if to say, *Den of vampires, what did you expect?*

"No one better lay a hand or fang on Hazel," Britt said sharply. "She's no blood doll, she's a master witch."

"A witch!" Marie Pierre gasped and clapped her hands together excitedly. "How did you guess a witch is precisely what we need. After what happened to Gerard, none of us feels safe. We need security."

I knew exactly where this was going.

"I don't do warding spells," I said flatly.

"Ah, she's saying we must haggle over the fee," Marie said, still talking to Britt, not me. Her attitude was infuriating. "Every witch has her price, no?"

I gave Britt a look that said in no uncertain terms, *hex no.*

"Uhhh, I'm sure an agreement can be reached, later," Britt said breezily. What? No, it couldn't. "But tell me, how are you holding up?"

"Barely, *mon cherie.*" Marie sighed. "I was the second person to see him." Her fingers around the teacup trembled as she landed it on the saucer. "What was left of him."

Britt winced, and discreetly pushed aside her blood vial. "We don't leave behind pretty corpses, do we?"

"Never mind, *cherie*, you get to be beautiful longer than anyone else." Interesting, she didn't say "we." Was Marie not a vampire herself?

"But, what happened that night?" Britt pressed. "When you found the … well, let's call it a body."

Did I want to know? Nope, I decided. A sweet, wonderful world of nope.

Marie sighed. "I was tempted to go into shock, but held myself together for the sake of Carina—she's the last of his progeny, and she was the one who discovered his staked corpse. Here in our very kitchen." She shook her head. "Poor girl, I'll never forget the look on her face. I'm grateful the other two newbloods were spared the sight. I buried him under a willow tree," she added, gesturing toward the sliding glass door to the backyard. "You are welcome to visit, whenever you feel lost without your maker's wisdom to guide you."

I was proud of Britt's poker face. "Thanks!"

"Can we talk to Carina?" I asked, temporarily forgetting that I was supposed to let Britt lead. Marie seemed to have some concern for the newbloods, which was nice and all, but had it even occurred to her that the person who "found" the murder victim could well be their killer?

Marie shook her head sadly. "She returned to her parents' house soon after. I have not seen her since."

"Her Ordinal parents took her back?" Britt blinked, and it hit me suddenly that she'd never once mentioned her own parents who presumably still lived in town. "Kind of surprised they're so chill and accepting. Glad it all worked out for her."

Oh, buddy. I wished we were in a different venue so I could give her a hug.

"Gerard, staked." Britt tsked and shook her head. "Did he have enemies?"

Marie Pierre sighed. "None at all. Perhaps a disgruntled former student here and there, you know how flighty and emotional young women can be."

So yes, enemies, I thought. Ones with excellent justification for hating him. Including Carina, who if his m.o. held true, was almost certainly a college freshman. It was all I could do to keep my fake sweet expression on and remain silent. Wow, was I glad Britt was leading this discussion.

"What about death threats?" Britt said.

"No…" Marie shifted uncomfortably. "Well, there was one.

He did not take it seriously, though. Nor did I, for which I kick myself now. But a week before I found him there, this arrived in our mailbox." She walked over to an antique writing table, opened its single drawer, and fished out a typed page much like the one Britt had received. The only difference was it made references to "undead bloodsucking monsters" plural, instead of singular. Britt's had even addressed her by name. But since Gerard was part of a family with multiple vampires, a more generic approach made sense, I supposed.

"Did you not share this with anyone?" Britt had already moved on to the meat of the matter. "Any authorities? Even after his death?"

"You are right, I should have." Marie Pierre swallowed. "Ever since that night, my every waking thought is for the newbloods. How to protect them and comfort them."

Eh. I didn't quite buy that. Some of her waking thoughts still seemed to be about Gerard and his magnificence.

"It sounds like you've had a rough time, Marie." Britt's voice was mild and gentle, which is how I knew she was being fake. Perhaps, knowing Marie as well as she did, Britt sensed that she would catch more flies with honey. "I know it's hard to talk about grief and loss, but if you ever want to share—"

"It happened just after midnight." Marie did want to share. Her sea-blue eyes looked haunted. "Carina and I were having a late-night chat, as we often do, and we decided to make hot chocolate. So we walked into the kitchen … and there he was. Or at least, there was a greenish-brown sludge with—"

"NOPE!"

They both stared at me.

"It's like you said, hard to talk about grief," I said.

"It really is." Britt got to her feet. Her eyelid was twitching. Almost like she was allergic to being in this house. "Thank you for the tea. Hazel and I will leave you to process what's happened and hopefully find some peace."

"Good to meet you, Marie." I sprang from my seat, eager to be on our way.

"Attendez!" Marie trailed us to the door. "What about my warding?"

Damn, I'd been hoping she'd forget it.

"You can negotiate terms later." Britt's voice was getting less warm and engaged with every statement. It was like her ability to fake it was just giving out. "Hazel, give Marie your card."

I handed her one of my Sage's Bakery cards and prayed she'd be too frazzled with grief to get in touch.

On the way out, we passed the media room, whose door had been closed before. Now it was open, and a pair of raucous female voices could be heard joking and laughing over the sound of whatever show they were watching. I'd have expected them to be sitting in a circle solemnly chanting, "I am grateful for the One True Life," but no, the two long-limbed beauties piled into a bean bag chair watching TV looked like ordinary teenagers.

Then again, so did Britt, though she had experienced as many years on the planet as I had. I'd always envied her for the fact that she'd never age, but now I looked at the situation in a whole new light.

It was sad. Really sad.

Max, hitching a ride in my hair, buzzed excitedly as I made my way to the door, running to catch up with Britt's vampire speed-walk. Interviewing the newbloods would have to wait.

All three of us couldn't wait to ditch this place.

CHAPTER SIX

KADE WAS WHIPPING up decaf espresso drinks for the handful of customers trickling in during the four p.m. lull when we three scooted into the back booth.

After that creepy visit to Gerard's, I'd called from the road to order three mocha chais and liberate a whole loaf of pumpkin bread from the glass while he was at it. That pastry was one I'd imbued with our special Second Wind spell, for reviving afternoon office workers.

Five minutes and about a thousand calories later, Britt's eyes still had a vaguely spacey look, but the magic was working.

"So what the deal with Gerard's wife?" Max stacked three slices of pumpkin bread and opened her mouth wide to bite into it, Big Mac style. "I flew into her tiny little bedroom and it's all Laura Ashley. Lace curtains on the one window. No way has a dude ever been in that room."

"Correct." Britt reached for a slice of pumpkin bread. "He would knock on her door and ask if she needed to feed, and she'd come out and drink his blood."

"Ew, she drinks vampire blood?" I asked. "Does that mean she's a vampire?"

Max's eyes had widened. "Or does it make her the ultimate Apex predator?"

Britt snorted. "Marie's more like a servant to our kind. She's a valet." She pronounced it so it rhymed with shallot. "Blood-bound to Gerard and his lineage."

We were still staring at her.

"Valet?" Max echoed.

"Blood-bound?" I said.

Britt sighed. "To make a very long story short, four hundred years ago, a turnip farmer in Alsace-Lorraine needed a wife, so he married a young girl from a struggling family. Unbeknownst to the girl and her family, this farmer was also a vampire."

Max wrinkled her nose. "I already hate this story."

"But rather than eating her up," Britt went on, "like you'd expect if this were a fairy tale, he began to feed the girl daily from his wrist. Within twenty-eight days, she had enough vampire blood running through her veins to enjoy some of his enchanted strength, speed, senses, and metabolism. All of which made her a stellar farmwife, envy of the whole parish."

"He gave her superpowers just so she could be the best little jam maker in Alcasce-Lorraine?" Max stared at her pumpkin bread sandwich, looking confused.

"Does anyone *really* make turnip jam?" I shuddered.

"It was a thing back then," Britt said. "Valets, not turnip jam. They're still a fixture in some vamp elder communities. The Northwest council frowns on it nowadays. But it's complicated because the valets themselves will sometimes speak up and claim they're *so* happy living this way. They love having many of the advantages of vampirism without any of the disadvantages."

"What disadvantages?" I said with a snort, and was surprised when Max and Britt both fixed me with a wicked side eye.

"Sunshine gives this woman killer migraines." Max sounded personally affronted as she spoke up for Britt. "She's targeted by hate groups, driven from her home. Forced to drink copious amounts of blood or she'll go into torpor. And you see *no* disadvantages?"

"Britt could eat this entire pumpkin bread and not gain an ounce," I said.

But that wasn't winning the room. I decided to cancel my cued-up rant about eternal youth, since now that I recalled there was kind of a major downside there too. That whole thing where you couldn't settle down in one place for too long or people would cop to the fact that you never aged.

"Hey, wait, didn't you say Gerard looked about fifty?" I asked, realizing suddenly that there was a hole in her story. "How come Marie Pierre looks my age, tops?"

"Because she was only twelve when she got married off to Gerard." Britt's voice softened. "He offered her parents three goats and seven chickens for her hand in marriage, and they really needed the chickens and goats." Britt's features wore a look I'd never seen on them before. Her mouth was a thin line, her eyes and eyebrows pulled down with sadness.

"I never thought about Marie Pierre as a victim," she admitted. "To us newbloods, she was the house mother. Super competent. Unflappable. She wasn't cuddly but she was always there for us. We looked up to her. But I guess it was always clear that Gerard didn't think of her as … how we modern people see a marriage partner. She was an employee, at best."

"More like his property," Max said grimly. "She had no rights. And she's not the only one, either."

"I beg your pardon." Britt stiffened in her seat. "Being turned is hardly the same thing as being a valet."

Max started to reply but I kicked her under the table. Wonder of wonders, she shut up.

"*I'm* not a victim." Britt's face filled with childlike uncertainty. "Am I?"

Instead of an answer, I passed Britt the last slice of pumpkin bread.

"Not even your cake could fix this," Britt sulked, but she nibbled at it anyway. "The only thing that would help me feel better is tracking down those stupid vampire hunters, so I can sleep in my own bed again." With a groan, she rubbed her back between her shoulder blades. I tried not to take it as an indictment of my futon.

"Hey, we three are working on catching them," Max reminded her. "And in the meantime, Graham will be protecting you, starting tonight."

Britt's shoulders slumped. "Almost forgot about your smelly grizzly bear ex."

"Ooooooh, rude, don't call him that. You could get mauled."

"She's kidding." I wasn't sure, but felt the need to inject some positivity—and more chocolate. I pulled myself to my feet. "Turtle fudge brownies coming up, on the house."

"You're a queen among bakers!" Britt called after me.

"Can I get another chai since you're up?" Max added.

"Get it yourself!" I shot back.

Kade was furiously typing on his phone, but when I walked up to the counter, he quickly pocketed his device. None of my business who he was texting, but I couldn't help but be curious. Did he have a girlfriend?

"How's it going, Boss?" he greeted me with his default expression, equal parts earnest and brooding.

He wore a long-sleeved grey Henley underneath his Sage's Bakery T-shirt, tattoos peeking out around his wrists. His slightly swollen lip lent a sultriness to his boyish face, but his black eye was, amazingly, almost healed from yesterday.

"Hell of a week," he said as if reading my thoughts.

"Yeah, but things are calming down finally." Positivity. I reached behind the counter and grabbed three brownies from the case. As I brushed past Kade, my arm touched his bicep and I caught the airy pine scent of his skin.

Sometimes I managed to forget that Kade was super-hot, which was convenient since he was Max's brother, my co-worker, and a really bad idea all at once.

Three different flavors of off-limits.

Walking back to our table, I forgot about Kade when I nearly bumped into a tall, well-muscled form in khaki.

"What's going on?" I blurted out.

Elliot's expression was serious, but even if it hadn't been I knew something was up. The man didn't come in for coffee after nine a.m., and he never ate pastries.

He motioned to our table. "I need to talk to all three of you."

From the moment Elliot pulled up a café chair beside me, I found myself sneaking peaks at his tan uniform, sleeves rolled up to reveal muscular forearms. Gun resting in its holster at his nipped-in waist. Elliot didn't seem to know what to do with his arms, so he rested them on the table. The woodsy scent of his buzzed black hair distracted me, just like in high school.

Till he spoke.

"Word on the street is that the vampire hunters have officially taken credit for the slaying of Gerard Chevalier."

"Oh no." I'd been holding out hope that those threat letters were a prank, Gerard's murder a simple case of revenge from one of his ex-pupils.

"Word on the street?" Britt frowned. "Who's your source on that? The local council of elders would have made an announcement to their ranks in FangLife."

"The hell is FangLife?" Max hooted. "Some kind of dumb vampire newsletter?"

"It's prestigious," Britt hissed. "They only send it to you once you've made it ten years as a vampire."

"In that case, congrats," Max said, while I was still doing math. "But if they haven't made an announcement, how do *you* know about it?" she asked Elliot.

"It's all over the internet," he said.

"Where, what kind of search did you do?" Max demanded.

He looked shifty-eyed. "Fine, I'll tell you. I've been interviewing crime suspects who happen to be shifters. Heard it from them first."

"Oh, you mean the Carnivora guys who robbed my bakery?" I asked. "And who might actually *be* the vampire hunters—given how much they hate vampires and those who help them find safety?"

Satisfaction swept over me when Elliot's brows lifted in surprise. "How'd you put that together?" he demanded.

"No thanks to you," I said. "Why *didn't* you tell us who they were? Don't you think I deserve to know who's got beef with me?"

"Not if it's being handled." His voice was cool and a little scary, half assuring me, half warning me off.

Max tilted her head back and groaned. "Don't take this the wrong way, Crow Bro. But last time, you kept us away from all the important intel and we *still* solved the case for you."

"And you almost got killed." His tight jaw belied his calm voice. "By the way, who rescued you three Miss Marples?"

I crossed my arms in front of me. "Maybe we wouldn't have needed rescuing if you'd kept us in the loop."

Elliot made a dismissive gesture with his hand. "I'm not getting into this with you. You three shouldn't be going anywhere near this case if Carnivora's involved."

"Elliot, my sire was murdered," Britt spoke up. "Can you

look me in the eye and honestly tell me his death will be properly investigated by your department?"

Elliot laughed. "I'm not looking into your eyes, nice try."

"Figure of speech," she snapped. "Will his death be looked into?"

He didn't try to sugarcoat it. "No. In the Ordinal world, there's no case. No body, of course, and no one's called him in as a missing person." He paused. "Are we even sure he's dead?"

"One of his newbloods discovered his body," I said, earning another gratifying look of respect from Elliot. "Let us follow that lead. We'll share our findings with you. And obviously we'll come to you if the evidence points toward Carnivora after all."

Elliot seemed to be weighing his choices. He turned to Britt. "Why the hell do you care what happened to that jerk?"

"Vampire reasons," Max said, just as Britt said, "Personal reasons."

He swore under his breath. "You won't get far before you're in over your heads."

Britt, Max, and I managed a gleeful three-way glance. In Elliot-speak, he'd given us the greenlight.

Just after nine p.m. that night, I was slouching at my dining room table in my softest sweater and comfy joggers, working my way through a stack of grimoires featuring warding spells, and a batch of spice cookies—sugar-rolled and drenched in molasses—when the doorbell rang.

"Bet that's my big furry bodyguard." Blasé, from her futon perch where she was streaming *The Golden Girls*, Britt clawed the air, miming a charging grizzly. "*Grrr, rarrr.*"

I opened the door to see a clean-shaven, thirty-something man with a wiry build and a serious expression. He wore horn rimmed glasses, steel-toed boots, and a blue flannel shirt open over a band T-shirt.

I was still chuckling at Britt's over-the-top miming when he politely wiped his feet on the mat. "Graham Rusk." He stuck out his hand for me to shake.

"I'm Hazel Greenwood."

"Good to meet you, Hazel. Did I miss something funny?"

"Not at all, come on in." I flashed a smile, thinking Graham's pleasant baritone wasn't grizzly sounding in the least.

He dragged a mini suitcase behind him. Its wheels squeaked. Then I realized he was still staring at me so intently I couldn't think of what to say.

"We were definitely not telling jokes," I said, feeling my palms go clammy, the first clue I was about to go into ramble mode. "And we weren't joking about you." *Crap*. Shut up, shut up now. "You know, I think we were both just expecting something different. Never mind. It was dumb."

He squinted through his thick glasses. "Different how?"

I looked to Britt, but her face was all blank innocence. She was also gooped up with a mint green masque, wet hair twisted up in a pink towel. Given that she was a vampire whose looks never changed, it felt like she was going overboard to show she had no interest in impressing Max's ex.

"Oh, I get it now." Graham's squint was growing up into a glare. "You expected me to smash your window. Gnaw on your sofa, bathe the leather in bear drool. That kind of thing?"

"*So* sorry. When you spell it out like that, super offensive. Sorry again," I whispered and ducked away, back to the table where suddenly the grimoires seemed more appealing.

"Don't mind Hazel, she's still unpacking her witch privilege," Britt spoke up from her *Golden Girls* marathon as Graham stepped into the living room. It took all I had to keep from shouting, *You were the one grrring and rarring.* "But in her defense…"

I smiled, waiting for her to tell him I was the nicest person in town.

"…she bakes a mean scone."

"You suck," I mouthed to her from across the room.

"Britt Salazar." She gave a nod when he approached. He did the same. Neither held out a hand. "Nice to meet you, I guess?"

"How nice could it be, under these circumstances?" He matched her tone of weary, griping resignation. "We stink to each other, and your life's in danger. If it can even be called a life."

"Just so you know, I prefer the term 'unlife,' but it's not like we'll be forming a friendship."

Graham nodded affably. "You can say that again."

He returned to the doorway and wheeled in a second ergo mini suitcase. Was it my imagination or was Britt sneaking glances at his lean jaw, his sinewy frame, the fit of his jeans? He turned to me. "Just FYI Hazel, I'm as civilized as you are. See? Got my toothbrush, floss, razor, cologne, copy of the *Grapes of Wrath*. Does that make me smarter than the average bear?"

Weirdly specific. "It's a classic," I stammered, and forced a smile, wondering if I'd ever felt this awkward in my own house.

"Brought a sleeping bag too," he said. "Max told me your place would be cozy, so I'm fine sleeping on the floor. But I do have a bed at home, with sheets and blankets and pillows."

"I *get* it. Glad you're okay with floor tonight, since floor's what I have." There was no backpedaling from my earlier gaffe, so I'd given up trying to make a decent impression tonight. Starting tomorrow I vowed to show Graham I wasn't the bigot I'd appeared to be.

Not that he seemed to be paying attention to me. His sparkling brown eyes were glued to Britt—or well, her iPad. "*Golden Girls*, classic. Mind if I join you? Not much else to do here."

Britt folded her arms. "Whatever."

I returned to my spells and spice cookies, though I couldn't help but keep sneaking glances their way every time they burst into laughter at something ridiculous Blanche or Rose did. Was it my impression, or were their heads drifting closer as they watched?

No way. Britt was a staunch proponent of the girl code and wouldn't dream of touching a friend's ex. Especially not a smelly shifter.

In my loft bed that night, I tossed and turned with nightmares about the robbers. In one, they bit the heads off my gingerbread witch cookies, spitting them out on the floor. I woke up in a cold sweat. My alarm clock read three twenty-three. Might as well get up and get ready for work.

Laughter rang out from the living room.

Were Britt and Graham were still awake, together?

That settled it: we needed to prove Carnivora were the vampire hunters, and fast. Not just to save Britt from an untimely staking, but to rescue my cozy, quiet, *witchy* lifestyle from being a casualty of the vampire-shifter war.

CHAPTER SEVEN

WHEN I TRUDGED over from the bus stop Thursday morning, Gran's beater car was parked behind the bakery. I raced to the back door entrance, my spirits lifting at the thought of finally getting some much needed one-on-one time with her.

"Gran, what a nice surprise!" I called.

"You're low on lavender, that won't do," she called back from the pantry.

She was tsking to herself as she perused the shelves of dried herbs, cannisters of flour and sugar, and various tinctures with her trusty clipboard and pen hanging from a little lanyard around her neck.

"No, we're not low on anything." I shook my head, feeling proud of myself for once. "Already checked inventory. I read a bunch of library books on small business management and I set up a binder with a weekly checklist. Lavender is checked."

"Don't believe your lying eyes." She flipped her white braid across one shoulder. "Better get some rose petals too."

Roses were out of season, and the only time we ever used them was for wedding cakes. Which were also out of season. "You feeling okay? Why'd you drive instead of teleporting?"

"Funny you should ask." Suddenly Gran looked shy, an odd look for her. "I made a doctor's appointment for next week. Was hoping you'd join me for moral support."

A pebble of anxiety formed in my stomach. Gran avoided doctors the way she dodged paying full price. "Sure thing, Gran. We can stop by and chat with Dr. Nguyen—"

"Not that young, fussy Ordinal." She hmmphed. "My appointment's with a magiopath."

"A witch doctor? I thought you didn't trust other people's magic being used on you."

"Desperate times call for desperate measures."

Right. Of course. Her waning magic. It's not like I was in denial, I just had so much stressful stuff on my plate that I was choosing to avoid thinking about it.

I threw myself into prepping the morning's fresh cookies, muffins, and croissants. Gran handled the savory scones and breakfast sandwiches. I talked her ear off, venting about everything from my struggle with teleportation spells to how I was sharing my house with a vampire and now a shifter, too. Gran chuckled and said my life sounded way more exciting than hers. The hours till opening zoomed by, and soon Gran and I were back in our old rhythm, juggling customers and ovens together as if she'd never left.

Around nine a.m., a young mother in yoga pants and a puffer coat stood in line, her infant asleep in a wrap across her chest. "Morning, Hazel."

"Morning, Nevaeh." She was a regular and I started to reach for her usual order, a morning glory muffin and a latte. "How's it going?"

"Great! In fact, my grandma Rose is turning a hundred on Friday. Can you make enough cupcakes for a hundred guests?"

I sighed. "Let me guess. Her favorite color's lavender."

I turned to Gran who looked smug as she assembled a plateful of macarons in a rainbow of shades.

"You can't just order what you're already out of," she explained, in a low voice. "You have to predict what you're going to need next."

"How?" I asked. "We're not clairvoyant."

"No. The kitchen is, though."

What?

"You ask the kitchen to predict its future needs before completing your inventory check. The answers will feel like a tingly itch at the edge of your mind."

I blinked. "I did not see that in the binder you left behind."

"Because it's not the kind of thing that's written into checklists. It's the kind of thing your mentor tells you to do, to give you a leg up."

I sighed. "Gran, let it go."

"I'd love to, but Yolanda can't let it go."

I sighed. I sure loved Gran, but the witch was impossible. "What makes you think hanging out with me would make any difference in that girl's life? I don't even know what I would say to her, how I could possibly help…"

"What I think is that magical kids radiate vulnerability. When a witchling isn't properly guided, she becomes a beacon attracting trouble of every sort."

As if Gran had manifested an illustration of her lecture points, who should walk into the bakery but Yolanda's bestie Amethyst—with her Beige Witch "mentor" Leia.

Leia was dressed like an L.A. fashion plate again, her curled hair and make-up annoyingly immune to the drizzle she'd just emerged from. Amethyst was wearing a pair of brown slouchy boots, and I didn't know if they were borrowed from Leia or a gift from her. They were talking and laughing as they marched up to the front.

"Good morning," I greeted them with my best attempt at cheer.

When Amethyst saw me, her grin turned into a scowl. *What is that about?*

"Two oat milk lattes please," Leia said. "We're having a mentor-mentee coffee date."

"I see that." I turned to Kade, who was already packing a shot into his portafilter. What was up with Amethyst? "Any pastries?"

"Do you have anything gluten free, babe?" Leia asked, cringing. "I hate to be a bother, and I mean I'm guessing not, since it's a small town and—"

"Right there." I pointed her to the GF section.

Small town this, wiznatch.

For the next hour, I watched the two of them out of the corner of my eye as they sipped their oat lattes and dipped gluten-free chocolate almond biscotti into them. What were they chattering on about? Did they really have that much in common? I tried to picture myself and Yolanda in their seats … and realized I couldn't think of three things to say to Yolanda.

Or maybe I just couldn't summon whatever delusional confidence made Leia think she could be a good mentor to Amethyst. Even if they weren't breaking the laws of magic, it was absurd. Right?

"A Beige Witch mentoring a Green Witch portents ill," Gran said darkly as I watched them hang out. "But it's better than nothing."

Ouch.

The sun was setting over the bay as I walked to the bus stop. It was cold as Blixen and I wanted to be home with a cup of tea and blankets as soon as possible. But a nagging unease tugged at me when I approached Purrfect Pancakes.

Much as I dreaded it, it was time I let Yolanda's mother know I wouldn't be available to mentor her daughter. I owed them both that, at least.

I wasn't expecting the diner to be busy around closing time, and it wasn't. The only customer in sight was a red-faced tourist looming over the cash register. Red-faced because he was yelling.

At Yolanda.

"Unacceptable, intolerable!" Banging his hand on the counter.

"My crêpes were so thin I could barely taste them, especially with that loud-flavored fruit filling."

"Crêpes are supposed to be thin, sir." Yolanda was making the mistake of trying to reason with Hate Man. Why wasn't she using a calming spell?

I caught Yolanda's eye and mouthed, *Are you okay?*

She nodded and kept talking. "And we make our own filling from local lingonberries in season, that's why it's so flavorful. If you have a problem with flavor—"

"I haven't even gotten to the biggest issue, young lady, don't you dare interrupt me." He was the one interrupting. "The sugar for my coffee was provided without packets, but in coarse brown lumps," he announced with triumphant horror. "Unsanitary. Archaic. Sugar. Lumps."

"My mom thinks it looks more trendy and upscale that way," Yolanda said patiently. "I'll comp your order, sir, it's no problem."

I had to hand it to her, this teenager handled a bullying customer better than I would have at her age. Maybe she didn't even need a mentor.

As the angry guy flounced out, a familiar grouchy voice announced, "Got it all. I'm posting this to the Bad Customer Wall of Shame."

I looked up to see Amethyst across the room, proudly holding her phone. Had she filmed the entire exchange?

"Good," Yolanda said, and smiled at me. "How can I help you, Hazel?"

"You can keep up the good work, that's how," I said, smiling back. "You're doing amazingly well at managing your life, Yolanda." I took a deep breath. "I'm afraid I can't be your mentor because there's nothing I could add to what you've already got. And I'm rooting for your success."

"Oh, I see. I understand." A weariness overtook Yolanda's voice and I hoped it was just the stress catching up with her, from dealing with the rude man. Not disappointment in me. "Thanks, Hazel."

As I turned to leave, Amethyst withered me with a stare, but that was just normal these days.

I meant what I said. So why, as I walked out of the pancake house after that quick—but far from painless—chat, did I feel the slightest hint of foreboding?

CHAPTER EIGHT

"**HEX MY LIFE!**"

I yanked off my apron in frustration. Instead of cacao, I'd just dumped four cups of cinnamon into the brownie batter.

It was 5:42 a.m. on Friday morning, and the day had already started off bumpier than a toad's butt.

I'd overslept and tripped right over Graham the shifter, who was dozing on my kitchen tiles. At least he'd been in human form when he snarled awake or I might have had a coronary.

Fresh snow flurries clung to my herb lawn; in my rush to catch the bus, I'd slipped on a frosty clump of thyme and snapped my boot heel. It was just me and Frances, the very taciturn driver, on the ride to work, and I spent the whole twelve minutes staring out the window stewing over Britt and Graham.

They were getting along better than expected, which was nice. But how long, exactly, was I supposed to live with the two of them? Hosting a supernatural slumber party in my living room was not sustainable.

I pushed aside the bowl of failed batter and considered curling up for a cat nap in bakery's the corner booth. Too bad Kade was already bustling around the dining room, making himself an espresso shot to start the day.

Resigned, I put the kettle on for tea.

I was about to set my mug of honeyed Earl Grey on the wooden kitchen island when I saw a steaming cup was already waiting.

"Double mocha." Kade appeared in the doorway, looking as sincerely surly as ever. A messy lock of auburn hair was falling over his left ear. "You look like you need the strong stuff today."

Coffee, for me? I stepped back as if from a flame. "Um … you shouldn't have." Tough to say which I hated more: bitter coffee or saying no to a kind gesture. How dare he make me rebuff him? Grouchiness levels rising. "No offense, but I'm a tea girl all the way." I held out the mug to him.

Kade crossed his arms in front of him. "And no offense, but I don't want you to pass out and hit your head on that mixing bowl." He sniffed. "Is that all cinnamon?"

"Don't want to talk about it," I muttered blearily.

"Drink the coffee." He brushed past me and disappeared into the storeroom, leaving me to gape.

At his sudden bossy attitude, I mean. Not his butt.

Maybe that too.

It was well-formed and muscular, as were his thighs.

I averted my eyes guiltily when he returned hefting a hundred-pound sack of coffee beans slung over his shoulder like it weighed nothing. I felt exhausted just looking at him.

Kade raised his scarred left eyebrow. "You haven't tried it yet."

Did shifters have x-ray vision? "How do you know?"

"You're still cranky and exhausted."

"I am not," I snapped, stifling a yawn. "Fine. One sip." I put the mug to my lips … and closed my eyes.

Sweet harmony. Coffee, vanilla, caramelized milk, and chocolate flavors blended like a barbershop quartet. Zero bitterness.

"Did I exceed your low expectations, Boss?" His soulful green eyes met mine and I broke contact fast, feeling too seen.

Did Kade *sense* that I'd had low expectations for him, too, not just the coffee? That seemed uncannily on-the-mark for a dude, especially one whose field of vision was forever partly censored by that sexy lock of hair.

I shrugged off his comment. "Not bad. I might even drink it."

"Just not bad?" He laughed. "You know it's the best there is. I'm a coffee genius."

Damn him. "Fine, you are. Now get out of my kitchen."

Amusement crinkled the corners of his eyes. "I don't have to do what you say, you're not actually my boss."

Man, did I regret telling him I don't technically own Sage's Bakery yet.

The next batch of brownies went smoothly, as did my pecan streusel coffee cake, Scottish oat scones, morning-glory carrot muffins, and twice baked almond croissants drizzled with white chocolate.

At seven a.m., Kade turned the sign around to Open, then saw my empty mug and did a little peacock strut. "Kaboom, Hazel's finally ditching weak tea."

"Wrong, tea and I are endgame." I picked up my neglected Earl Grey and took a performative glug. It tasted as drab as a rain puddle. "Just having an off day," I muttered, setting it down.

"Really? I didn't notice." The teasing left his voice. "Not that it's any of my business but is everything okay? You don't seem quite yourself."

I bit my lip. Maybe it was the caffeine messing with my brain, but for the first time, I felt the urge to spill my guts to Kade. In some ways, he'd be the perfect person to listen to my messy life woes because he'd been there.

But I settled for generalities. "Roommate problems."

"Ugh, the worst." Kade gave me a sympathetic look, then dipped a scoop into the sack of coffee beans and began packing the grinder.

The bakery hit its first morning slam—the line was reaching out the door—and I busied myself handing out warm goodies to the parade of teachers, firefighters, gardeners, nurses, and other morning people who patiently stood in line. Kade's espresso machine purred, and the scents of toasted pecans and brown sugar mingled with coffee in the air. He was surrounded by a contingent of women who seemed to have taken great pains with their outfits, hair, and makeup. Lately the entire female Blue Moon Bay retirement community seemed to be hooked on lattes and cappuccinos.

Before we could recover from the first rush of the day, our door chimes rang again and the entire police department of Blue Moon Bay filed in.

Which wasn't as impressive as that sounds, given that it's only Sheriff Gantry, Deputy Elliot, and two other officers. But they did look more serious than usual. Officer Potts wasn't even playing *Candy Crush* on her phone.

"I need your help, Hazel." Elliot's angular face was grim as he marched up to us. Before I could bask in my infinite smugness at the irony, he continued. "There's a crisis going on in the Green Witch community. Yolanda Hyacinth was kidnapped last night by a vampire."

A few minutes later, I was sitting next to Elliot in his police car, staring at his phone screen.

I'd already watched the grainy ransom video four times, and each time, it just made me more sick to my stomach.

Yolanda sat tied to a chair, still wearing the jeans and purple hand-knit top she had on the previous evening. Her mouth was duct taped shut, and her big brown eyes gazed up helplessly.

A familiar, grating voice intoned, "Greetings and salutations, Mrs. Hyacinth, or should I say Mrs. *Green Witch?*" The camera shifted to reveal the speaker—the horrible red-faced tourist who'd yelled at her irrationally about sugar lumps … only he was fanged out. "Your witchling here tried to escape me with some dumb spell, but her skills weren't up to the task. Pathetic."

She needed a mentor, I wailed inwardly.

"She's as bad at magic as you are at running a restaurant. Wake up, sugar lumps aren't charming, they're unsanitary." He was like a pit bull about that sugar lump thing. Jeez, I'd thought they were pretty cute. "I was walking back to my hotel when I realized it's going to take more than one free nasty coffee and the pleasure of one-starring you on Travel Advisor to make myself feel whole. That's why I decided to come back and take Miss Yolanda here hostage. If you don't give me …. ten thousand dollars … I get a tasty witchling dinner on the house. You have forty-eight hours to pay me in unmarked bills." He rattled off a locker number and combo at Swole Tim's Gym downtown, which would be anonymous and accessible 24/7. "And another thing about sugar—"

"That's enough, his voice makes my teeth itch." Elliot switched off the video. "All right, you said you saw this guy yesterday?"

I nodded, my stomach in knots. "Do you really think he would drain poor Yolanda? And what's with the low ransom number?"

"I don't know." Elliot raked his fingers through his hair, frustration plain on his face. "I can't get any kind of read on this guy."

"It feels like things are spiraling," I said. "First Gerard gets staked and the vampire hunters threaten every newblood. Now a vampire kidnapper? What's happening to Blue Moon Bay, Elliot?"

"I don't know." He clearly hated to admit it. "Listen, before we go in and talk with Jacinta together, I need to know everything you know. When and where did you see him, what was he doing?"

I bit my lip. "He was in Purrfect Pancakes, yelling at Yolanda. She seemed to have everything under control, though. I was impressed by how she handled a difficult customer. I had no clue he was a vampire, let alone that he was capable of kidnapping the poor girl."

If only I'd stayed…

"Hang on, you saw them interact? What time was this?"

"Five-thirty-ish."

Elliot's sharp eyes narrowed. "That's closing time. What were you doing there?"

I shrugged. "Personal business."

He gave me an impatient look. "Aren't we past that?"

"Fine, it was magical business. I needed to tell her mother I wasn't going to be able to mentor Yolanda."

"Why couldn't you mentor her?"

"I'm too busy, okay?" Why was even Elliot getting on my case about it? As if Gran wasn't bad enough. "Also I've never mentored anyone and it seemed intimidating. Obviously I regret my choice now."

Yolanda clearly needed someone to look out for her.

"I shouldn't have asked," he said gruffly. "You didn't cause this evil vampire to kidnap the kid. We just need to figure out what's going on and how to find him. Did he appear threatening?"

"No, just like a loony old coot. Who's finicky about service."

"Well, he probably is that, too. Just, also, lethal and with fangs. On the bright side," he added, "if there is any bright side, ten thousand dollars should be easy for her mother to come up with given how successful that restaurant is."

"Wait, you mean you're going to let her pay it? You're not going to give him fake bills and then have the whole police department ambush him, like on a TV show?"

"One shifter and three Ordinals ambush a vampire?" He snorted. "I don't love our chances."

"The shows I watch haven't explored that scenario." Poor Yolanda. This was a nightmare. My heart was pounding. Maybe coffee was a bad idea, after all.

"I'm letting the rest of the department follow some dead-end leads while I do everything I can to get Yolanda back to her mom. That might mean getting every ex-member of Carnivora to hunt this guy down, it might mean working with the local vamp elders if they'll deign to work with me … or it might mean paying off the kidnapper. I need to be prepared for anything."

"Got it." And I did, suddenly. His job wasn't that of a small-town deputy, but more like a quadruple agent who had to speak many languages and learn many cultures.

"So, will you come with me to talk to Jacinta? I feel like she might be more comfortable with a fellow witch in the room."

Talk to Jacinta when I could have possibly prevented her daughter's kidnapping? Last thing I ever wanted to do. "Of course. I'll let Kade know he's in charge of the cash register."

Jacinta was sitting on the floor in the middle of her office above the restaurant, bawling. Amethyst, still in her work apron, knelt at her side, rubbing her arm. Jacinta's eyes had dark circles. She'd probably stayed up all night worrying and crying.

"My baby," Jacinta wailed. "My baby's been taken by vampires."

"I'm so sorry, Jacinta." The guilt was worming through my guts. "I can't imagine what you're go—"

"Goddamn bloodsucking monsters!" she hissed.

"Ma'am." Elliot fixed her with a stern look. "That's hate speech."

"Yolanda wouldn't want you talking like that," Amethyst added quickly. "Just because the kidnapper happens to be an undead citizen…"

"Undead demon, you mean!" Jacinta growled.

"Oh no, demons are a different thing," I said. "As in, from a different dimension. Trust me, I was engaged to one."

Elliot's eyebrows disappeared under his police cap.

"Let's not get sidetracked," I added quickly. "We should focus on getting Yo back as soon as possible."

"How?" Jacinta threw her hands up helplessly. Yarn-wrapped bangles jangled from her wrists. "You think I have ten thousand lying around? My debts alone—"

"Jacinta!" Amethyst threw her arm protectively around her boss's shoulder. "You don't need to tell us your bank account's life story."

"But, couldn't you just borrow money against your business?" I asked. "Purrfect Pancakes is an institution around here. You inspire all of us witches, you're a—a—"

"Single mother success story?" Jacinta suggested grimly. "The restaurant's humming along okay, but look around you."

Confused, I looked around Jacinta's office. "Well, it's super homey in here. I'm digging the macramé wall hangings." All six of them. "Wow, is that a whole shelf full of découpage photo boxes…?"

"There's no dancing around it, Hazel, I've got a bad crafting habit," Jacinta snapped in a desperate voice I'd never heard from her before. Normally she sounded so prim and proper. Was it all a front? "One that's been sucking the life out of my bank account." She looked down sadly at her chunky, handmade sunset ombré knit top.

"It started off innocently, with tissue paper flowers for one of Yo's birthday parties. Next came the knitting, then macramé, and finally découpage. I'm in too deep now. I've been trying to go to Crafter's Anonymous meetings, and it was working for a while. But then…" With a sigh, Jacinta yanked open the top desk drawer, whipped out a small remote control, and clicked a button. The wall of shelves zigzag-parted in the middle to reveal a hidden room, more like a large walk-in closet. Piled to the brim with paintbrushes, jars of clay, knitting needles, sponge stamps, hot glue guns, popsicle sticks, pipe cleaners, feathers, knitting needles and crochet hooks of all sizes, and a giant pile of yarn in every color.

It was like a sad mini-Michaels in there. The ugly shadow of creative possibility.

"I relapsed." Jacinta hung her head.

Surely it was wrong of me, amid all the tragedy, but a part of me was having trouble stifling a rogue giggle at the craft closet.

Elliot was giving me a pointed look. "Craft addiction is a real and serious issue in Blue Moon Bay," he said, talking straight to me. "All those yarn stores we have are notorious for luring people into dark places. Like this horrifying closet." He slid the door shut with finality, then addressed Jacinta. "I'm sorry for what you and your family have suffered through."

"Jacinta, you're a pillar of the Green Witch community," Amethyst reminded her, sounding more poised and adult than I normally gave her credit for. "I'm sure everyone who goes to the meetings you host would like to contribute money to help Yolanda."

"Shoot, that's absolutely true." I reached for my phone. "I'll set up an online tip jar right now."

Jacinta cheered a bit. "You think people would donate?"

"Of course they would." I typed as fast as I could, then texted Max so she could share it to her blog, which was how things got done here in town. New post notifications went out to half the population of the Bay, so by the end of the day everyone would have read it.

In fact, I could hear the bell-like tones of a push notification on my own phone as well as Jacinta's and Elliot's. Amethyst was a rebel, as usual.

I clicked the link on the notification to donate immediately. Then stared at the screen. "Um … this can't be for real."

"What's up?" Elliot said.

I turned the screen to face them.

Congratulations, your goal has been met!

Within the last thirty seconds, an anonymous donor had already donated the full amount.

"Really?" Jacinta wiped tears from her eyes. "You mean it's all been taken care of? We can pay the ransom?"

"One person gave it all?" Elliot looked to me for confirmation.

I nodded, not wanting to tell him more till we were alone.

"Some of our customers have deep pockets," Amethyst explained to him. "I bet it was one of the guys from Onyx Pact. The drummer and the bass player both go crazy for Purrfect Pancakes."

"They certainly do, bless them!" Jacinta looked a little cheered up.

"We'll be in contact," Elliot promised. "We're going to do everything we can to get Yolanda back to you safety as soon as possible."

"It wasn't Onyx Pact, was it?" Elliot asked me the moment we were back outside. "I know you can see who the donor is, even if they're anon to the public."

I handed him my phone wordlessly.

"The payment was made by a Marina Polonsky." He shrugged. "Name doesn't ring a bell."

"Drew Kensington's assistant," I said. "There's more. She included a note from him below."

"*Not all of us are evil,*" Elliot read. "*Sending my prayers to the witch community, Andrew Kensington.*" He gave me back the phone. "He just outed himself as a vampire." Elliot sounded totally confused. "What possible motivation would he have to do that?"

"I think it's very mature of him, to be honest." The last time I'd seen Drew Kensington, he wasn't even out to his assistant, but sneaking bites from her neck and then using compulsion to make her forget. Hopefully he'd come clean and apologized for that? "Instead of hiding behind his billions, he's risking his safety to advocate for vampires."

Elliot looked decidedly unimpressed. "Or he's an idiot."

I tried again. "Or he's worried about the reputation of vampires in Blue Moon Bay. I mean, who's going to care that they're being hunted if people just think they're a bunch of evil kidnappers? They could use some better PR."

Elliot shook his head. "Vampires aren't like you and me, they take the long view on everything … except survival." He was walking so fast I had to run to keep up, male behavior I normally attributed to jerkiness. But in this case, he seemed unaware his long legs had sped up. He was talking faster too. "Vampires are solitary creatures who stay out of each other's way. Like spiders. Except spiders are way more personable, and delicious."

I rolled my shoulders in disgust, but I didn't want to interrupt his stream of consciousness. For the first time, I felt like I was privy to Elliot's mind's inner workings. The door that always seemed nailed shut was ajar. And I was starting to sense, for the first time, that Elliot did in fact share his kind's wariness about vampires. What other cards did he keep close to his chest?

"Now, the elder council is all made up of vampires over a thousand years old," he went on. "That's often how long it takes for them to seek each other's company. Younger vampires don't often know who else is town *is* a vampire. And they rarely out themselves to humans unless it's a situation of very high trust. Yet suddenly we have vampires coming out of the woodwork to kidnap humans? And other vampires coming out to pay the ransom? That's not how the world works. Not the world I know."

"The world's changing," I said.

"Shifters don't like change," he confided. "Neither do vampires, normally."

I was shocked to hear him admit the two sides had anything in common.

But the biggest surprise was waiting for us at Sage's Bakery. Britt, sitting practically in Graham's lap, was waiting for us at a table loaded with chocolate croissants and an entire pitcher of hot cocoa. How'd she get Kade to give her a pitcher? He was immune to compulsion. Maybe she just asked nicely.

"Drew Kensington's assistant Marina just called me," she said, sounding flabbergasted.

"She says we have to put aside our differences and our fear of being hunted ... for Yolanda's sake. We're *all* invited to a supernatural community meeting at the Kensington house tonight."

CHAPTER NINE

"I JUST DON'T SEE why a witch needs to be at a vampire's meeting," I said nervously to Elliot as we sped away from downtown in the squad car.

"You wanted in on Yolanda's case." The crow shifter's slightly hooded eyes crinkled with amusement. "They won't bite you, Hazel. It's against vampire law to kill a Green Witch. They'll find your presence calming."

"So *that's* why you brought me along?" With so many vampires and shifters packed in one room, he had to keep violence from erupting somehow. It was equal parts reassuring and insulting. Peak Elliot. "You're using me as a human tranq. Or peace sign."

"No…" He feigned being affronted, then his smirk won out. "Maybe a cute little white dove, clutching an olive branch in your beak."

"Ha ha, thanks." I made a show of rolling my eyes at him, then looked out my window at the winding hills. Not all my stomach butterflies were about the meeting at Drew Kensington's mansion, or the twisty turns of Blue Moon Heights Road.

No, for the first time since we slow-danced together ten years ago, I was close enough to smell Elliot's buzzed black hair, his peppery shampoo. His skin had an earthy wood and amber scent that was objectively irresistible. Despite the circumstances, sharing a car with a man this hot was distracting the hex of out me. Almost felt like we were on a date…

"Can't you put on the flashy lights and go faster?" piped up a grouchy voice from the backseat. "I don't want to be late to a meeting that's about rescuing my best friend."

Oops, I'd almost forgotten about Amethyst sitting in the back.

She'd begged Elliot for a chance to help with the rescue effort, so he let her take Jacinta's place tonight at the meeting. Understandably, Yolanda's mom was too broken up and panicked to leave her house.

It was probably the first time she'd ever passed on a community event.

"Trust me, this thing's not starting at seven," Elliot assured her in his usual gruff tone. "My people are genetically incapable of showing up on time, and vampires hate repeating themselves. Being late's the one thing you *don't* need to stress about."

In the mirror, I watched Amethyst's eyes widen in disbelief as she took in this classic Elliot pep talk. Dry, informative, grim as hell. She fixed him with a sultry, rebellious bad-girl stare, and looked deflated when he didn't even notice.

After a few moments, Amethyst flipped her teal hair and muttered a spell. At once, two shimmering, ethereal scalloped shells cupped her ears. Magical headphones. Each of us lost in our own thoughts, we wound our way through the hills to the police radio's soundtrack of static and cryptic murmuring.

Not for the first time, I wondered what possessed a guy like Elliot to sign up for a law enforcement career. In high school he'd been a slacker, quiet but eerily intense. Skulking in the back row when he bothered with class. Hanging with delinquents like Kade de Klaw. His silent nonconformity and good looks meant he starred in half the scandalous rumors that went viral in the gossip cesspool of Blue Moon High.

But those rumors had to have been false. He was probably never a drug dealer, or an assassin, or an international jewel thief. As far as I knew, Elliot had never been in trouble with the law. Still, what motivated him to put on a uniform every morning and *be* the law?

I was dying to know, yet I held my tongue. Of all the intel the crow hoarded, he was tightest-lipped when it came to himself.

The gate was wide open when we pulled up to the sprawling Kensington's property. Ten acres or so landscaped to look like a Northwest forest in miniature, clipped and curated, a deer-filled pocket paradise of cedar, Western Hemlock, and Sitka spruce.

If he was welcoming every shifter and vampire in town, Drew must have figured, there was little point in keeping up security.

Elliot parked in the roundabout, directly in front of the modern Pacific-Northwest-style mansion with its light-filled window walls and rooftop gardens. Amethyst unbuckled her seatbelt early. The car emitted a scolding beep and she cursed a blue streak at it.

A stunning, androgynous housekeeper clad in sleek black scrubs let us into the grandest of foyers, featuring twin koi ponds bridged with vertigo-inducing glass floor panels down the room's center, offering a look into the huge subterranean pool and ballroom below. Fortunately, neither was being used at the moment, or that glass would be my skirt's worst nightmare. Water burbled through fountain pumps and drummed, forceful yet serene, from the massive waterfalls built into white marble caverns sculpted to evoke the caves of Patagonia. This ostentatious entryway was brand new and had to be the work of that Beige Witch Leia.

Okay, fine, it was cool. Really cool.

While the housekeeper, who sported a kaleidoscope of butterfly tattoos on their wrists, led us across the glass gauntlet to the front hall. Amethyst kept stealing dazed looks at the expensive-looking, fat, orange and white fish. Judging from the large SUV she drove, her Ordinal family wasn't poor, but Kensington opulence was its own universe.

I was surprised when Butterfly Wrists ushered us into a salon decorated in the signature 1980s *Dynasty*-era style Estelle Kensington was known for. Apparently, Beige Witch Leia hadn't gotten around to updating this room yet. Voluminous dusty rose drapes still hung from the enormous bay window. Bold, red-and-gold paisley sofas lined the window wall, with oversized gold-striped beige cushions covering the floor in front of them.

Elliot was dead right about the meeting not starting on time. Drew was nowhere to be seen yet. Supernaturals were still filing in, one by one or in small groups. They either gravitated to the floor cushions or to standing by the shorter wall.

Elliot perched on a sofa and I sat on the opposite end of it, wanting and not wanting to be distracted by his closeness.

Amethyst slumped onto an oversized floor cushion, where to my surprise the scruffy waiter at the Drunken Barrel was lounging in a puppy pile with the raven-haired rockabilly chick who womaned the cash register at Wagmore Pet Supply ... and a whole crew of sullen looking types in ripped jeans and leather jackets. I felt gut-punched at the sight of a familiar square face, and an equally familiar head of bright green hair.

Bad enough that the two bakery robbers had made some kind of deal with Elliot to get themselves out of jail. What were they doing here, at Drew's meeting? They *hated* vampires.

Elliot's face tightened almost imperceptibly. Carnivora's presence had caught him off guard too.

At this rate, it would take more than my oh-so-calming presence to prevent bloodshed.

Especially since Carnivora didn't exactly love me.

I waved to Max who was straggling in with Kade, both

clutching coffee cups, and settled on a couch together. Britt—who I'd finally given a housekey to—arrived with Graham, wearing identical looks of resignation. They peeled off in opposite directions instantly, Graham curling up on a floor cushion while Britt leaned against the far wall scrolling her phone.

"It's gonna be okay, Am." I looked up to see the young, curly-haired robber comforting Amethyst. "We're gonna get Yo back."

Amethyst looked down. "Thanks, Jasper."

Those two seemed to know each other well. Could they be classmates? When I was in college, I'd had no idea who the local shifters were. I didn't even know about Kade and Max; it was something you didn't talk about.

But times were changing.

"I promise you we'll get your friend back." The square-faced robber spoke up, his voice low and chillingly familiar. "We'll end that bloodsucker. Send a message to the others."

An angry murmur went through the room and Elliot's brows shot up. Things were off to a stellar start.

"I appreciate you, Torrin," Amethyst addressed the green-haired robber. So, she knew him too. "But I'd also appreciate you using more respectful language. And not lumping all vampires in with the kidnapper."

My jaw dropped. Did she just tell the shifter gang leader to watch his language? Laughter and boos exploded from the floor cushion section, but the solo wallflowers clapped.

Must be the vampires; I didn't recognize the other four besides Britt.

Torrin snarled. "Whose side are you on, witch?"

The temperature in the room had plummeted to Antarctic levels. He'd stopped just short of calling her a traitor—maybe he was willing to give her the benefit of the doubt since they knew each other. (How?) Still, Amethyst gazed back at him, resolute. Her bravery thrilled me—and filled me with terror. Were we going to have to get a Graham to guard her, too?

I felt a tingle in my scalp and remembered one of my Green Witch vows.

I shall not let down a sister in need.

"Amethyst isn't your enemy," I said to Torrin, hoping my voice didn't shake. "Don't try to bully her. She's just trying to do what's right."

"Shut up, vamp lover."

At his hate filled dismissal of me, the room buzzed with discordant anger.

But even as Torrin's sneer chilled my bones, I couldn't help but feel he was laying it on a bit thick. *Vamp lover?* That same feeling I'd had at the bakery came up: was this a performance? Or was Torrin's hatred that over the top?

"Leave both the Green Witches alone." Elliot was on his feet, addressing Torrin in a tight growl I'd never heard before. "They're not part of our war."

Our war? Was he referring to the historical tensions between vamps and shifters, or did Elliot have a personal stake in this?

Stake was a poor choice of words.

"Not part of the war, right." Torrin's face twisted with contempt. His words dripped out slow and soft, full of insinuation. "Everyone's a civilian these days, huh, *Deputy*?"

The hex was that about?

Elliot wasn't going to let the gang leader bait him like that, was he?

"Leave the Green Witches alone," Elliot repeated, ignoring Torrin's attempt to rattle him.

"Or what, you gonna peck my eyes out?" Torrin sounded bored.

Elliot shrugged. "If that's what it takes."

The two shifters stood glare to glare. You could have heard a credit card drop as the room waited to see who would blink first.

Yep, we two Green Witches were doing a bang-up job with that peacekeeping mission … sarcasm.

Luckily, before Elliot threw down—with a fellow shifter, no less—Drew's assistant Marina clacked into the room in a grey pantsuit with matching heels. She began passing out leather folios equipped with ruled notepads and roller pens. All Kensington Industries branded, with the company's new triangle logo … or was it a fang?

Not even the shifters could help but be impressed by the top shelf corporate swag. Several Carnivora folks held the leather to their noses to sniff deeply and made sounds of animal pleasure.

Then a cool breeze floated through the room and Drew Kensington's imposing figure filled the doorway, wearing jeans and a black sweater that looked like they'd cost thousands. The billionaire was sculpted like a work of art, with the prettiest pecs and straightest teeth money could buy. Drew, who'd been a vampire for less than a year, was given to exuberance and flowery language, but tonight his gorgeous face looked somber.

Moving as a finely honed machine, the two of them hefted the octagonal ornately carved coffee table and moved it to the front of the room where Drew hopped on top of it and sat cross-legged, as if were his own patch of floor.

"Welcome, friends." He flashed a perfect, fanged smile at our motley group. "I want to thank you for joining us, despite it being the dinner hour. And despite the ancient supernatural war between our two kinds."

Weak applause from the new vampires. Stony glares from the Carnivora gang.

Torrin snapped, "We're only here for the money!"

What money? I turned to Elliot. His expression was blank, but a flash of anger in his dark eyes told me he'd been caught off guard again.

"I hear you, fellow obligate carnivores." Drew didn't look the slightest bit flustered. "Rest assured, the juicy rumors are true. Tonight we're here to pair up capable shifter muscle with local newbloods. Protection from the vampire hunters … for cash. Everyone wins."

I blinked. It was like a paid, organized version of what we set up with Graham and Britt.

Wait. Torrin was about to let his crew accept money to protect the thing they hated most, vampires?

Was *that* why he was going above and beyond to make it clear he hated them?

"Not everyone wins," Elliot spoke up, not bothering to hide his irritation. "What about Yolanda Hyacinth, the kidnapped witch? We're supposed to be putting together a rescue effort, with ransom."

"And I'll be sure to get that agenda item, as well, Deputy." Drew flashed a 1000-watt smile but Elliot met his eyes without intimidation.

Shifters—immune to compulsion.

"I'll make sure you do."

Drew's smile lost approximately 250 watts, but he recovered and nodded to the woman on his right. "Sheryl, would you like to speak for the elder council?"

All eyes turned to turned to the pudgy, middle-aged, white woman standing in the northeast corner of the room. An *elder vampire*. My blood ran cold at the thought. This school lunch lady type had been drinking human blood since before Columbus sailed the ocean blue. She could probably kill all of us without working up a sweat.

"The council just held an emergency Zoom call," she said in a musical mélange of a voice. She sounded like she'd gained and lost a dozen accents in her time. Some perhaps no longer existed on Earth. Ordinal linguists would have a field day studying her. "We discussed the possibility of providing an escort detail of one of our members to accompany the Vigile—I mean, Deputy Elliot—to the ransom exchange."

Vigile? I'd have to ask Elliot what that meant.

"A security detail of one single vampire?" asked a leather-clad shifter. "Damn, you old corpses are stingy."

Sheryl fixed him with an otherworldly smile as if she couldn't decide whether to admire the young shifter's cheek or bite it off.

"Not just any vampire," she corrected. "One elder can easily put down a nobody like this kidnapper."

"How can you be so sure he's a nobody?" Elliot said. Good point. "Did you run his image through your digital scrolls?"

"Of course. Nothing came up. He is just some unregistered newblood. Trash."

She said it with such derision that I made a note to ask Britt how newbloods went about registering themselves as vampires. I'd had no idea it was so important.

Horror of horrors, Sheryl turned to me. "I assure you, honored *magicka,* he is an aberration who flouts one of our most sacred laws. He'll pay for threatening a Green Witch."

Cool, they really did take that rule seriously, I thought, though I was careful not to meet the elder's eyes directly.

"Good talk, Sheryl." Drew clapped his hands, though he was the only one doing it. "Key learnings: we vampires live by our mission statement, and we add value to Blue Moon Bay."

Several Carnivora members jeered, and Torrin called out angrily, "You lie, bloodsuckers! Vamps killed my brother."

Elliot's eyes narrowed. I suspected he was making a note to ask about this brother. In case it was true, which I very much doubted given the speaker.

When Marina cracked open a buttery leather briefcase full of cash, though, they all shut up.

Drew smiled, showing fangs. "Deputy Elliot, do I have your approval to move on to the next item on our agenda? The part where I pay these fine furry folks their cash?"

Elliot nodded his satisfaction and told terrifying Sheryl that he'd be in touch to coordinate.

One by one, reading from a list, Marina matched up newbloods with a shifter bodyguard. The pairs were asked to stand together, which lead to a lot of flared nostrils and pointed sniffing.

"Brittany Salazar," Marina called in her Russian accented English. "Your bodyguard will be Torrin Mongusta of the Meerkat clan."

Britt's gaze jerked away from her phone screen as the leader of Carnivora leered up at her. "Looks like you're mine, bloodsucker."

"Naw, I got this one assigned to me already." Graham sounded bored and disaffected as ever, but Torrin took a step back. Maybe he knew Graham could shift into an enormous grizzly. "I foolishly agreed to do it as a favor to a friend." He glared at Max—who shrugged—then turned to Drew. "Since you're handing out Benjamins like candy though…"

"My good man, consider yourself paid!" Drew clapped, and Marina tossed a tied stack of hundreds to Graham. Was that why he'd spoken up for Britt, to get his cash? Or did he genuinely care enough—now that they'd spent time together—to want to keep protecting her even when someone else was available.

If Britt was relieved or grateful to Graham, she didn't show it. Went back to playing *Candy Crush* or whatever she was up to on her phone.

Max and Kade weren't paired with anyone, I noticed. Drew had made this deal with Carnivora members only. He wasn't just trying to broker a peace deal, I realized. He was trying to buy peace outright. Would it work, or backfire in all our faces?

"That's only the first ten percent, my friends," Drew promised. "You'll get paid the rest when the vampires hunters are caught and Yolanda's brought home safe."

The shifters murmured with excitement, and I hoped the prospect of more cash would be enough to keep them from simply staking their charges.

"Excuse me." The softly terrifying voice of Sheryl interrupted my thoughts. "Am I to understand that the weak young vampires present tonight will be joined by brawny shifters? In that case, I withdraw my previous offer of a council member for security. The whole group of you together would surely best him."

Drew looked the closest to dismayed that I'd ever seen him. That is, he looked mildly nonplussed. "Interesting how you reswizzled the deal, Sheryl! Could I change your mind? Is there maybe a cause dear to your blood that I could donate to in your name…?"

"Oh, that's adorable." She laughed and smoothed her wrinkled white T-shirt. There was a small hole in the belly. "To think you could buy me off like these common animals. Oh, Drew! Should you make it there, I'll toast to your century day." Still giggling, she sped out of the room, appearing as a blur to my eyes.

The moment the door slammed behind her, Britt pocketed her phone and looked up. Had she only been waiting for Sheryl to leave?

Drew turned to face Elliot's glower.

"Batting a thousand with that compulsion tonight, huh?"

"The art of negotiation is subtle," Drew said smoothly. "I'll reach out to her people tomorrow, following all the proper protocols."

"You do that."

Drew looked to Marina for relief. "Any other agenda items?"

She shook her head. "We now open discussion to the group."

Britt raised her hand. "We need more bodyguards," she said in a no-nonsense voice. "The newbloods at Marie Pierre's house are defenseless."

"In *whose* house?" Drew looked confused as Marina went over her list, flipping the paper over for good measure.

Britt explained. "There are half a dozen girls at Gerard Chevalier's ... my old sire who was killed by the vampire hunters, *in that same house*. They've been taught nothing, they have no one to look after them except a valet. They're sitting ducks in there." Britt's voice broke, and I suddenly felt bad for getting so angry that she'd cavalierly signed me up to ward Marie's house. She was legit worried about those girls. Probably saw herself in them. And she was right, they were all sitting ducks.

I looked up just in time to see an odd look on Torrin's face.

"You think some old school valet's going to let a shifter in the house?" Torrin said bitterly.

I hated to admit it, but my robber had a point.

"Hey, Britt, don't forget there's another way to protect the girls at Marie's," Max piped up. "Wasn't Hazel going to ward the property?"

All eyes followed her gaze. To me. My cheeks felt hot with anger.

It was time to speak up for myself. For witches' rights. "No. No, I don't do warding."

"But why not, Hazel?" Britt's adorable small forehead wrinkled, like she found me more frustrating than one of those tricky new compostable produce bags at the co-op.

The whole room seemed to be awaiting my answer. Even Elliot appeared gobsmacked by my resistance, his dark stare trained on me like I was some fresh enigma he couldn't wait to solve at any cost. He was, in other words, no help.

Gulping, I turned to appeal to Amethyst, the only other witch in the room. But she was first-gen and didn't know our customs.

"Hazel, why don't you want to help those young girls?" She tilted her head in suspicion, and I just knew she was mentally accusing me of anti-vampire prejudice.

Even as her buddy Jasper denounced me as a vamp-loving traitress.

For crêpes sake, a witch couldn't win in this town.

"I—I said I don't do warding spells," I stammered. "Only desperate witches do that kind of soul sucking work. I mean, it's not *literally* soul sucking," I added at their expressions of horror. "At least I assume not." I'd never known anyone who would admit to having done it.

"What exactly is so terrible about warding work?" Graham asked, not unkindly. "Is it painful, hard, disgusting, humiliating? Or just boring."

"I don't want to get into it." I was bad at explaining things, especially things I didn't understand. But was it my fault no one ever told me *why* warding was bad? It was one of those things the Green Witch community never talked about, but everyone agreed you just didn't do it. "Trust me," I said, "it's unnatural and exhausting and no one should have to do it."

"I'm a middle school vice principal," said an older female vampire, to collective oofs. "Just saying."

"Vet tech," offered a shifter. "I do surgeries at the animal hospital in Astoria."

"I work *four* jobs," announced the bar waiter, who come to think of it had also been the valet at Drew's wedding. "You think any of them are a blast?"

"You think robbing people's fun?" demanded Torrin. "Actually, it is. It is fun." His friend high-fived him and I seethed silently, thinking of Gran's bakery defiled. "But I'm also a hospital orderly, changing bedpans and whatnot," he added, frowning. "So, I got no sympathy, witch."

I was feeling good and defensive now. "Warding sucks more than *all* y'all's non-magical jobs, okay?" I snapped, though I had no idea if that were true. Because again, I had no idea, period. My mentors had thrown me to the wolves on this. "Why do you think witches charge ten thousand a gig to ward?"

At the mention of money, Drew brightened considerably. "We have a saying here at Kensington Industries," he announced. "Appreciation cures frustration. To honor your hard work, Hazel, I'm going to pay you twice that going rate."

I gulped as Marina began counting it out. She wrapped a squeaky rubber band around the thick stack of twenties.

"Every witch has her price," Marie Pierre had said.

What was my price for one stupid little warding gig? The task needed to be done. It was for the greater good. Twenty K would buy a brand-new Viking range for the bakery.

All these vampires and shifters were staring at me.

I held out my hands to catch the money stack sailing toward me. But my breathless self-justifying paused when I remembered the pesky fact that I didn't know any warding spells. Or even anyone who did.

Now what?

Elliot folded his arms and shook his head slightly. Had I disappointed him by accepting the cash?

If so, he was the only one.

"Look at you, nice hustle!" Britt gave me a look of surprised admiration. "You really were playing cutthroat for the higher fee. And now you can invest in a comfier futon for your living room.

Guests will appreciate it," she added with a wink that would have been adorable if I wasn't so mad at her.

Britt had no idea what a mess she'd gotten me into. Neither had Max when she brought it up tonight. I wanted to yell at them. I wanted to pause the world and reflect on why in the steaming cinnamon buns of hex I'd never told my friends the truth. That warding was a heavy, shameful, taboo topic among witches … okay, that was why. I avoided heavy topics like I avoided kale.

Sadly, I didn't know a spell to pause the world and every pair of eyes in the salon was fixed on me. Suspicious shifter eyes. Pleading vampire eyes. Elliot's penetrating gaze was the worst. I knew he'd be interrogating me about this later.

But I had to do something before I burned up under the fire of all those glares.

Blushing hot, I stuffed the money in my purse. Still wasn't sure what I'd do with it.

"Another community problem solved … by supernatural synergy," Drew intoned. "Coined. Supernatural synergy. Marina, take a note on trademarking that."

She scribbled with an e-pen onto her tablet.

Elliot's face was blank, his hands folded in his lap, but I knew him well enough to know what he'd thought of Drew's idea of synergy. I looked around the room at the shifter and vampire pairings and saw pointed air-sniffing and looks of revulsion.

How long till this temporary peace blew up, and then what would become of Yolanda, and the newbloods in this room?

And unless I went against every fiber in my being and warded Marie Pierre's house, what would become of those innocent young girls?

CHAPTER TEN

NIGHT WAS FALLING over Ocean Street as I hurried along the sidewalk beside the sandy beach, dotted with chowder stands and ice cream shops. A herd of striped surreys rested under a rental shop's awning. Two beach firepits were ringed with local high schoolers gamely roasting smores and sipping hot cocoa from thermoses—spiked with whisky, no doubt, unless things had changed drastically since I was one of them a decade ago.

Ocean Street was the Bay's lifeblood, a lavishly maintained thoroughfare where retro streetlamps softly glowed, and oak trees glittered with fairy lights year-round, the backdrop for a billion vacation memories. But only a few blocks to the east, the charm faded fast.

Side streets devolved to cobble stone pathways too narrow and snakelike for a car to pass, poorly lit and bordering on sketchy. That's where I was headed tonight.

Rather than interrogating me on the car ride back, Elliot barely said a word. Maybe because Amethyst was in backseat chattering a blue streak about how this controversial warding thing seemed sooo lucrative. That her new plan, which she was going to run by her cool mentor Leia tomorrow, was to drop out, become a pro warding specialist, and only work five days a year. I'd glanced up to see Elliot's probing gaze searching my face; he'd stopped the car in front of my house. The squad car lingered with the lights on until I was safe inside, which made sense given that my purse bulged with a $20,000, mob-wife cash stack.

I'd watched from the window till he drove off before I jumped back out, crossed Filbert Street to the bus stop, and hopped the last bus downtown.

I stumbled over a chipped cobble stone as I wound my way up a moonlit spiral path that barely passed as an alley. For the third time, I whirled around, paranoid that someone might be behind me. Getting mugged wasn't what I was worried about. No, what scared me was the thought that someone I knew might see me performing the most dubious of errands.

I scanned the storefronts, grateful for the tacky neon lights that went against the Bay's grain. A sign for Lara's Lingerie made me duck, out of sight of the vitrine. Lara was a Beige Witch who came to Mother's holiday bashes and flung around discount coupons for her magical corsets. They whittled an apple shape to an hourglass but felt as comfy as sweatpants. Using such a product went against my Green Witch vows, but on top of it all, Lara was a major gossip. If she spotted me out here, I'd soon be drowning in concerned texts from my sister Bea.

I hurried down the next block, where iffy establishments closed in around me. I tried not to gag at the smell of smoke and burning grass, telltale scents of Grey Magic.

Finally, in-between Hexxed Vixxen Videoz and Potemkin's Home Staging, I found what I was looking for.

Git-Er-Done Gigging.

I pushed the heavy glass door.

"Good evening." A silken-voiced woman glanced up from her tablet at a desk whose dark wood was so polished it showed her reflection. She wore a navy blazer and a strand of pearls, black hair in a bun. "How can I help you Git-Er-Done?"

"Well, first of all, I'm not exactly the client," I said, noting her slight British accent.

"Ooh, a new Green Witch." Fiona, according to her name card, looked me over like a steak. Her looks suggested Beige Witch, but I could pick up a faint burning grass scent from across the desk. So, Fiona was a Grey Witch. Made sense, given her profession—running a magical temp services operation that preyed on witches down on their luck.

"Don't worry, sweetie," she simpered. "Loads of gigs opening up if you need to make a little extra for the holidays. You big-hearted Green Witches are always giving too much, and, well, going broke. Bless your hearts."

"Oh, no. I'm not looking for a gig for *me*." Too late, I hoped my tone didn't convey my full horror and disgust. "I have a referral. For a warding job." I pushed the card with Marie's contact info across the desk. Since the desk had zero friction it flew and landed in her lap. "Sorry."

To my surprise, she picked it up and pushed it right back at me. "I've talked to this bonkers bird already. She's got no money, tried to haggle me down to 1950s prices." She made the crazy sign with her finger twirling around her ear.

I tried not to show how taken aback I was. How could Marie Pierre be broke, when she lived in a beautiful house and employed a maid. Perhaps Gerard's will hadn't been read yet? Surely even that spectacular screwup wouldn't leave her penniless, after centuries of loyal service.

"She's not the one paying for it, I am." I flung the card back. "I'll give you double the standard rate to have Marie's house warded properly."

Her jet-black brows arched up. "Double?"

I yanked open the magnetic closure on my purse, pulled out the stack, and plonked it on her desk. "Cash."

"Right. I'll have a gig witch out there in no time." She picked up the money pile with hushed reverence. I swear I thought she might have to fan herself with it. She flipped her tablet screen to face me. "Let's have you fill out a client profile."

I held my arms in front of me. "No thanks, not necessary."

"Miss, I need to be able to reach out to you when the gig is complete." She looked scandalized, like I was the amoral one. "All I need's your name and contact info. It takes seconds."

"It's not about the time." I didn't want any record of this transaction. And I sure didn't want my name in her nasty little files.

"Then, what, are you just too lazy to fill it out?" Fiona taunted as I turned to walk away. "You Green Witches are all insane, I swear…"

Eager to leave her stinky presence, I threw open the door and marched out.

And crashed head on into someone standing on the sidewalk just outside.

A woman in a dark cloak and hood. Cinnamon-red dyed hair framed her face as she blinked up at me in open-mouthed surprise. "Hazel?"

"Jacinta." I stared back at her, face burning as my brain processed the jackpot of awkwardness I'd hit.

Caught red-handed, exiting a shoddy establishment that exploited witches. By my community leader … whose child was just kidnapped.

Jacinta's eyes looked red from crying, but she was calm and composed now. In fact, she looked pretty much like she always looked, but I wasn't fooled. I knew how much Jacinta loved Yolanda. They'd always been close, a complete family and of themselves.

I remembered the first day I met them both, the same day

I spoke my vows and officially became a Green Witch. Jacinta was a hardworking young widow who'd poured her heart and all her savings into opening a diner. Yolanda was her little girl eagerly serving coffee, gripping the carafe with both her small hands. Always at her mom's side. Tears filled my eyes.

"I am so very sorry for what you're going through," I stammered. "We're going to do everything possible to get Yo home safe … and…"

I stopped, aware that she was looking more uncomfortable with every word out of my mouth. Shut up, Hazel. The woman said she was too fragile to even leave her house.

What was she doing *here* then?

Oh no…

"Thank you, Hazel," she said finally, her face as red as my own. "Er, goodnight."

Of course, she wanted me to go. So she could do what she had to.

"Goodnight, Jacinta."

I turned and walked back down the cobblestone road, so the leader of the Green Witches wouldn't see me see her walk into Git-Er-Done Giggings, to pay off her sad debt to Crafters Cave.

It took me an hour to trudge home. By the time I reached Filbert Street, the harvest moon shone high in the sky. My arches ached in my boots. And I'd had plenty of quiet time to curse my remedial skill level in stupid, *stupid* teleportation.

Too tired to hike all the way to the stone garden path, I walked across my lawn, kicking up an herby scent of creeping time with every step.

The ominous sight of a pale envelope taped to my front door only made me groan in irritation.

I tore it open just to confirm it was what I thought. Yep, the by-now-familiar typed screeds of the Vampire Hunting Society greeted me: blah blah traitor, we know you're sheltering fangs, we'll get to you right after we rescue the kidnapped witch and execute her captor … all it did was make me roll my eyes. Maybe it was my recent foray into the sketchy part of town, but at this point the slayers' schtick was getting old. Were these people total amateurs, expecting me to be quaking in my granny boots at the same insults and threats when I had bigger fish to fry? Like an actual, fanged kidnapper?

Okay, so it *was* kind of a new twist that they'd come to my home. At night. Letting me know they knew where I lived.

But, whatever, they were gone now. My porch swing's eerie rocking was just the wind.

A rustling in the filbert hedge behind me made my heart skip. I whirled around and thought I saw something—an animal?—dart between the thickly planted trees, but it zipped out of sight.

The hairs on my neck were standing up. As I stood on my porch on the verge of an anxiety attack, I caught a whiff of some dark, primitive scent in the night air.

Musky and wild. The smell of pure malevolence.

That's when I heard hysterical shrieks coming from inside my house.

Pulse hammering in my ears, I plucked an Invisi-mint out of my purse, unwrapped, chewed, swallowed, waved my hand in front of my face to make sure it wasn't a dud. And steeled myself to enter a possible crime scene.

My dim entryway looked normal enough, and the wild scent

was fading from my nostrils. Then another round of shrieking pierced the air, coming from the living room.

I grabbed the ceremonial antique broomstick off its hook and ran down the hall, silently wishing I'd thought to grab it *before* going invisible. Hopefully a floating broomstick would be terrifying to whatever evil creature was menacing Britt.

There, on my rug in front of the couch, was sprawled a preternaturally huge bear with thick golden-brown fur. The grizzly, unlike a typical wild animal, seemed fully engrossed in whatever show was playing on the screen of Britt's tablet and would bellow occasionally as if in reaction to onscreen antics. Britt, meanwhile, was laughing like a banshee at the same show, her fangs plainly showing, her satin-PJ-clad back resting against his fur. In between peals of crazy laughter, she reached into an open Costco flat of blueberries resting on my coffee table, grabbed a handful, and tossed them one by one into his waiting maw.

At the sight of those saw-like teeth, I groaned. "Oh, it's just you two idiots."

And instantly I turned visible.

Britt spun to face me, looking more annoyed than embarrassed. A naked Graham was now in place of the bear, looking equally teed off. And with killer abs, I must say. Britt tossed him my cream chenille couch blanket. I made a mental note to dry-clean that thing—and send the bill to him.

"If I may ask, what the unholy hex is happening in my living room?"

"Relax, Hazel." Britt snapped the plastic flat of blueberries shut. "We didn't see you after Drew's meeting, so we assumed you'd gone to bed even earlier than usual."

"We texted you to see if you wanted to debrief after the

meeting," Graham said quietly. "You didn't reply. We assumed you were asleep."

"I told him about how you never go out to do fun things," Britt added helpfully. "And you don't have a boyfriend and we're like your only friends."

"I have other friends," I said automatically. "The garden store girls, Gran … other people…" I trailed off.

Listing my grandmother as a friend made Britt's case for her. I couldn't muster the necessary indignation to argue any further. Instead what I felt, worming through my guts, was guilt. Not because I'd missed their texts, but because they saw me as so innocent. Sheltered and sweet. Everyone did.

What would they think of me if they knew I'd been out doing shady deals in the skeezy part of downtown, pawned my warding gig off on some poor witch too desperate for cash to say no?

I wasn't sure what *I* thought of me.

Before I could spiral into self-recrimination, I remembered the creepy note in my pocket.

"Welp, so much for all your super senses." I pitched the note onto the coffee table. Which, I couldn't help but notice, had some animal drool on it. "You two were so busy flirting, you didn't notice someone left this."

At the mere sight of the typed page, Britt hissed and massaged her temples.

Graham snatched it off the table and instead of reading it, sniffed the paper like a bloodhound.

"What are you picking up?" I asked, eager for clues.

"Hmm." He sniffed again, deeply. "I'm getting … mostly … paper."

Britt snorted and shoved the page under her own nose, then

held it away from her like a dirty diaper. "Paper, are you kidding me? Try testosterone and gamey shifter sweat."

"So, like me?" Graham suggested, giving her a teasing look.

"Way worse, babe. Like you on steroids."

"So that could be half the members of Carnivora," I said, totally noticing she'd called him babe.

"Does it matter who delivered it?" Britt said. "Torrin's the gang leader, he must have ordered them to. He's responsible."

"Unless he's got a rebellion on his hands," Graham said, frowning. "Or paws."

"I'll take it to Elliot in the morning," I said, feeling twice as exhausted now that the adrenaline had worn off.

I bagged the letter, in hopes of preserving the scent, and plopped down on the couch to shuck my boots.

In the bathroom, I brushed my teeth and changed into my "Eat Sleep Cupcakes Repeat" nightshirt. Then I headed up the loft steps for bed, calling over my shoulder, "You can get back to your … whatever."

Unfortunately, they did.

The lack of a wall meant I'd barely slipped on my fluffy, cloud-shaped eye mask before their voices began to drive me nuts.

"That meeting was depressing," Britt said with a sigh. "Why don't vampires take better care of their childer? We newbloods are left defenseless, especially if…" She trailed off. "Especially some of us."

Odd. What had she been about to say, before she thought better of it?

"I think it's 'cause vampires suck," Graham replied, and then added, "*Ow!*" I'm pretty sure she'd punched his arm.

"I suppose shifters all look out for each other?" Britt sulked. "Like one big happy zoo family?"

"No, it ain't perfect on my side," Graham admitted. "But our mom taught me and my brother what it meant to be a bear. Her parents taught her. Their parents taught them. We raise up the next generation of cubs with as much wisdom, strength, and love as we can before we send them out into the world."

"Love, ha." Britt sounded wistful. "I'd have settled for an orientation packet with a wallet card tip sheet. Gerard taught me nothing. He didn't *want* me to survive without him."

"That undead ass." Graham swore. "You deserved better, Britt."

Agreed. And now go to bed, both of you. Please.

She was silent for a minute, giving me hope.

Then she said, "I'm starting to think he's not alone. Listening to Sheryl from the council tonight, old vampires expect most of us newbies to get picked off."

"A weeding out process." Graham's voice was thoughtful. "Where only the most ruthless sociopaths survive."

"I wouldn't go *that* far," she said.

"Please," he scoffed. "We're talking about freakin' vampires. The unbridled id of late-stage capitalism."

"You know what? I liked you better furry. And nonverbal."

"Grr, roar," he deadpanned.

She giggled. "Want me to toss more blueberries in your mouth?"

"That *was* more fun than it had any right to be," he said grudgingly. "Which describes every minute I've spent with you."

"I could say the same of you, grizzly."

Well, hex it all. Amethyst was going to have to teach me her stupid headphone spell. Because no way was I going to lie here every night listening to these two flirt.

Had they forgotten about that whole eternal war thing, for toad's sake?

Or the lack of walls in my house?

Most importantly, had Britt forgotten he was Max's ex?

"Graham." Britt's voice was suspiciously husky. "Would you maul me if I kissed you right now?"

My eyes flew open inside my sleep mask. Not that there was anything to see up here in my loft bed and hopefully there wouldn't be downstairs either. Graham would give a hearty laugh at her *ridiculous* suggestion, and they'd cue up more *Golden Girls* ... right?

Instead, he growled, "Come here, undead girl."

I heard a sharp intake of breath, a low moan, and then I swear on a stack of Gran's chocolate chip cookies, *the vampire and the shifter were kissing passionately.*

If those hunters didn't break in soon and put me out of my misery, it was going to be a very long night.

CHAPTER ELEVEN

THE NEXT MORNING at dawn, two hours before opening, I was frosting lemon drop cupcakes on four hours sleep. I was feeling groggy as a bat in the sun, despite chugging a double mocha, when a banging at the bakery's back door startled me to alertness.

I locked eyes with Kade, who was leaning over the counter scrolling through wholesale coffee bean catalogs on his tablet.

"Don't open that door." I yanked off my gloves and dug into my apron pocket for my cell phone. Given the crazy tension with Carnivora last night, I wasn't taking chances. "I'm calling Elliot."

"Robbers don't knock." Kade's mouth twitched. "In my experience, having been robbed. Or, robbing."

"What if it's an *invasion*?" I shuddered and flipped through my contacts. Ah, there was Elliot's number. "Carnivora sees me as a traitor," I reminded Kade, hitting dial. "What do you think they do to traitors?"

"If they're coming for you, why would they announce it?"

The knock came again, super loud.

"Psychological warfare." *Damn you, Elliot, pick up.*

"Right." Kade nodded like he was humoring an insane person, then pointed toward the door. "I'll just go see who it is."

Moments later, Elliot stormed in with Kade on his heels. At the sight of his chiseled, angry face, I dropped my phone back into my apron pocket. I wasn't going to let him see how bad he'd rattled me.

"You really don't need to knock like it's a drug bust." I hoped he couldn't hear my voice shake. "What's going on?"

"You two tell me," he shot back. "How many people did you talk to about that meeting at Kensington's?"

Kade didn't hesitate. "Zero, dude."

"No one," I echoed guiltily. Did Elliot know I'd been to the shady gig store?

"Neither of you told a soul about what happened in that meeting."

"Bro, who would I even tell?" Kade snorted. "Everyone I know was there." He didn't seem to appreciate being interrogated by his old friend.

Neither did I.

"Stop treating us like suspects," I snapped. "Tell us what's happened so we can try to help."

Tilting his head, Elliot gazed narrow-eyed into the distance, like he was weighing ten different variables. Or maybe he just wasn't used to hearing commands from me.

"All right," he said finally.

Moments later, the three of us were seated around the blue corner booth.

"This video was anonymously file-dropped to my phone fifteen minutes ago." Elliot put his phone on the table and hit play on a grainy video, a closeup of the cackling vampire. The room was dark, you could barely make anything out, but that old cranky-pants voice was unmistakable.

"Well well well, looks like somebody in that lil tourist trap town's got deeeeep pockets. I'll be needing a hundred thousand dollars now. I know you got it."

I slammed my hand on the table as Elliot hit pause. "He's

asking for ten times the ransom! Wait, you thought one of *us* leaked info … to the kidnapper?"

That was insulting, also nuts.

"Not directly." Elliot had the grace to look embarrassed. "But word got to him somehow that Drew was throwing cash around."

I shook my head. None of this was computing. "How could anyone from the meeting be communicating with that crazy vampire?"

Kade and Elliot exchanged wry looks.

"It's hard for someone like you to fathom the criminal mind," Elliot began.

"Wow, that's not condescending at all," I said.

Kade looked pained. "It's just … Some of these sketchy shifters would sell their grandmothers for a slice of ransom pie."

"I don't doubt it. But, not what I meant." I was so over everyone seeing me as a sweet, totally naïve witch when I was actually ahead of them in the sleuthing. "If someone from that meeting was able to leak news to the kidnapper, it means he's dialed into the community. He's not a random tourist. Not the lone whacko he appears to be…"

Understanding registered on Elliot's face. "It would mean the case wasn't what we thought at all."

"Exactly."

Kade rested his hand on his stubbly, square chin. "Do we know for *sure* he's a tourist?"

Elliot squinted at me. "You saw him, right?"

"I saw a rude customer … didn't know he was a vampire at the time." I thought back to the customer who'd yelled at Yolanda while Amethyst filmed it on her phone. That guy sure acted like a tourist, but it didn't add up. "He's not broke if he can afford to spend his time visiting cute seaside towns, eating every meal in a restaurant. So why would he risk his unlife to kidnap a Green Witch for ransom?"

"What if he doesn't know it's taboo to harm witches?" Kade shrugged. "Sheryl did say he was a rookie newblood, right?"

"She said there was no record of him, whatsoever," Elliot clarified, his brow furrowed.

"How complete are those vampire records?" I asked.

Elliot shot me a piercing glance. "Most vampires between the turning ages of ten and five hundred years have been registered in the scrolls. Some newbloods slip through the cracks, but few of them last long enough to matter."

"Oof." So, Britt was right; vampire elders seemed content to let newbloods get picked off.

"Before about 1600, all bets are off," he went on. "There must be hundreds of unregistered rogue elders roaming the planet, and some are real loons."

Kade pushed a rusty lock of hair out of his eyes. "So, dude is either a weak lil baby vamp or an ancient outlaw."

I shivered, not wanting to imagine that Yolanda was in the hands of an unhinged, ancient evil. "How do we fight an old vampire?"

"We need the elder council's help," Elliot said bleakly. His voice hardened to bitterness. "We had it—till Kensington pulled his stunt, bribing those gang members. Bunch of broke shifters will do anything for cash. Even help vampires."

I followed his train of thought to the next station. "So you think some shifter's helping the kidnapper, for a cut of the ransom?"

"I think we put tails on all the Carnivora members who are 'protecting' newbloods." He pocketed his phone and eased out of the booth. "Kade, you willing to do some surveillance work?"

"Unbelievable." Kade shook his head in disgust. "You have some nerve, walking in here accusing us of blabbing about the case—and now you want me to be your spy? If Torrin so much as dreams I'm the fly on his wall, he'll squash me."

A chill ran down my spine. I'd heard that once you were in a gang, there was no getting out alive. "Do they think you're a traitor, too?" I asked.

"No," Kade and Elliot said at the same time.

Elliot nodded to Kade, like, *you* talk.

"I was never initiated into Carnivora. They have no hold on me. That's mostly thanks to Max. After I got arrested, she broke down in tears and begged me not to go back when I got out." Kade paused and raised his eyebrows at Elliot, who cleared his throat.

"It's common to have local kids be affiliated with the gang," Elliot said stiffly, "but never officially join."

Was it uncomfortable to talk about his friend's checkered past when he himself was a straight-arrow cop? The two of them were acting pretty awkward, and I found myself wondering sadly if being on opposite sides of the law had damaged their lifelong friendship beyond repair.

They'd been like brothers once.

"It's a phase for some shifters," Kade added. "If we walk away at that point, we're seen as non-combatants, off limits as long as we stay out of the gang's way. Which I *was* doing … until they robbed this place. If I get caught spying, I'm not walking away with just a black eye."

"I know." Elliot folded his arms across his chest. "So, you're going to make me beg for your help, furball?"

Kade shrugged, the lock of auburn hair falling right back into his face.

"How about apologizing?" I said, forcing myself to go on despite Elliot's glare. "For acting like such an arrogant jerk cop when you came in."

Elliot let out a sound of pure, fire-breathing grump.

"I'm sorry," he said through clenched teeth. "When the stakes are this high, it's hard for me to trust that people won't act like idiots."

"Hmm." I chewed my cheeks as if considering, which earned me another fire-breathing groan. "And?"

"And you two are not idiots, most of the time," he went on grudgingly. "You don't deserve that from me. I'll make myself do fifty extra pushups tonight, okay?"

He was only joking with that. Making fun of me. Nevertheless, my brain was now playing a big-screen movie of him in a pushup position. Did he do them every night, before bed? What did he wear to bed? A warm blush spread across my face.

"Um … you're forgiven," I said belatedly.

Kade nodded his satisfaction. "Fine, I'll spy on Carnivora for you … *birdbrain*."

Maybe that friendship was salvageable after all.

Kade slid out of the booth and stood, facing me. "If they swat me to death, do not replace me with an automatic espresso machine. I will *haunt* you."

When Kade was back in the kitchen, Elliot turned to me, all business again. "What's the latest on your investigation of Gerard's true death?"

"The Vampire Hunting Society claimed credit, remember?" I said, wondering if he was trying to catch me out. "So now we're just investigating them. And honestly, Carnivora are our top susp—"

"Hazel," Elliot cut in. "Them claiming credit doesn't close your case. It's hearsay, not evidence. Talking big to build a rep. In most cases, the killer is a family member. Have you done follow-up interviews with his widow and his newbloods yet—especially the newest one, who found his remains?"

"Uh, it's on my do-list," I said, mentally adding it to my to-do list. He was right and I felt embarrassed that I'd made such a beginner's mistake. A Goody Two-shoes Mistake. "So, they could lie about committing murder, just to brag?" The thought boggled my brain.

"Of course, they could claim credit for killing JFK." Elliot was enjoying his victory too much. "They could type it on a quirky old typewriter and it would be creepy as hell but it wouldn't make it true."

"Crap!" The creepy note from the vampire hunters. "I almost forgot to show you."

I slid out of the booth and went to go retrieve my purse from its hook on the coat rack. When I returned, Elliot was standing by the cold case, sneaking a glance at the fresh cinnamon rolls that I knew he'd never allow himself to taste.

"The vampire hunters left this at my front door, around midnight." I reached into the main pocket and held up the note, rolling my eyes. "Their threats are so dumb and repetitive, right?"

"They came to your *door*?" His voice was soft, but disturbingly so. A bit like last night when he was talking to Drew. "Why am I only hearing about this now, Hazel?"

I chuckled like I wasn't unnerved by having Deputy Elliot James's cold fire gaze aimed right into my soul. "It didn't occur to me to call you in the middle of the night."

"Yet you just called at 4:57," he lobbed back.

"Yeah, to a baker that's morning! Also, I thought I was in danger."

He tilted his head like he wondered if he'd heard right. "And you didn't think that last night?"

"I … had it well in hand." In my mind's eye flashed on an image of last night's floating broomstick, like a mental hangover. Maybe I'd never be graceful, but I was used to looking out for myself. I'd been doing it all my life.

"What's a baker doing up at midnight anyway?" His eyes bored into me, demanding answers.

"How's that your business?"

"I don't like it that they were at your door." His tone made a shiver run down my back. It was like he'd slipped off the good—if grumpy—cop mask and underneath was an animal. Wild instinct. Deadly defenses. "I'll make damn sure it never happens again."

Gulping, I nodded. I had no idea how Elliot planned to guard me from future harassment, but I believed him. He'd looked scary for a moment.

Then the menace was gone, and he was just Elliot again. Grumpy, lawful Elliot. Kade handed him a drip coffee on the house. They shot the breeze for a few minutes about who-knows-what dude stuff while I finished up the cupcake frosting and slotted the tray with my latest masterpiece into our cold case.

Calm again, Elliot bused his mug like a gentleman and whirled to ask me a final question. "So, you really going to ward Marie Chevalier's house?"

I groaned. "I knew it!" He was just waiting for the moment we were alone so he could give me the third degree.

He pressed closer, his dark eyes twinkling with curiosity. "You were dead set against it, but you took the money."

"They threw it at me."

I waited for him to tell me I should have thrown it back. That even in that tense room I should have had the guts to say no.

"Hazel? What makes warding so terrible for witches?"

His genuine, personal question caught me off guard. "I … don't know."

"What?" He looked at me like I was an unsolvable mystery, equal parts annoying itch and tantalizing appeal. "How can you not know?"

"It's so bad witches don't talk about it." Guilt pinged me, for outsourcing it to some desperate witch who couldn't say no. "Bet that doesn't make sense to you, does you? You'd never be satisfied not knowing something."

He shook his head. "If it were me, I'd ask your grandmother."

"I can't do that to her." Picturing Gran's worried face made my heart hurt. "She'll know I'm asking for a reason."

Elliot's gaze stayed locked on me as he leaned in. His wood moss and amber scent was like a drug, sending my senses into overdrive. "Then go ask someone who's less perceptive and caring than your Gran."

I heaved an exaggerated sigh. "Get out of here. I don't like when you're all intense and bossy."

Lies. His muscles looked even bigger right now as he loomed over me with his smug, logical authority.

"You know I'm right," he said with a shrug.

I waved him out.

Then mustering all my willpower, I pulled out my phone and texted Mother.

CHAPTER TWELVE

"**HAZEL! OVER HERE!**" My older sister Beatrix leapt from her chair to wave at me with both arms outstretched, as if without help I might fail to spot her and our mother at their prominent beach view table.

I hurried across the polished stone floor of the intimate dining room. Bea always set these mom-and-daughters dates, once a quarter or so, at some trendy, upscale restaurant that was popular with tourists and other ordinals. Even though they were technically witches, Mom and Bea fit right in at such places.

Sometimes that still made me jealous.

Even though this time I had been the one to initiate this lunch at the last minute, Bea took over the planning after two texts, and I let her. Because honestly she was way better at it.

"Sorry, am I late?" I glanced at my watch. Was it wrong?

Bea's text had instructed me to come at one, but they were midway through a share plate of BBQ jackfruit lettuce wraps.

"No, you're not late, Hazel," Mother said soothingly. "It's fine. You're fine."

"We're just having a nice chat here, nothing to get upset about." Bea smiled and patted the seat next to hers.

They'd obviously texted each other privately and agreed to meet earlier so they could chat without me but didn't want to admit to it. That was why they were acting like I was a crazy person for asking. I was used to their ways, and it rarely even got me down anymore. I was proud of that.

For the first seventeen years of my life, I believed I was terrible at magic. I couldn't do what my mother and Bea did, decorating a room to look like a magazine. I couldn't give myself good hair days 365 days a year, like my little sister Cindra could. While not nearly as powerful as Green Magic, it made you look amazing. It turned out what I wasn't good at was their kind of magic.

I settled into a dove-grey leather armless chair and cracked the menu, reading it close to my chest since there wasn't room to put it on the table … because of Cindra. Her photo frame, that is. My little sister Cindra wasn't dead or anything. She lived in London, where she made a paltry but glamorous living as a hand and foot model. Still, Mother insisted on bringing her photo to lunch with us. It didn't cut into my elbow room *that* much.

"Ooh, the taco omelet looks good," I said.

"We *knew* you would say that!" Bea chuckled, exchanging a look with Mother. "We're getting the roasted kale bowls. Light and healthy."

They always ordered the same thing.

"So? How's your grandmother?" Mother prompted. "Still wearing her hair like an elderly Apache princess?"

Dad's mom turning out to be a Green Witch was a surprise that had hit her only after the wedding. My mother's upbringing as a Beige Witch was so sheltered she hadn't known much about other colors of magic and referred to Gran by the offensive term "kitchen witch."

"Gran's doing great." A big lie, but one I considered an act of loyalty. Gran would rather die than endure their Beige pity, the sad faces and aww sounds and heart tapping. The care packages.

"We love to hear it." Bea smiled, curling her fingers around her matcha latte cup. "And uh … well … how are you holding up, with everything that's been going on?"

"The question caught me off guard. "Oh, fine, I mean, yeah, there's a lot going on but, it's not really about *me* per se…" Wait, how did they know about the Vampire Slayer Society and Yolanda and the warding? "Oh! You mean Bryson. That we split up."

"*Of course* that's what she means," Mother put in. "Hazel, only weeks ago you were engaged to be married. Then you flew into a rage in the middle of Thanksgiving dinner, accusing the poor man of being … well, I don't remember what exactly."

A demon. He was a demon.

I silently thanked Britt's compulsion for keeping my family's memories hazy on the details of that breakup. "I'd really rather talk about something else."

"Honey, we know you're struggling." Mother mirrored my crossed arms and leaned in with a stiff smile that I'm sure she'd learned from some YouTube video on feigning empathy. "You don't have to pretend, we're family. We know he's on your mind all the time. You're sad and lonely, no romance in your life. Feeling like a failure. Having a hard time keeping up with laundry?"

I looked down at my slightly wrinkled but still cute button-down shirt in time to see a flit of light—and kazaam, my shirt was glamoured smooth. Bea's signature magical scent Glossier You spiced the air.

"Oh, you didn't have to do that…"

"I wanted to, Hazel," Bea smiled warmly. "We're here help get you back on track. That's why you reached, isn't it?"

"Oh … no." I laughed before I could stop myself. They'd clearly been talking about my breakup incessantly since Thanksgiving. Now they were out of details and were hoping I could supply some. "I reached out so Mother could tell us everything she knows about warding spells."

"Augh!" My mother touched her perfectly-rouged cheek as if I'd slapped her. "Why would you mention the W word?"

"Hazel, you're unbelievable," my sister hissed. "How could you blow up a negativity bomb in our faces?" She gestured to her porcelain skin. "So bad for our pores."

I ignored Bea's ranting. "You always told us never, ever, ever to take a job warding a location. You said it's miserable work and it's beneath us."

"Well, it is, both," my mother huffed. She was beginning to hyperventilate.

"Okay but why?"

Bea shook her head at me. "Do you not see you're upsetting her?"

"Mother, do you actually know anyone who did a warding job and had a bad experience?" I pressed. "Or is it just some superstition or something."

"All right, since you've asked this extremely personal and indelicate question. My great aunt Hilda was in dire straits during the Great Depression. She was a beautiful young woman with perfect hair. Well, her family was hungry, so she took a few jobs warding rich men's houses from evil spirits, and afterwards…" Mother balled up the napkin with her rose-gold manicured hands. "Well, she…"

"Go on," I said, feeling hopeful.

"I just can't say it."

"Stop trying to make her say it, Hazel."

"Her hair was a mess!" Mother exploded, the horror of it sagging her face. "From that day forward, her clothes were wrinkled and her face was puffy and her skin was splotchy, she had lipstick in her teeth and her perfume signature never smelled quite right anymore."

"Okay, well that's not *so* bad." I reached for my herbal tea, which was cold because Bea ordered it for me before she'd told me to show up.

"Not so bad?" Mother's voice was shrill. "The poor thing ended up marrying a short man and their children played badminton. Not football. Not even soccer."

What? As always when I listened to Mother I found myself lost in a sea of toxicity, struggling to find a molecule of sanity or sense.

"Hilda…" I mused. "Isn't that the aunt you said I remind you of?"

"What's *that* have to do with the price of lip filler?" Mom's elegant features twisted, like she was too distraught to deal with such a silly question. "The point is, her magic was *broken*."

Bea and I gasped.

Silence fell across the table.

Could this be true? Did warding spells damage your gift, or was Mother confused? Such a brutal injury would explain why warding was a tragic subject among us witches. But could a witch's magic ever really die? I'd always felt like it was part of us, from cradle to crone.

But was I willing to bet a stranger's magic on that feeling?

"I have to go." I stood on wobbly legs, panic pumping through my body.

I didn't bother to look back at their wide-eyed bewilderment or to see if Mother was arranging Cindra's photo in front of my cold tea, which I knew she totally was.

This time I chewed an invisibility mint before I hoofed it back to the iffy part of downtown. As my ghostly boot stomps echoed down the cobblestone sidewalk, I regretted wasting a mint. This part of town was dead in daylight. Hexxed Vixxen Video was boarded up. So were half the stores on the street.

Fortunately, Git-Er-Done Giggings had its neon sign blazing. I threw open the door and declared, "I want my money back. I'm canceling the warding gig."

Fiona stared at me from across the gleaming mahogany desk, which for all I knew was just a glamoured cardboard box. "Found your long-lost sense of ethics did you, Green Witch?"

"I didn't know warding damaged people's magic." I refused to be intimidated by her tailored navy suit jacket and peach silk layering top. "That's unacceptable."

Fiona rapped her blood-orange, oval nails on the desk. "Cost of doing business, love," she said. So Mother had been right. "But don't be such a downer. It's not only *damage*, it's change. And change is good."

I gaped. Could she be any more glib about people losing their sacred gifts?

"You cancel that gig." I'd found my moral center again. "I'll stand here while you do."

Fiona's voice took on a cloying, saccharine tone. "I'm afraid that's not possible, miss. That gig has already been assigned and scheduled for fulfillment." She presented sparkling white teeth. "Imminently."

My heart fluttered. "Tell me who you assigned it to."

"Not possible, not happening," she repeated in the same singsong voice, like an evil Mary Poppins. "Read your contract next time, sweetie."

My blood boiled. "Don't call me sweetie. Who did you assign it to?"

"Oh, let me just pull up our company database and furnish you with that private client info. Joking," Fiona added without any mirth whatsoever in her tone. "You're batty if you think I'm going to let you put the kibosh on my gig, *sweetie.*"

With a wiggle of her blood orange fingers, Fiona commanded the door to open. Suddenly a powerful gust of wind erupted in the air between us, propelling me toward the door. The scent of burning grass filled my nostrils as I gassed for air struggling to stay on my feet, but the force was too strong. I fell backwards, landing on my butt on the cold hard sidewalk.

Yep, Grey Magic—called it.

"Private client info" indeed. Hex my life, I had no choice but to pay a visit to Marie Pierre tonight.

CHAPTER THIRTEEN

I HUNG A LEFT turn to climb the hill toward Sunset, in Britt's Mini Cooper. It was four-thirty and the sun was in fact already setting over the horizon as we drove, washing the sky in peach and purple hues. Graham had insisted on joining us, for protection. But so far all he'd contributed was making out with Britt in the backseat.

"You guys, I feel like a limo driver on prom night."

No response, making my point.

"He's supposed to be your bodyguard," I growled. "Not your boy toy."

Britt detached herself at last from Graham's lips. "Having a super rough December here, Hazel," she said. "Also, I haven't kissed anyone in two entire years. Don't begrudge me this bear."

"Maybe she's jealous? You said she was extremely single."

"I know you *think* you're whispering, Graham," I sniped at my second forced roommate. "But I've got bad news. Your quiet voice? Is loud."

Britt raked her nails through his sandy hair, looking dreamy. "Aw, I love your loud grizzly voice…"

"Well, *I* don't love keeping secrets from Max."

My record scratch of a comment made Britt wince. "Low blow, Hazel."

"Mood killer," Graham intoned.

Hex me, they were annoying. Bet they wouldn't be acting so lovey-dovey if Max were in the car instead of off being interviewed on some travel podcast. As she often was, being the voice of Blue Moon Bay. "Have either of you thought about what you're going to tell her?"

To her credit, Britt looked sober. "I don't quite know yet," she admitted. "But it's my problem, not yours."

"You mean our problem." Graham grabbed Britt's chin and pulled her in for another steamy kiss.

As I turned onto Marie Pierre's street, I thought again of how depressing it was that the last person I kissed was a demon milking me for energy. I stole a glance at Britt—her big brown eyes lidded in bliss, dark hair wrapped around Graham's thick fingers. I wasn't jealous exactly. But I wanted to feel what she was feeling.

For a split second, I recalled the ferocity in Elliot's eyes this morning. His oak moss and amber skin scent. What would his lips taste like on mine?

It was such an arresting thought that I didn't have room to be nervous till Britt and I were settled at Marie Pierre's kitchen table, awaiting tea and cookies that no one particularly wanted.

Graham had introduced himself—*as Britt's boyfriend!*—and parked his butt on the sad yet ostentatious velvet chesterfield in the living room. He'd be near enough if needed, but not so close Marie would sniff him out as a shifter.

Not that Marie seemed to suspect a thing. She was completely engrossed in mentoring her new maid, offering guidance and direction with every order she barked.

"Faster, Bronwen." She snapped her fingers at the lanky young woman who was hastily setting the table with actual, polished silverware. "The oolong is ready for steeping. You must not neglect one task for another, my dear child, or you'll get behind."

My dear child? Her over-familiarity made me squirm in my seat. Till I glanced over and saw this maid looked familiar. Wispy, candy-pink bangs brushed the sides of her forehead, framing a pixie face adorned with long lashes and raspberry lips.

"Excuse me…Bronwen?" Britt's voice was overly composed, like she was trying to hide her emotions. "Aren't you one of Gerard's newbloods?"

The pink-haired girl looked to Marie as if checking if it was okay to answer.

"Yes, I am training her," Marie said, her posture still and her voice tinged with sadness. "I want her to acquire the skills to work in service. The study of Film Lit is no longer a luxury that we can afford for someone in Bronwen's position."

"Her position?" I blurted out.

Marie regarded me with a mournful expression. "Since Gerard's passing, we've all had to lower our expectations, myself included. It's a difficult time for us all."

Britt and I exchanged a skeptical glance. Marie's concern for Bronwen's future employment seemed rooted in a genuine desire to help her, rather than any personal vendetta. But how could Gerard have left them poor?

"Money's such a delicate subject," Britt began. "But Gerard left a will, surely—"

"His soul could not have been more generous." Marie clasped her hands and gazed up reverently, as if at Gerard in vampire heaven. "The house and everything in it are mine, community property. But he is not declared dead and may not be for a very long time. There is no human body, of course. And his fake ID will not withstand the scrutiny of a missing persons case. It can take years to declare a person dead and in the meantime we are penniless."

"Oh, Marie, that's brutal." Britt reached out to comfort the valet with a gentle arm pat. "But hey, if any of you ever wants a beer-slinging-type job at the Drunken Barrel, I know someone who knows someone."

"Oohlala, what a fate at my age." Marie sighed heavily and turned to me. "Is it possible I am under a curse?"

"Sure, could be a minor hex." I wasn't sensing witch magic on her at all, but a decade of customer service had taught that most people just wanted to feel seen in their pain. And to get a groveling apology. And free cake. "Even a mini hex can be mega stressful." I put on my cashier empathy face. "*So* sorry you're having to deal with that."

"How are you dealing with it?" Britt added.

"I'm surviving, barely." Marie gestured to her ash-blond chignon, little black dress, and bold patterned silk scarf as if they represented craven squalor. "But you are not here to ask about my well-being." Her deep blue eyes narrowed. "What do you want to know?"

"You said Carina moved back in with her human family," I spoke up. "We need their contact info. Last name, address, and phone number."

"You expect me to know any of these things?" Marie blinked in confusion, as if I was asking her to recite obscure Tibetan poetry. "And why do you want to bother that poor girl?" She gasped. "Don't tell me you suspect her."

Britt's voice was calm but firm. "We can't rule her out, Marie. According to you yourself, she's the one who found his body."

"According to ... what does *this* mean?" Marie demanded. "You suspect me now?"

"Of course not." Britt touched her arm again.

I thought back to Elliot's reminder that family often murdered family. Marie seemed to worship Gerard, yet Britt said he'd treated her like a mere employee. Wasn't it possible she'd gotten sick of that dynamic? After several hundred years, maybe she wanted to bossing others for a change … like she was doing with Bronwen?

I felt sorry for the long-ago version of Marie who was Gerard's child bride, but the Marie in front of me? Was def on my suspect list.

"Carina's an innocent girl," Marie insisted. "And I don't just mean with regards to the murder. Her head is as fluffy as a poodle's. Gerard, in his infinite prudence, did not always choose eternity's children for their wits. Don't dilly-dally with the cookies!" she added sternly.

Bronwen stood at the counter with tongs in her hands, a strained look on her pretty, young face. Had she been eavesdropping?

She resumed placing chocolate chip cookies, fresh from the oven, onto a glass platter. A golden-brown cookie fell off the tongs and shattered on the tile. She cringed, cursing under her breath. "Sorry."

"Don't worry about it," Britt said. "Is it all right if we take up ten minutes if your time? We have a few questions to ask all the newbloods."

Bronwen looked at Marie, who frowned.

"These girls don't know anything about his death that I haven't shared with you," she said. "Why upset them even more?"

"Marie," Britt pleaded, "we're the only ones trying to bring his killer to justice. To bring you all some peace of mind. A sense of security."

"Peace of mind is not what I am lacking," Marie said stiffly as Bronwen appeared with the cookies and tea balanced on a tray. I found myself praying she wouldn't drop anything. "I have no reason to believe it was anyone but the vampire hunters who took credit. As to security—aaaahhh!" She cried out as if stung. "What is this now, paper towels—for our guests?" She fixed a look of pure disappointment at Bronwen, whose shoulders shrank as she passed me a folded paper towel. "Your generation, I cannot understand."

The girl ducked her head. "Sorry, Marie."

Why did I have the feeling Bronwen said those words a lot lately? I reached for a cookie and set it on my plate, determined to say they were delicious no matter what.

Marie tutted. "*Mon dieu*, where was I?"

"Security," Britt said with exaggerated gentleness. She was treating Marie with kid gloves, and I had the feeling this was how everyone ended up treating her.

"Ah, yes!" Marie's face brightened considerably. "I have the most amazing news on that front. Some anonymous donor is paying a witch to ward this house."

"A witch who isn't Hazel?" Britt shot me a look of confusion.

Crap, why hadn't I filled her in on the warding drama? When it came to opening up in the midst of crises, I was no better than Elliot.

"That's *great*, Marie." I glared daggers at Britt to shut her up and took a sip of oversteeped oolong.

"*Oui*, I was moved to tears by their kind gesture." Marie's lips curved up in a shy smile. "It's proof that some in this community still cherish us."

It was hard not to notice her veiled lament. Was it the elder council, embracing modernity's encroach, who didn't appreciate valets in her view? Or someone else?

"So, when's this fabulous warding spell happening?" Britt had recovered from my blunder and was playing along. I was thankful my friend was quick on the uptake.

"Soon, Monday morning." Marie's eyes sparkled with relief and a joyful anticipation seemed to radiate from her. It was plain that her unwarded house had been a heavy burden, one she was now on the verge of releasing.

Which made me feel the tiniest bit conflicted about my plans to sabotage the whole thing.

Come Monday morning I'd be here, come hex or high water, doing my best to talk some poor witch out of harming her own magic.

Please don't let it be Jacinta. I wasn't sure I could survive that level of awkwardness.

I bit into the cookie and nearly gagged. The bottom was black charr, the inside raw flour. No wonder I was the only one eating them. I didn't blame Bronwen for this travesty; the kid wanted to be studying film, not baking.

Surreptitiously, I tucked the cookie into my paper towel. When I folded it over a second time to cover the cookie, I looked down to see ink stains on the paper.

Bronwen met my eyes, her expression too neutral.

Not stains, it was blue cursive writing smeared by the absorbent towel.

A message. Secret. For me.

Heart pounding, in one move I crumpled the towel with the cookie still in it and tossed the whole mess into my newish black purse while Britt stared, bemused.

Marie's skinny brows shot up toward her platinum hairline. "What on earth?"

"Had to get one for the road," I explained, hoping the sweat beading on my forehead wasn't too obvious. "They're so delectable."

Marie pointed her finger at me and looked at Bronwen. "Now *that* is true politeness."

One hour later, the whole gang was huddled around the bakery oven for an emergency meeting armed with provisions. I'd conjured up a dozen fresh, flaky croissants infused with a focus spell to keep us sharp. Meanwhile Kade fired up the espresso machine and whipped up frothy macchiatos for himself, Elliot, Britt, Graham, and Max. To me, he handed a piping mug of cocoa with marshmallows.

Indulging in croissants at ten p.m. might be considered blasphemy by some, but this was Blue Moon Bay, not Paris or Rome.

I put down my hot chocolate and read Bronwen's paper towel note out loud to the group again. It had taken me fifteen minutes to decipher it due to the smeared ink:

> Carina didn't go home. She ran away the night Gerard was killed. Marie goes to confession Tuesdays at noon.

"Concisely written." Elliot nodded with grudging respect as he poked a straw into the premixed protein shake he'd brought over.

"And brave," Max added, just as grudgingly. "Going behind Marie's back to send you a message."

"But is the message *true*?" Kade said and crunched his croissant pensively.

"I can only think of one reason why Marie would lie about Carina's whereabouts." Britt looked distressed and stuffed another croissant in her mouth for comfort. "To keep her off our suspect list. Running away after the murder? Looks real bad."

"You did say she was protective of you newbloods," Graham said without looking at Britt. "Albeit in a creepy, colonial way."

Max shot him an odd look. From the moment she'd dashed

in—late, since her podcast interview ran over—Graham and Britt hadn't so much as brushed elbows. No doubt they understood they'd give themselves away with a mere look or touch. The sparks radiating in the air between them made me want to run through the kitchen screaming, "They're kissing!"

Instead, I mused aloud, "If Marie's protecting Carina, then she can't be the killer. Marie would draw the line at shielding her husband's murderer. Wouldn't she?"

"What if Marie's the killer?" Kade suggested. "And Carina's a witness who fled the scene."

"Or maybe Marie staked Gerard *and* staked Carina for witnessing it," Elliot said.

Kade groaned. "You always gotta one-up me dude?"

"I just can't see Marie staking him," Britt said. "I lived with those two and there was zero tension between them. She did his bidding, he gave her blood. End of story."

"If Gerard and his childer are her only source of lifeblood, she's in a precarious position." Elliot eyed the croissants like they were his personal enemies, then drained his protein shake. "Are the newbloods going to keep giving her blood forever?" He looked at Britt. "Would you give her blood?"

Britt frowned and bit her lip. "To keep her from dying? Sure, I guess."

Max whistled. "Marie better hope Bronwen and the other girl are more enthusiastic blood donors than you."

"I guess we'll learn more on Tuesday," Elliot said. "While Marie's in church."

"Two whole days till we can interview the newbloods?" I gave Elliot a significant look.

He tilted his head down slightly. "I'm afraid there's no way for me to use my legal authority here, Hazel. There's no Ordinal case, as

I said. But since we're all here ... Kade, want to give us your update on Carnivora?"

"Right." Kade cleared his throat. "So tonight I was tailing Jasper, and let me tell you. All that boy does is hang with his idiot crew and drink beer at the Howling Hogshead. They talk about girls, talk about getting high. How their parents don't get them. It was like spying on my teenage self. But the kicker is, they all had their vampire protectees with them—and they were pretty much getting along fine. No one attacked anyone."

"So, what, the hatred's all talk?" I asked.

"No," Elliot, Kade, Graham, and Max answered at once.

"But I do think they play it up," Kade added. "You have to, or you're seen as weak. I'm sure they were more relaxed because Torrin wasn't there."

"The gang leader was missing?" Elliot said.

Kade shrugged. "I got the impression he's been skipping late nights at the bar lately."

"The better to leave creepy notes at my door," I said.

"It had to be him." Elliot's jaw tightened. "From now on, I'm Torrin's shadow."

I shouldn't have been surprised by his vehemence. But after the dinner with Leia thing, some part of me thought I'd misjudged more than his level of romantic interest in me. It was comforting to see his urge to protect me was real.

"Anything of note about the conversation at the bar?" Elliot asked.

Kade scratched his beard. "They talked for hours. How do I know what's important?"

"Go with your gut," Graham said, stealing a glance at Britt. "I always do."

"Well, okay," Kade said, "some of the girls they talk about are local witches. Jasper's dating Amethyst, for example."

"*Our* Amethyst?!" I k*new* she was going out with inappropriate boys.

"But he's worried gang politics are going to tear them apart," Kade went on. "Apparently, that's what happened with a former gang member, Orion, and his girlfriend Ree. The girlfriend was an alpaca shifter. Carnivora doesn't accept herbivores. It broke them up."

"Which sucks for them, I'm sure," Max cut in. "But did you really risk your wings for a high school soap opera?"

"I guess you're right," Kade said, sounding sheepish. "It's probably not front-page news."

Then Elliot did something he rarely did. He smiled.

"It is front-page," he said. "Because Orion was Torrin's little brother. He disappeared a month ago, the night of the full moon. Ever since then, Torrin's been telling anyone who'll listen that vampires killed his brother. And it's only in the last two weeks that the vampire hunters started sending threats."

I glanced at the wall at my Seasons of the Witch's Garden calendar, last year's stocking stuffer from my sister Bea who was at least trying. "The night of the full moon is when Gerard was killed."

"And Carina ran away," Britt added.

"You think Torrin's brother has something to do with Gerard and Carina?" Elliot asked.

I snapped my fingers. "What'd you say Orion's girlfriend's name was?

"The alpaca shifter?" Kade blinked. "Ree."

"Carina!" we all said.

I shivered again. "We're getting somewhere, but I don't know where."

"We need to interview rank and file gang members to learn

more about Orion and Carina," Max said. "I can talk to Scruffy tomorrow."

"And I'll follow Amethyst tomorrow," I said. "She's connected to just about every thread. She's dating a Carnivora member. She's best friends with Yolanda—and, ooh, they both had to be in the same film class as Carina, since we know Gerard used his courses as a dating pool. She mentioned having a vampire friend!"

"Don't you love this feeling?" Elliot caught my eye. "Something's starting to come together."

"I think I prefer the feeling where everything's already together," I admitted. "But at least we finally caught some sort of break. And we have a plan."

CHAPTER FOURTEEN

THAT'S WHAT I thought, until the next morning.
Elliot's back was ramrod straight as he speed-walked through Sage's Bakery at ten-thirty a.m., rudely ignoring my fresh pink raspberry cakes, my gingerbread cookies, and my cranberry pecan scones drizzled with orange glaze. A clutch of blonde, yoga pants clad toddler moms glanced up from their crumb-covered children to admire the taut line of Elliot's jaw, which looked like it could crush diamonds. He ignored them too.

Instead, he locked eyes with me where I stood wiping the busing counter with a hot, soapy rag.

From five feet away, I could feel the fury pouring off him, but his voice stayed low and calm. "There's a new video from the kidnapper."

My heart caught in my throat. *Yolanda.* I set my rag down and called to Kade that I was taking a break.

At the corner booth, Elliot scooted closer to me, which would have made my breath quicken if my heart wasn't already thumping at a wild canter. Had the kidnapper hurt Yolanda? Did our splintered community fail that poor girl, wasting too much time bickering? What if, God forbid, he broke vampire law and harmed her?

The witch I was supposed to mentor.

Guilt hung like a cloud over me as Elliot pushed his tablet

toward me and hit play. I wanted to squeeze my eyes shut but forced myself to watch.

I was expecting to see the grizzled vampire's ruddy, scowling face, as in the first two videos. Instead, a khaki sleeping bag twisted like a worm on a dusty, black and white tile floor. Draped over the bag's opening was a mop of dark hair. The sleeping person turned and made cute little sleepy sounds, and I gasped in relief. It *was* Yolanda. The bag crinkled as her breaths went up and down, slow and regular.

I exhaled a huge sigh. "It's a proof of life video," I said, and silently gave myself props for bingeing all those TV cop dramas. "She's okay, thank God."

"For now." Elliot pointed to the screen. "Listen."

"Isn't she precious?" The kidnapper's loud, crackly voice intoned sardonically from off camera. "I can hear that young blood humming, bet it tastes like birthday cake." Gross. My hands felt hot with anger and revulsion. "If you don't want your witchling to be dessert, you'll get me my money by Saturday night. Midnight. Oh yeah, and the price went up again. It's two hundred K now baby, or…" He made a disgusting wet slurping sound, and the vid was over, frozen on Yolanda's angelic sleeping face.

I turned to Elliot in disbelief. "How are we going to get two hundred thousand dollars to him by midnight?"

"Already solved that piece." Grim satisfaction colored his features. "Kensington's agreed to pony up the cash. Sheriff's department personnel will put it in the gym locker as required."

"Wow, Drew's being so generous."

"Generous?" He gave a short laugh. "He's cleaning up his own mess. He tried to leverage a crisis in our community to gain influence. He threw money around, and word got around. And now, the ransom keeps going up."

I nodded slowly, though for once Elliot's logic wasn't adding up. Something about Drew made him see red, and I wasn't sure if it was the fangs or the billions. "You still think the kidnapper had an accomplice at the meeting?"

Elliot nodded. "I'm almost sure of it."

"Who would wish this kind of misery on the Hyacinth family?"

"Maybe it's not about the family." Elliot sounded like he was trying out a theory. "Maybe it's about survival." His gaze wandered out the window, narrowing on a tree heavy with snow. "Brand new vampires face long odds. Most human families reject them. Their sires … not always helpful." I thought of Gerard and shuddered. "They're isolated. Desperate. If I were a newblood vampire, I'd be willing to form ties with someone unsavory."

I thought back to those three nervous wallflowers at Drew's meeting. Sure, it might be logical to suspect one of them, but I couldn't see it. Carnivora, now those guys I could see aiding and abetting a gross kidnapper—except that they hated vampires. There was the chic, polished house staff, though they seemed to be all ordinals. So who did that leave, other than my friends and me?

Amethyst. That night, she'd pouted at Elliot, been grouchy about a seatbelt, and spoken up boldly for social justice toward vampires. She was acting too normal for someone whose best friend just got kidnapped. But what would her motive be?

"Anything jump out at you in the video?" Elliot interrupted my thoughts.

"Yeah, that floor," I said, realizing it was bugging me. "Not only was it filthy, but nobody makes those weird octagonal tiles anymore, except to be all retro."

The moment the words were out of my mouth, I regretted how, well, *Beige* they sounded. Elliot was a cop, investigating a serious case. Why would he care about décor?

To my surprise, his eyebrows raised with interest, stylus hovering over his tablet screen. "Go on…"

"Um, okay. Clearly no one's washed those tiles in years." I saw Elliot scribbling notes on his tablet and got so excited I began to ramble. "And the room looks huge. Too huge for a house, even a huge house. Because only rich people own those, and—"

"They'd hire a cleaner." Cool, he'd followed my ramble-logic. "So, our kidnapper's got Yolanda holed up in an institutional space. An old, unused one." His brow furrowed. "Not too many places in town fit that bill. We'll find where he's hiding her. Tonight."

"Does it have to be here in town?" I asked.

"No," he admitted. "But it's a good bet, if he's counting on the money to be delivered to that locker at Swole Tim's."

He didn't say the part I was thinking. That if the kidnapper had moved Yolanda to another town, there was little chance of us tracking them in time to raid his hiding place.

It was a bet we'd have to take.

"Oh." Elliot snapped his fingers as another thought seemed to occur to him. "Did you notice the vampire wasn't on screen this time?"

Good point. "Maybe he was holding the phone to film Yolanda?"

"No, his camera's clearly on a tripod. No shaking."

Now that he mentioned it, the video's quality was surprisingly good. The clarity of Yolanda's features in the dim room meant he must have played around with lighting. Something else dawned on me. "When he was talking, the sleeping bag stopped making crinkly sounds."

Elliot scribbled in his notes app again, immediately seeming to get where I was going with that. "Editing his voice in later is a fairly sophisticated thing to do, technically."

"Right? If he's some crochety elder who just got turned, how does he know so much about making videos. Someone has to be helping him."

Someone like a film student? There was so many to choose from. Bronwen, Carina, and Amethyst, for starters. Amethyst had even filmed the vampire before—when he first showed up at the diner.

Elliot shook his head. "I should have realized sooner that he had an accomplice."

I'd never heard him admit to a mistake before, but he didn't take long to dwell.

"All the schools in town have basements," he said, all business again. "So does city hall. The courthouse. The library. As soon as you can get off work, we'll split up and get the de Klaw twins to help us look around, in stealth mode."

"Sure thing." Max and Kade could both shift into houseflies, so they could investigate without being discovered. Though, they could be swatted. "Max and I can check out local schools."

He nodded his approval of the plan. "Kade and I will check out other buildings, meet back here at ten."

It was almost a shame, I thought, walking back to my post at the register, how you never got to appreciate the moments when your life was action-movie thrilling.

Because you were too busy being terrified.

CHAPTER FIFTEEN

FAT RAINDROPS WERE leaking from the starless sky onto the Mustang's windshield when Max pulled into the student lot at Blue Moon High.

I slotted my plastic cup of bubble tea in the drink holder next to hers and was flattened by a rogue wave of nostalgia.

Other than the ten p.m. darkness, it felt just like when we were seniors here. Sneaking off campus for a break from the mean girls who hounded us.

Real jerk types, like *Britt Salazar.*

Max didn't share the warm fuzzies.

"Blue Moon, True Moon, vic-to-ry," she sang sarcastically. "Hate you forever, vicious hell-school," she added.

In the last few hours, Max had shifted into fly form six times to examine the floors at Blue Moon Bay Middle School and the three elementaries it fed into. As well as the Catholic school. And the weird New Agey school that no one knew much about because only Ordinals went there.

No dice.

Some had dingy floors, but none that matched the black and white tiles in the video.

I was about to say I didn't blame her for being in a bad mood, that I was in a bad mood too and would be until Yolanda was safe and sound.

But when I turned there was no one in the driver's seat, just a pile of clothes.

A fly buzzed around my ears, and I rolled down my window to let it out.

A transom window near the eaves of the gym building was cracked open. I figured that's where she'd head first, but of course I lost sight of her within seconds.

Leaving the engine running, I waited nervously for Max to return. We'd agreed that if she did discover where the vampire was holding Yolanda, she'd fly straight back and we'd together call for backup.

Still, now that the plan was in motion, I seriously doubted Max was capable of leaving an innocent kid tied up in some corner. She'd be more likely to shift into bobcat mode and try to gnaw the vamp's head off.

Barring miracles, I'd be out a best friend.

A sudden movement on my right made me jump. A grandpa raccoon was waddling toward the dumpster on the sidewalk next to the parking lot. Then a light blinked in my eyes—just a streetlamp with a failing bulb.

Fifteen minutes that felt like an eternity later, the fly was back. Buzzing at me to lower the window again.

I felt pretty stupid, taking orders from a housefly. But it was my only real contribution to the mission.

While I was at it, I scooped up Max's clothes and moved them to the dash just as she materialized in the driver's seat, naked. I turned away while she did a deft pretzel dance putting her outfit back together.

"Wrong kind of flooring," she said, before I could ask. "Let's go, I hate this place."

Max looked bone-weary and I felt let down as she drove north toward Blue Moon Bay college, our last stop.

Unlike the high school, this campus was jamming at ten-thirty.

The parking lot was half-full and a steady triangle of raingear-clad students streamed between it, the library, and the food court which I vaguely remembered stayed open till midnight with a skeleton crew.

"Ah, finals week," Max said fondly.

It was almost a party atmosphere.

"I don't remember loving to study *that* much," I said, glancing at Remington Hall, the staid Victorian building where I'd taken over a dozen business classes. "Though, maybe it's because I really never got to pick my major? Gran just told me what my destiny was."

"Hey, you were lucky she did." Max's tone was bitter. "Some people spend years waffling between majors. Some never find one and drop out. They wake up one fine morning and realize they've chewed up every course syllabus, while they were an animal, and puked it up."

"Weirdly specific example." I stared at her. Till this moment I'd had no inkling that was why Max dropped out. I figured she'd paused her education because her blog was taking off. But her voice carried regret … was she still wistful about not graduating?

"Augh, look at that Ordinal idiot." Max gestured to a Humm-Vee that was double parked outside the auditorium. "Womp womp, too big to park."

I was pretty sure Max was just changing the subject, but I stole another glance at the Humm-Vee. "It's not just Ordinals, Amethyst drives one." It was her dad's and he was an Ordinal, but I wasn't going to undercut my own point.

Max's eyes narrowed. "Isn't that her right there?"

A girl wearing a fuchsia rain jacket with the hood up was rushing up the path from the food court, her gait uneven. As she approached, I saw why. Her small frame was weighed down with bags: a plastic one in each hand, a satchel dangling off each shoulder, and a hip bag worn tight across her chest.

"Speak of the devil," I said, unclipping my seat belt. I opened the car door and ran toward her. "Amethyst!" I called.

Amethyst blinked. "Hazel? What are you doing on campus?"

I sidestepped the question. "Can I help you carry all these … ah, what *are* you carrying?"

"Just my books." Her eyes shifted to the left. "And dinner."

Now that we were up close I could see and smell that the two plastic bags in her hands were from Guac'n'Roll, the taco joint in the food court.

And they were full to bursting.

How many tacos could one witch eat?

Is something I wasn't rude enough to ask.

"That's a hex-ton of books," I said instead. "Want me to carry one of your bags to the car for you?"

Amethyst's lips twisted into a cruel smirk. "Oh, how sweet of you," she spit out in a voice dripping with false kindness. "So now you suddenly want to help the younger generation of witches, do you? Is that because you feel guilty for not mentoring poor Yolanda when you had a chance?"

Her words were a slap in the face. I took a breath and reminded myself she was a teenager, and she was hurting.

"To be honest, I do feel guilty," I said. "But that's not why I'm offering to help."

I'm offering because you're acting really sus, and I think you might be the key to everything.

"It's kinda late, Hazel," Amethyst snapped. "Gotta go."

She pushed past me and staggered to her behemoth car. Its driver side door was touchless, by magic or by tech. Without stopping to pull the satchels off her shoulders, she got in and the Hummer zoomed off.

"What was that about?" Max had caught up with me. "And why was she carrying like fifty pounds of tacos? Jealous."

"Maybe she's got a dozen friends waiting in the car?" They'd fit.

Max shook her head. "Nah, I checked. Not unless they were ducking down or locked in the trunk."

"Ha."

"What? She was acting shifty."

"Has been for weeks now," I said. "I just don't think a Green Witch who's into social justice and fairness would lock her enemies in a trunk, and then feed them tacos."

"Mmm, tacos…" Max was extra distractable when she was hungry.

"We should tell Elliot we saw her and that she was acting odd," I said, "when we're done with this pointless floor crusade."

Max winced. "Speaking of which, do we really need a fly for this last one? Library's open so you can just go invis, right?"

I dug in my purse for my tin of mints. "I got this."

The hardest part was avoiding crowds on the way into the front lobby. It was easy to sidestep the front desk and hop the turnstile without tripping any alarms. From there I strolled into the stacks.

They were as endless as I remembered them. A whole world of knowledge to lose yourself in, though it could be awkward if you stumbled on a couple who were lost in a different sort of knowledge.

But the flooring? That was new. Gone was the white vinyl that carried whispers and made every shoe clack. Each floor I walked had been upgraded to some kind of premium rubber. It was eerily quiet but as an invisible witch I appreciated the extra cover it gave me. I could walk right past people like a library ghost.

And truthfully, that's what I felt like. Not just because I was invisible, either. That warm feeling I'd had earlier, that little had changed since Max and I were seniors? Being surrounded by college kids—with their backpacks and their world-weary laughter and their bizarre flirting rituals—was reminding me that college kids were … kids.

I didn't belong here anymore.

I was itching to call it but knew I couldn't tell I found a way into the basement. I walked around till I spotted a technician repairing a light fixture on the ninth floor. I swiped her keys from her belt and pushed a button for the service elevator.

And boom. Dingy black tile. It was here.

Only problem was, Yolanda wasn't. The place was empty, except for a rat that skitched across my path. I screamed and clamped down on my urge to curse in words. Last thing I needed was to turn visible here.

My phone burbled and I read the screen in disbelief. It was a file drop.

Of course, another video.

My heart was hammering in my chest—how close did the kidnappers have to be to send that?

I ran to the elevator and waited till the door closed safely behind me before hitting play.

This video was even more spare than the last. No proof of life. No reassuring images of Yolanda. It was only trees, giant conifers. Had the vamp moved her to the woods?

"You tried to get something for nothing," a theatrical, grouchy male voiceover began. "Life doesn't work that way. Once you've paid me, I'll send you the coordinates to get your witch back. The price is now half a million."

My phone burbled with a text from Elliot.

The floor matches the college library basement. Be careful.

I forwarded the video to him. And I couldn't resist sending a selfie too: "Way ahead of you."

He shot back another text: "**Get the hell out of there. I don't want to have to rescue you twice in one month.**"

Oh damn. Rude.

CHAPTER SIXTEEN

THE CORVID WOODS was a three-thousand-acre wilderness, home to black bears and much scarier elk. But to Kade and Elliot? It was their backyard.

It took the two shifters less than five minutes to watch the video and then ID *from memory* that *particular* stand of spruce trees.

Midnight found us all crowded around the bakery's corner booth, staring at a projector painting the wall with the landscape of those precise GPS coordinates.

And by "us all" I really do mean *everyone*.

Elliot. Me. Britt and Graham, who wouldn't so much as look at each other with Max literally standing between them. Drew Kensington, who'd clearly never set a gold Versace sneaker in a common bakery before. The Carnivora gang, sullen-faced, with their vampire charges. Who also looked sullen, after having been forced to endure a week of the Carnivora lifestyle of beerhalls, darts, casing local businesses, and late-night gossip.

Torrin was even edgier than usual. His hands were in the pockets of his leather jacket, and he glared out the window as if the full moon or Gran's flowered curtains personally offended him. I wasn't thrilled to see him *or* Jasper in my bakery, which they'd tried to rob. Unfortunately, we needed all hands on deck if we were going to take down Yolanda's kidnapper tonight.

Elliot was locked in a heated debate with Drew over a plan of attack, and Kade was busily brewing coffee to fortify everyone as it slowly sunk in for me that Yolanda's rescue was happening. *Finally* happening.

We were going to raid the vampire's stronghold in the woods and get our girl back, safe and sound. Assuming it wasn't too late.

And assuming we could ever stop bickering amongst ourselves.

"How do you *not* see it? Approaching from the North is superior." Drew's million-dollar face was perplexed as he squinted at Elliot. "The wind muffles any sounds, blows our scents in the opposite direction—massive win."

"Drew, buddy, I know you've never done this before." Elliot seemed to take pleasure in pointing it out. Drew had begged to be involved, since it was technically his fault that Sheryl revoked her offer of a century-old vampire for backup. But Elliot wasn't about to let him take over.

"In an ambush like this," Elliot went on, "the wind's not high on our list of problems. Being seen is. We split up, one group sneaks in from the East, the other crouches in the underbrush over here coming from the Southwest…" He bent over to draw on his tablet with an electronic pencil, and two diverging lines appeared on the projected map. The room was hanging on his words and I wasn't gonna lie: he was even hotter when he was in his crime-fighting element.

"That plan gives us the most visual cover," Max said, thinking aloud. She, too, knew the woods like the back of her hand. And the back of her paw.

"I just need to get a clean shot at his heart," Elliot said, "before he's got visual ID on us. That'll incapacitate him for long enough for the rescue team to dash in and grab Yolanda, and the stake team will follow." At our silence, he added, "That's how cops think," like a mic drop.

"With all due respect, this is not your typical police ambush." Drew flashed a smile at the group of us. "You need to think like a vampire, am I right?"

Some vampires clapped in agreement, or maybe just vampire solidarity.

"Wrong." Torrin pounded the counter. "You. Have. To. Think. Like a criminal."

"Glad someone said it," Jasper added. "We're trying to knock him down and take what he has, yeah? Keeping out of sight is everything. The cop's got it right … for once."

"Young man, you underestimate how good our hearing is," said the vampire who had been a vice principal. "Some of us can echolocate like bats and dolphins."

Torrin recoiled. "Well, that's just friggin' creepy."

She held her ground. "Would you talk like that to a dolphin shifter?"

"No, ma'am. They're cute. You're an unnatural monster who shouldn't exist."

Protests rang out from everyone who wasn't Carnivora.

Britt's voice rose above the din. "We have a witch in the room!" All eyes turned to me as she continued, "Hazel, can your magic help either of these plans?"

I thought it over. "Logistically, it's easier for me to create a cone of silence for us," I said, "than to glamour everyone invisible and keep them invisible for as long as they want."

"Oh, well, that changes things," said vice principal vampire. "If the kidnapper can't hear us, then Deputy Elliot's plan makes sense."

Her neck-tatted Carnivora bodyguard clapped her on the back and Drew shrugged like it didn't irk him. Which is how I knew it did.

Scruffy the waiter from the Drunken Barrel spoke up. "What if we don't want a witch to silence us?"

"She's not *silencing* us, bro," Torrin said. "She's keeping our words from being heard by the kidnapper."

I stared at Torrin. Did the gang leader just defend me, sort of? Only to put an irritating new member in his place–Scruffy had to be a raw rookie, surely?—but still. I wanted to replay the moment over and over.

But Scruffy wasn't satisfied. "What if I'm philosophically opposed to witch magic?"

"Then leave," Elliot said flatly. "The door's right behind you."

"Wait … what if Scruffy's right?" a second Carnivora member spoke up. "This witch has been known to side with the undead."

"Seriously?" I said, as the predictable murmurs kicked up. Not this "traitor" garbage again.

Graham's chilling roar shut down the room.

"Suck it up, kids." Graham cast a glower straight at Scruffy. "Take it from a Poli Sci professor. If you don't want to be an evil dictator someday, your purist ideology must bow to the greater good."

"Yeah, so both of you zip it or we'll put *you* in a cone of silence." Torrin looked annoyed that Graham stole his thunder. "We need Hazel to do her witch thing, got it morons?"

Weird how it took him that saying it for me to realize … they *did* need me. I was playing a vital role in this battle. *Battle? I'm not built for battle.* I lost track of the conversation as my breath sped up. I was a baker, just a baker. What was I doing here, surrounded by much stronger beings, preparing to fight for the first time in my life?

I had to, though. For Yolanda. Couldn't let her down a second time.

There was no room for failure.

While everyone was busy telling Scruffy to get over his oh-so-pure self, I slunk to the back kitchen. Panting shallow breaths, I leaned against the counter to steady myself.

"Earth to Hazel!" Kade was holding his hand up in front of my face. "Your mocha."

"Sorry. I was zoned out." I took a deep breath—too deep. I felt dizzy. "Well, freaking out. Panicking."

Kade nodded like that was all normal. "It's scary stuff," he said gently. "Ambushing a vampire."

"You look calm," I accused.

"I'm just used to ever-present panic. It's like an old friend." He handed me the cup.

I held it in both hands, letting it warm my fingers. "Tell me it's going to be okay," I begged. "That Yolanda will be okay."

He gave a short laugh. "I'm better at coffee than pep talks."

"Can you *try*?"

Kade bit his lip. "In high school, Dad would always promise me I was only going through an awkward stage and any minute now I'd wake up and find I'd grown up. Into a normal, stand-up guy, like Dad himself. Made me feel better. Till one night I woke up and … I'd shrunk. I was buzzing and flying through a strange landscape in the night, blinded by the light of the full moon."

"Holy cupcakes."

"Yeah, the pep talks stopped making me feel better after that. I felt kinda betrayed, even though it wasn't Dad's fault. See, he didn't know things don't always turn out okay. But I do. And so I never make promises."

I stared at him. "You could have said she'll *probably* be okay."

"Oh, yeah, true." He cleared his throat. "She'll probably be okay."

"Thanks," I said sarcastically.

"I can't say it with any more conviction, or it'll sound like a promise."

I tossed a dishtowel at his back. *You did turn out to be a stand-up guy,* I thought. But I didn't get a chance to say it out loud, because he turned back to his espresso station just as the front door chimes dinged and the buzzing in the front room turned to stunned silence.

I ran back in to see Drew's assistant Marina standing in the doorway. She was carrying a giant yellow duffel bag—which wasn't good. She was supposed to have dropped it off at the police station along with two other identical cash-stuffed bags, for the officers to place in the kidnapper's locker at Swole Tim's Gym.

Elliot got to the point. "What happened at the drop off?"

"It went not quite as smooth as silk," said Marina, a fashion designer by training and by passion. "More like polyester satin in a house with cats. I deliver three bags to the police station. I wait with Officer Potts. I help her with Sudoku, while Sheriff Gantry and Officer Murthi drive away to place the money in the gym locker. I expect them to stay and monitor the premises, but they come back! They say it did not all fit so they … brought back the third bag." She held it up, her eyes flashing rage. "*Why* did they simply not place it in the locker next door with a small note?"

"Because they're incompetent idiots," Drew said with feeling. "'Good enough for government work' does not mean good."

Elliot didn't argue, for once. Just swore under his breath.

"Shoot." Max's hand flew to her mouth. "If his accomplice tells him the money looks light, I hope the kidnapper won't take revenge on Yolanda."

An angry, low buzz filled the room. The thought of that gross kidnapper hurting Yolanda minutes before we could get her to safety was too awful to contemplate.

"Don't you worry," a trembling female voice spoke up. "That

evil bloodsucker's not going to live long enough to count the money if I have anything to do with it."

I looked up to see a frail, older woman who was the shiest of the newbloods. To my surprise, all the Carnivora shifters high fived her.

"You heard the lady, let's go rescue a witch!" Jasper yelled, and the whole room roared with one voice.

CHAPTER SEVENTEEN

PROVING THAT THE kidnapper was a low-energy old man at heart, his hideout's coordinates were barely a mile from a trailhead with ample parking. At 12:42 a.m., our caravan of half-a-dozen cars and several motorcycles arrived in the Raven Lot. The weather was doing that Pacific Northwest freezing rain-snow-sleet combo they call a "wintry mix."

Wintry mix, like seriously what kind of b.s. is that?

I zipped up my puffer coat to my chin and pulled up its quilted hood. I was already freezing, and we hadn't even done anything yet.

"I want to do the cone of silence before I go invisible," I said. "It won't take long, but we need to stand in a circle."

"You heard her," Elliot barked, "gather round!"

Scruffy threw me a contemptuous look, and I was definitely worried he would spit in my rosé the next time I went to the Barrel for drinks. But he joined the others as they formed an awkward oblong around me.

Reaching into my belt bag, I pulled out a half-pint jar of crushed herbs and nervously scattered them in a circle. Stress, in my experience, upped the challenge of casting a spell. But what I *hadn't* factored in was the power of nature to put a Green Witch into trance. The grass shimmered where my herbs touched it, and the face in the full moon winked. The trees all around me swayed closer and whispered, "You got this," in the most unbelievably calm, tree voices.

"Step forward thrice," I commanded like a witch who knew what she was doing … and was shocked when they all did indeed take three steps closer to the center of magic. Me.

Now we were a real circle, and I could speak the ancient words:

"Within this hallowed dome, our voices freely roam.
The secrets herein blest, no enemy shall wrest."

I prayed I wouldn't have to use the thick, pointy wooden stake Elliot had issued me moments before I glamoured myself invisible.

"So how do we know the spell actually worked?" Torrin demanded as we trekked through the forest as part of the Southwest faction, a.k.a. Team Stake.

"Of *course,* it worked," Drew Kensington snapped, "she's a professional. Hazel would no sooner ship a dud spell than serve a sub-par wedding cake."

I flinched at the memory of Drew's ill-fated wedding, but I appreciated the sentiment. "Thanks, Drew," I called from my invisible spot at the rear.

"Also," Max added, "I gather it's a pretty basic spell."

"I wouldn't say *basic,* I mean it's not as simple as shifting," I said.

And then regretted being petty at a time like this.

Torin still looked doubtful. "Maybe we should stop and test it, to make sure."

"We can't stop now, young man," said the vampire vice principal. "What's gotten into you?"

What *had* gotten into Torrin? Back at the bakery, he'd gloriously shut down Scruffy in my defense. Now he was suddenly unsure of my casting skills? Even if it were possible to test the spell, stopping would put us behind the other group. We all needed to arrive at the spruce stand at the same time.

"Have I ever questioned *your* ability to intimidate people and break windows?" I asked.

Torrin paused, then shrugged. Maybe he was just unnerved at being dissed by a disembodied voice.

Half a mile in, we had to go off the trail and I was deeply regretting my cowardly choice to glamour myself invisible. It was nearly impossible to hike through slushy, leaf-encrusted mud at a fifteen percent grade without twisting my ankle when I couldn't see said ankle.

No one else seemed to be struggling, and why should they? They all had Godlike superpowers. Once again I felt my vulnerability as the only somewhat-regular human in the group.

We crunched through endless leaves until we could hear the Eastern group's feet crunching over frozen grass up ahead.

"We're very close to the hideout!" Elliot's voice rang out, startling me. Weird how it didn't sound like where the crunching footsteps had come from. Was my spell distorting the sound's location?

Okay, fine, something *might* be wonky about that spell … but I wasn't going to share that thought with Torrin.

"Rescue group is crouching immediately to the west of the copse," Elliot reported. "Stake group, are your weapons ready?"

My heart was tap dancing inside my ribcage. "Ready!"

"Taking my position to aim for the suspect's heart!" Elliot yelled. "When you hear shots—"

"Ew, what is that horrible smell?" Britt interrupted, just as a young female voice took over the night air through what sounded like a loudspeaker:

"*Greetings,*" the voice intoned. "*From your friendly, local vampire hunters.*"

Oh no. Oh *no*. Had we fallen into a trap?

"Who the hell are you?" Elliot yelled.

The young woman only continued in a world-weary tone: "*As you can see, we've freed the young witch.*"

I crept up to peek between the trees. There indeed was Yolanda's sleeping bag, the tips of her dark braids easing up and down with each sleeping breath. *Breath*, she was breathing. Alive! A lump caught in my throat.

"*We watched you fail,*" the loudspeaker voice said. "*And understood we would have to take over. To do the job you should have done, again.*"

Something about that voice's cadence sounded familiar, but I couldn't place her. Was she using voice distortion software, or magic? Come to think of it, I could also smell a perfume, heavy with coco notes. I'd assumed it was one of my teammates, but was that what Britt meant by the smell?

Could it be…? Was a Beige Witch behind all this?

"Let's go!" Torrin's voice jolted me out of one adrenaline haze into another. He shoved his charge, a middle aged vampire guy who I was pretty sure worked at the library, forward. "We're not your bodyguards anymore. We align with the hunters, shifter pride forever!"

The other Carnivora members in my group took off running after their leader. Rustling and crunching from the East, as well as loud protests, let me know the same thing was happening in the other group. They were leaving us here.

Was that the play all along?

"Oh, my heavens!" the trembly-voiced vampire lady wailed. "They've delivered us straight to the hunters."

"*Outrageous*," Drew spat. "I paid them good money to protect innocent vampires."

"You're free to write a bad review," Graham said wryly.

"So-called Vampire Hunters, show your faces now!" Elliot demanded.

"I think they're hiding behind Beige Magic," I said.

"Why would a Beige Witch join the Vampire Hunters?" Britt sounded betrayed, and I remembered she'd been friends with several Beige Witches in high school.

Max said three words that it clearly pained her on all levels to speak: "I don't know."

I didn't either. Nor did I understand how they knew where to find Yolanda's kidnapper, given that he and his accomplice just moved his hideout tonight.

Had the accomplice stabbed him in the back? Or the front, for that matter.

And how was Yolanda still dozing through this confrontation? Had the kidnapper compelled her to sleep or was she, too, under a witch's spell?

Any hopes that the Vampire Hunter girl would shed light on these mysteries died when the loudspeaker clicked. I heard frantic scrambling through the brush. The smell of perfume grew uncomfortably strong.

Then I was knocked down flat on my butt.

Not by the perfume smell—by another invisible witch who ran right into me.

More annoyed than hurt, I pulled myself to my feet. "I think she's gone."

"So's the vampire kidnapper." Elliot was standing only a few steps away from Yolanda's sleeping bag. "The hunters did do our job for us. See?"

We all drew closer, then recoiled *en masse*.

At Elliot's feet was a smoldering pile of greenish-brown, jellylike sludge. Gagging, I averted my eyes. Suffice to say *that* was the source of the awful smell Britt had noticed.

At the sight of the vampire corpse, the newbloods resembled startled emojis. Their facial muscles contorted in a mask of fear, as if they were trying out for a horror movie and overdid it just a tad.

A young, male voice piped up from several yards beyond the spruce copse. No loudspeaker. No distortion. Just an angry yell.

"Behold, the vampire Walter J. Veruca!" he cried. "Please note, this is the second vampire we have cured this community of. The first was Gerard, another disgusting menace. One by one, we will free this community of dangerous and unsavory vampires. We're the Vampire Hunting Society, remember us!"

With the snap of a twig and crunching footsteps on frost, he vanished.

"Anyone else find it weird that he kinda used that speech to build their brand?" Max said.

"Did anyone recognize that young man's voice?" Elliot sounded desperate. "Speak up now."

Kade, Graham, Britt, Drew, the other vampires, and I all stared past each other with distant gazes that showed the weight of too many shocks in too little time. No one said a word.

The sleeping bag rustled and a soft yawn rang out. Yolanda's eyes popped open.

"Whoa!" She blinked in groggy confusion at the motley crew huddled around her in the moonlit forest. "Where am I? What's going on?"

I ran to her side, forgetting that I was invisible. "It's okay, Yolanda! You're safe. You're coming home."

Rather than being spooked by the reassurance from a phantom,

Yolanda smiled her familiar sweet smile. "I've been dreaming about that for days," she said.

Elliot seemed to study her face. "How long do you think you've been asleep?"

Yolanda's eyes traveled upward, like she was trying to think clearly. She was already sounding less groggy.

"The last thing I remember," Yolanda said, "is that mean customer looking into my eyes back in Purrfect Pancakes and telling me to fall into a deep sleep."

Britt let out an astonished gasp. "Babe, you should *never* look into a vampire's eyes!"

Yolanda's eyes widened. "That guy was a vampire?"

It struck me, and maybe the others too, just how innocent Yolanda was.

"Hey, you've been asleep for nearly a week," Max said. "You must be so hungry!"

"I bet your mom will make you her best magic pancakes ever," I said. "Bursting with healthy Green Magic."

Everyone laughed except Yolanda, who incongruously broke into sobs.

"She's been through a lot," Elliot reminded us.

Finding Yolanda alive and well was an oasis of joy. A victory over the divisive forces that fought to tear apart our town. But only a couple of hours later, I sat up in bed with a start, so panicked it took several gasping breaths to orient myself.

I was in my peaceful loft in my cozy house. All was quiet, except for Graham's snoring.

I was safe. *Yolanda* was safe. The vampire kidnapper was dead. So how come everything felt absolutely wrong?

Yolanda's homecoming had been both sweet and tearful. She and Jacinta flew into each other's arms in the doorway of their apartment above Purrfect Pancakes. Mother and daughter squeezed each other tight in such a vice of affection that I was honestly anxious for their ribs.

When they let go, Jacinta breathed the sigh to end all sighs.

"Thank God you're home, sweet girl!" she said. "And thank goodness for the Vampire Hunters."

Everything about that sentence went *clunk, wrong* in my brain. The hunters weren't heroes. Them gaining clout among shifters and witches was frightening.

Yet at the same time, who could blame Jacinta for being grateful her daughter was home safe?

Yolanda, apparently.

She winced. "Mom … they're not that great. They're vigilantes who happened to be helpful once. I think in some ways, they're as bad as the kidnapper."

"How can you say that?" Jacinta demanded. "He was an evil bloodsucking monster!"

"Mama, stop. You hate it when people say 'wicked witch,' how's this any different?"

Jacinta frowned in confusion. "Well, of course it is. But let's not argue tonight, unless it's about what kind of pancakes I should whip up."

Max, Britt, and I hung around while Jacinta frantically made pancakes for everyone. They smelled like butter, sugar, and chocolate chips. She was probably too drained and exhausted to add Green Magic.

"You should call Amethyst," Jacinta nagged her daughter. "She's been worried sick."

Had she really? I wondered "Wait, where *was* Amethyst when the kidnapping happened?" I asked, remembering she had been upstairs in Purrfect Pancakes after having filmed the bad customer incident. "Why didn't she hear the vampire dragging you away?"

Yolanda looked confused. "I … I don't know. I was unconscious."

"Sorry, of course," I said. Why was I interrogating the victim? It was Amethyst who had quite a bit of 'splainin to do.

We had then said goodbye to the two, leaving them to bicker gently on.

But now, waking up in the night, I marveled at how rational and articulate Yolanda sounded about her own kidnapping. How could someone who'd just been kidnapped be so stinkin' philosophical and nuanced about it all? Most people would be in shock, taking years to process it. Yolanda's resilience was inspiring. But it was also … well, if not suspicious, then odd.

Even odder than what happened to the ransom money, which, if you listened to Officer Murthi tell it, was, "Nothing. Nothing coulda happened to it. No cars drove up to Swole Tim's Gym all night. No people ever went through the doors, front or back."

Be that as it may, he could not deny the locker was empty. Someone had snatched the two duffel bags and spirited them out of the building … and that someone also knew enough to block the security camera with spray-paint.

"So what happened to the money?" I wailed to Elliot on FaceTime as Graham drove me and Britt home from the police station at two a.m. "Did the accomplice take it?"

Elliot wearily shook his head. "What do you think, Hazel?"

"I think the accomplice is one of the Vampire Hunters!"

"I do too," he said.

It was a surprisingly comfortable feeling, albeit currently stressful, to work so closely with Elliot. The way our minds worked dovetailed nicely.

"Gosh, how many of them *are* there?" I asked.

"More than I thought." Elliot paused like it pained him to go on. "More than I can handle. I hate to say it, but I need to ask for help from the elder vampire council."

So even though I longed to climb back into that healing, rainbow light of the moment we found Yolanda, as I lay in bed trying to soothe myself back to sleep, I couldn't shake the sense that nothing was really solved and nothing was as it seemed.

CHAPTER EIGHTEEN

I'D BEEN WAITING approximately fourteen years for Elliot James to ask me out.

But on Sunday, the day after Yolanda's rescue, he finally strung together words that sounded like a dinner date. And it was far from magical.

"You're coming with me to Farm to Beachhouse. The vampire elder council's meeting there tonight, and I need their help with the hunter situation."

I shivered, not just from the chilly evening air. It had started to snow just as I was locking up the bakery, moments before Elliot caught up to me on Ocean Street heading to the bus stop.

"You've got to be kidding," I said. "Why not bring Graham?"

If the meeting went south, the grizzly could probably remove their heads.

Elliot gave me a patient look. "It has to be you."

"But why?" Despite my terror at the thought of being surrounded by thousand-year-old undead, I was flattered Elliot chose me as his second. "I guess I did solve a murder before you," I preened, admiring my nails, which Britt had painted for me last night. Green, of course. "And I *am* something of an expert on vampires these days—"

"It's 'cause you're neutral," Elliot interrupted, his patience wearing out.

Right, the whole Green Witch thing.

"Neutral." I stuck out my lower lip and blew on my bangs. "You really know how to make a girl feel special."

He gave me a *whatever* look, not deigning to acknowledge my snark.

Farm to Beachhouse wasn't just any old fancy, all-local-and-organic restaurant that my mother drooled over. Sure, it boasted a Michelin star and a killer view of sunset on the boardwalk. Sure, people went crazy for the fried golden beets and sun-dried tomato focaccia. But the place also belonged to Max and Kade's parents, Noor and Aaron Dweck. It was a labor of love for the foodie farmer couple who had taken me in during my senior year and fed me warm, delicious meals while I lingered at Max's house to avoid my own family.

No part of me envied the Dwecks and their success. Becoming local celebs hadn't changed them one bit, and Farm to Beachhouse's popularity was well-deserved.

Still, there was something a little surreal about how my teenage comfort food was now the town's chic date spot.

The first wave of the dinner crowd was already gathering. Several well-dressed couples stood under heat lamps outside, waiting to be called in. As we entered the waiting area, a trio of bankers in suits filed in behind us.

At the firepit bar, stylish patrons sipped wine and enjoyed a view of the moonlit beach boardwalk. The bartender was chatting up a pretty woman in a fuchsia bodycon dress and sky-high heels—a look that made me feel underdressed in my Sage Bakery T-shirt and a blue, slub cotton maxi that was the skirt equivalent of sweatpants.

I did a double take. The pretty woman was Leia Lin.

Weird, how at every step of this investigation, I ran right into that Beige Witch.

Weird, bordering on suspicious. Especially now that I had reason to believe a Beige Witch was somehow mixed up with the Vampire Hunters. The timing didn't quite line up—she hadn't arrived in town till weeks after Gerard's death.

Or had she?

You could never be sure of anything, with a witch whose magic was all about preening and playing dress up. *Who even knew what the real Leia looked like?*

Or acted like. In some ways, a Beige Witch was like an overgrown teenager, trying on views and values like outfits. And looking fierce in all of them. No wonder Amethyst had clamored to have Leia for her mentor over solid and sensible Lorelei.

The start of a theory was bubbling in the cauldron of my mind, but unfortunately Elliot stood mere inches away, smelling great and being super distracting. Instead of his tan uniform, he was dressed in date clothes. A black jacket, crisp blue button down, and jeans that didn't look like he'd they'd spent time in the woods or in a tree. His cowboy Chelsea boots looked like Italian leather.

I unzipped my parka and turned to face Elliot. "I need to blend in. Give me your jacket."

His eyes narrowed slightly. It *was* kind of a power move.

"If you'd given me a heads up," I said, "I'd have dressed differently."

"I like how you're dressed."

"Well, I guess that's the important thing," I quipped.

He stared at me for a moment, then took off his jacket and draped it over my shoulders. His touch electrified me, but I tried not to let on.

"Does the council always meet at cool restaurants?" I asked.

He shook his head. "Normally they meet at each other's mansions, eat what their chefs cook, drink from blood dolls, and play board games. But shifters aren't allowed at those meetings, explicitly. This was the only place they might be willing to parley."

I laughed. "To 'parley'?"

"Talk to the other side." Elliot paused. "My kind."

"I know, it's just … like that's so … pirate talk. Ar, ye matey."

"It's a war." He gazed back at me, not sharing my amusement. "To us shifters, it's no joke."

I faltered. "Okay."

I knew what he meant. Even before the hunters came along, the enmity between vampires and shifters in Blue Moon Bay ran deep. I just hadn't grasped until this moment that Elliot had a personal stake in it.

So to speak.

Feeling more than a bit off-balance, I trailed after him toward the host stand where a stunning, blue-haired hostess devoured Elliot with her eyes.

"What can I do for you?" she purred to him, ignoring me.

As usual he seemed perfectly clueless that a woman was throwing herself at him.

"We're with the Juventus party," he said blandly. "In the private dining room."

There was a private room? How come I never knew that?

The blue-haired temptress looked him up and down. "Of course," she murmured. "Follow me, I'll take you down to the wine cellar."

She spirited us through the kitchen and down a set of back stairs to a cool, stone-walled basement lined with wine bottles and oak barrels. The décor here was not trendy but classic, old-fashioned. A Persian rug on the stone floor, in cream, wine, green, and gold hues that felt timeless. There was one long oak table that looked fit for a medieval castle, and seated at one end were three people.

Just three.

No security. But why would you need it when you were a thousand-year-old vampire?

No blood dolls. They were probably waiting at home, setting up the board games. The image made me chortle, but Elliot's glare wiped the smirk off my face.

As a whole, the vampires didn't look like my idea of the wealthy, immortal elite. It was disturbing how all over the place they were, thematically and aesthetically. The terrifying lunch lady, Sheryl, was there, a stain on her shirt that stretched over her tum. And a round, jolly, balding man in a Lululemon half-zip, joggers, and Hoka sneakers, who I could easily imagine barefoot in a friar's robes a millennium ago. A youngish-looking woman in a puff dress and slouchy jean jacket wore her long, mushroom-brown hair in a mass of Cypriote curls on the top of her head, like a Roman statue.

Was she an actual ancient Roman chick?

They went silent when we walked in, an unnerving silence that made the hostess scurry back upstairs without waiting for us to be seated.

The possibly-Roman chick broke the silence. "Who is your companion, *Vigile?*"

Elliot nodded to me. I was glad he didn't presume to speak for me, but nervous about introducing myself to these ancient creatures.

"Hazel. Greenwood. I work at Sage's Bakery down the street? Actually, I co-own it, or will own it…"

The old ones' eyes narrowed, as if to say, *Get to the point.*

"I'm a neutral Green Witch," I blurted out.

All tension evaporated like butter on a sizzling pan of golden beets.

The friar patted the seat next to him and poured me an actual goblet of ruby wine. "Hazel, you must try the Burgundy." He had a faint British accent and totally crooked teeth.

I opened my mouth to demur but made the mistake of meeting his jolly, crinkled eyes. This homely vampire was suddenly the most charismatic man in my world.

Too starstruck to refuse, I sat down beside him and accepted the glass. As I drew it to my lips, Botticelli angels swam through my vision, and Mantovani violin music hummed in my ears. I wanted to weep. Because this wine tasted so good it had ruined me for the cheap crap I could actually afford. *Forever.*

No one offered Elliot a seat. It was downright weird to see *him* being disrespected.

"You may ask your questions, then be on your way." The Roman chick addressed Elliot as if she were his queen, which I reckon did not sit well with the shifter. But he was putting up with it, more or less. He knew he was in enemy territory.

"We're here to enjoy ourselves, after all," she added, "not solve your problems."

"About that." Elliot cleared his throat. "I wanted to alert you to a problem *you* might not be aware of. This Vampire Hunting Society is bigger, more powerful, than we'd realized." He paused dramatically. "And they've claimed a second kill. I thought you'd want to know."

Elliot's tone implied, *You're welcome.* But the vampire council's reaction was not of gratitude but amusement.

"We heard they put down the silly kidnapper." Roman chick—I'd begun thinking of her as Flavia—gave a golf clap like a hummingbird's fluttering wings. "Congrats to them. Killing a newblood might even be a fair sport for those burdened with a pulse."

"Hear, hear." Friar Tuck raised his glass. "To fairness and sport!"

It was distressing how likeable he was when I didn't think about what he was endorsing. Or that he'd probably feasted on people's eyes back in the Middle Ages when even humans ate weird stuff.

"So, you're not at all concerned." Elliot's voice was calm, but his face looked on the verge of twitching with frustration. "That a Vampire Hunting Society is racking up kills and gaining clout."

"What should be our concern, precisely?" Sheryl ripped a piece of focaccia and savored it. "Mmmmm. Mmmm…"

"Consider them part of the ecosystem," Flavia said. "Culling the weak. Let's face it, this town is too small to support so many vampires, and you can't get anyone to move out. It's too idyllic here. The sweet little downtown…"

"The sunsets," Sheryl agreed dreamily. "Salty sea air."

"Good food and wine," the friar added, and the trio clinked glasses.

But I couldn't force down even one more sip, and not just because I'd already emptied my goblet. I felt sick. Britt was totally right. The elder vampires not only didn't care if the newbloods died, they secretly kinda preferred it.

"Your community values are noted." Elliot's irritation wasn't far below the surface now. "But your lack of concern is misguided. The hunters aren't just culling your herd for you. Gerard Chevalier was hardly a weak newblood."

At Gerard's name, all three elders slumped in frustrated deflation.

"Oh, him." Friar Tuck sighed and stabbed an oily, fried disc of a golden beet.

Flavia muttered, *"Tramas putidas."*

"What does that mean?" I ventured. "Does that mean nobody here liked him, either?"

Sheryl the lunch lady was sharp enough to follow the look in Elliot's eye. "Don't overthink, *Vigile*. It wasn't we who staked that fool, Chevalier. Would have been within our rights to execute him eventually, but we'd agreed to a more modern approach first." Contempt twisted her mouth. "He was recently placed on a Performance Improvement Plan. Just twenty years ago."

"What are you talking about?" Elliot snapped. "What were his crimes and why weren't we told about them?"

Flavia cleared her throat. "Some years ago, this council censured Gerard for creating newbloods without following protocol. It was no one's business but our own."

"We cautioned him to cease and desist his activities," Friar Tuck explained, pouring himself more wine. "Guy just kept coming back with lame excuses."

"He told us the law was different in his time." Flavia looked disgusted. "As if we are not familiar with change ourselves. It's not the Middle Ages anymore, buddy, look around." She gestured around the ancient-looking wine cellar, and grimaced. "Perhaps I did not choose the best location to illustrate my point."

The others laughed and threw back their wine.

Elliot and I sat at the bar minutes later, side-by-side and debriefing. "Did *anyone* on the planet like Gerard?" I asked rhetorically.

Elliot had ordered a double shot of whiskey, Mr. Low Carb. Still buzzed from the fine Burgundy, I was sipping ice water.

"I can think of only one person," Elliot said. "Marie Pierre."

"She doesn't count," I scoffed. "His blood was all that kept her young and beautiful. Not to mention, alive."

He gave me an appraising look. "Since when do you know about valets?"

"I'm a fast learner, Elliot." The friar's wine was making me bolder. "Really, you can stop underestimating me anytime."

"What makes you think I'm underestimating you?" He gestured toward the hidden stairs to the wine cellar. "I brought you to a vampire council meeting. I let you in on the kidnapping case."

"Because you needed a witch! You should have let me in because I'm good."

His eyes twinkled with amused fire that belied his nonchalant response. "Sure, okay."

Was he being infuriating on purpose?

I returned to the subject at hand. "So, Gerard was breaking vampire law," I said, "when he turned Britt and the others. Are they entitled to any compensation from the council, or from Marie?"

Elliot's amusement faded. "It works the opposite way," he said. "They're unregistered newbloods, the lowest rank of vampire there is. No record of their existence in the scrolls. No vampiric penalty for killing them."

I shook my head as the implications sunk in. "I'm starting to think whoever killed Gerard did us all a favor."

"Just 'starting to'?" Elliot downed his whiskey and flagged the bartender to ask for another. "It's highly likely his own kind whacked him, by the way. An execution. For being … noncompliant."

"Then what about the Vampire Hunting Society?" I wondered aloud, glad the people around us looked too engrossed with their dates and exquisite meals to eavesdrop. "You think the council staked him and then paid them off to take credit? Maybe they even created the Vampire Hunting Society and funded it!"

"No. Not the council's style to play around like that. Threatening newbloods is beneath them." Elliot sounded certain, and I wondered if there was anything hotter than a man who knows exactly what he's talking about, because he pays attention all the time.

"If anything," he went on, "they must be annoyed at the hunters for drumming up interest in Gerard's murder. You heard Sheryl—they don't want us digging around. She said it would have been their right to execute him. They want us to drop it."

I thought about what he'd said. The vampires wouldn't play around. "What happens if we don't drop it? I mean, to us."

Elliot leaned over, his expression teasing. His woodsy cologne tantalizing. "Are you worried they'll invite you over to play board games, Hazel?"

I crossed my arms. "I was hoping you'd say nothing bad could happen. Because I'm neutral."

"Well, they won't kill *you*," he said with bleak cheer. "But if you cross them, they might make you wish you were dead."

I shivered. "Not reassuring."

"I'm a crow, we don't blow sunshine." He clinked glasses with me. "Welcome to the war, witch."

I rolled my eyes. Could he *be* any more patronizing?

"Do me a favor and try to think back to how you felt," I said, "when all of this was new to *you*. And confusing. And scary."

His smug smile only got smugger. "What happened to, 'don't underestimate me, Elliot'?"

Before I could think of a zinger to properly shut him up, his phone beeped. He peeked at the screen, then silenced it and drank his second shot.

"I'm going to hang out here a while," he said, setting the shot glass back on the bar. "Aaron and Noor will be in later, and I haven't said hello to them in a while. What about you, gonna stick around?"

I grinned. "Is this your convoluted way of asking me to have dinner?"

"No, I just kinda want to know when I'm getting my jacket back," he deadpanned.

But there was a twinkle in his eye and his words didn't matter. The way he was looking at me right now did, like I was the world's most entrancing witch. Like he was through underestimating me. Like he could spend the whole night like this, bantering back and forth until the last riposte transformed into a kiss.

My heart quickened to an untamed waltz as I met his gaze.

Though a less-mature version of me would have wondered if there wasn't a hotter woman standing directly behind me.

Then I heard a soft, charming voice. "Elliot."

"Hey, you're early." Elliot's posture straightened. "We said eight, right?

I turned around very, slowly, knowing what I would see but hoping until the last second I was wrong.

Leia stood at the corner of the bar, reaching out her hand to flirtatiously touch Elliot's arm.

"I know, I just couldn't stay in my boring apartment," she said, giggling. "I was so looking forward to seeing you and ... Oh, hi Hazel!"

My face burned. Had I gotten everything wrong?

Everything?

Elliot crossed his arms and turned to me, for once tongue tied. "Hazel, it's not what you..." He trailed off, then restarted. "I met Leia a week ago and we started talking—"

"Great, I'm happy for you." Normally I didn't interrupt people ever, but adult Hazel was no longer in charge. If I had to hear the story of how they met, I wouldn't be able to hold it together. To pretend I was anything but stunned and devastated. "Have fun you two." With a big fake smile, I took off the jacket and handed it to him. "Don't forget to order the golden beets. People go crazy for them."

He called my name and I ignored it, high-tailing it for the door. On my way out, I flagged the blue-haired hostess and arranged to buy them an order of focaccia. It was my last classy adult move before teenage Hazel, the bullied and forgotten middle sister, was running the show while fueled by hurts that were a strange mix of old and new, like the restaurant itself.

Marching up Ocean Street in the bitter cold, I knew exactly what I was going to do before I did it, because I knew teenage Hazel very well. She would dig into her purse for an invisibility mint, shuffle back home, and stay up late reading a grimoire while snacking on her own baked goods. She'd ignore her roommates carrying on a thrice-illicit courtship downstairs. She'd ignore confusing Elliot and his weirdness. She'd ignore everything except getting better at magic, because magic never let you down. Magic helped Gran and the community.

Damn it, Elliot, why did it have to be that Beige Witch?

CHAPTER NINETEEN

I PREDICTABLY SPENT THE evening binging on grimoires and bad chocolate, and when my alarm beeped from under my pillow the next morning, I was so deeply in communion with the ghost of Hazel Past that I half-expected to find myself late for sophomore PE.

Washing my bleary face in the bathroom, I allowed myself a moment of gratitude. Elliot was choosing to date a Beige Witch instead of me, and that sucked. But I was a free adult witch with a fabulous job.

One crap thing about working at Sage's Bakery, though, was having my work alarm go off at a time that could easily be described as night.

Living alone, it had quite never sunk in for me what a giant bummer it was not to get to sleep in past dawn … till I was forced to tiptoe through my dark living room past the bear-snores emanating from Graham's XL sleeping bag. Britt's petite, satin PJ-clad form lay spread-eagled on my futon, looking like she died of relaxation. Meanwhile I was already in work-appropriate clothing.

And a puffer coat.

And earmuffs.

Powered by resentment and lots of milky tea, I shuffled outside at four-thirty a.m. and eased the front door shut. A blue piece of paper fluttered like a fall leaf onto my porch.

Dread-butterflies dancing, I scooped up the page and breathed a sigh at the benign moon logo on the letterhead. It was only a notice from BMB Metro Bus. Phew.

No, wait, not phew. They were canceling early-morning bus service effective today, due to a driver shortage.

Dear Bakery Lady, I'm retiring to Maui to volunteer with a sea turtle rescue, someone had scrawled in ink at the bottom of the page. *Safe travels, Frances. P.S. Might be time to get you a car!*

It was more than she'd said to me in two weeks of rides. *Godspeed, Frances. Save those baby turtles.*

I'd have to rescue myself.

My gaze narrowed on Britt's gleaming, dove grey Mini Cooper preening in my driveway, dateless until her nine p.m. waitressing shift at the Drunken Barrel. Oh, I'd get me a car all right.

I marched back inside—no point trying to wake the undead girl—and swiped her keys from the coffee table.

A low growl made me fumble and drop them.

"What are you doing?" Graham stood behind me suddenly, fully dressed. Deadly calm.

"M-my bus was canceled," I stammered. "I have to get to work. You don't want to see what the people in this town are like without their mood-boosting muffins and stress-melting cookies." I took in his flannel, jeans, and boots. Dude slept fully dressed? *Actually, that makes sense for a bodyguard.* "Wait, you just growled at me ... but you're in *human* form."

"Got your attention, didn't it?"

I rolled my eyes at him. Would shifters and vampires never get tired of trolling me?

"You're right about the cookies." He reached into his pocket and pulled out a set of keys. "Take my truck." He tossed them to me. "You can keep driving it to work while I'm here. Least I can do for all your hospitality."

I willed my jaw to return to a closed position. "Wow, thank you, um. Don't *you* have a job to go to?" I thought of his lumberjack flannels and boots. His ancient truck. Was he losing a week of logging wages to take care of Britt? Or cowboy wages? Or whatever rugged thing he did for a living.

"Nah, it's dead week," he said, looking a bit sheepish. "I teach Poli Sci over at Reed."

Graham was a *college professor?*

"I asked my TA to proctor the final next week," he went on, "Don't worry, I got her a stack of gift cards with the cash that rich vampire threw at me. Student instructors don't get paid enough. Hey, what's *that* look?"

"Look? What look?" I made my face go blank, unaware I'd been broadcasting anything. "I just thought you were some kind of outdoorsman. The way you dress…"

His brown eyes narrowed. "You think I'm a poser."

"Hey, none of my business." Not gonna lie, I was relishing this moment. *Me* being the smug one.

"Well, my outdoor hobby kinda is your business, since you're about to drive my truck." He put his hands in his pockets, looking pained. "The smells … can linger."

Smells? "Really, I don't need to know!" I frantically waved him off. "*Please don't—*"

"Hauling deer carcasses, there's a lot of blood." Too late. "Hunting elk is worse. Let's not even talk about moose…"

"No! Let's not."

In the end, I cranked down the windows and drove with my scarf wrapped around my nose and mouth to drown out the thick, metallic scent that followed a successful hunt. The local deer were sulky, entitled pests who'd nibbled a hole in my herb lawn, but that didn't mean I wanted to picture Graham hunting them in bear mode.

Unfortunately, I couldn't stop picturing it the whole time I was in his truck.

Breathing in the fresh, pastry-filled air of Sage's Bakery was a privilege I'd been taking for granted. In the kitchen, I inhaled deeply and nodded to Kade, who was across the room funneling cinnamon, nutmeg, vanilla powder, and cocoa into shakers for our coffee bar.

He met my eyes for a moment and I tried to ignore the energy crackling between us.

An elegant white demitasse waited for me on the counter.

"What's that," I asked Kade hopefully, "a very tiny mocha?"

He wagged his finger at me. "Mochas are only a gateway. You're ready for the next level."

"Oh, you're confusing me with someone who loves bitter-tasting awfulness."

He pouted. "It's a dry cappuccino, with our finest roast."

I took the tiniest sip and made a face. "I like my drinks wet."

Secretly? It wasn't that bad. Complex flavors, caramelized milk and velvet foam, a sprinkle of nutmeg, but it just wasn't my thing. After dealing with Elliot last night, I had to admit it felt good, empowering, to be able to hold my own with Kade.

"You're the worst." He didn't look the slightest bit upset. "You know, it's kind of adorable though." His green eyes sparkled with trouble. "How you're like, almost scared of anything not sweet."

"Shut up, I'm not *scared*." I felt a blush rise at being called out. Sure, I preferred sweet-tasting things. I was a baker. Not a kale farmer.

"Your cheeks get bright pink when you're embarrassed." He

shook his head as if in wonder at me. "Man, you really have no idea … how cute you are."

"Okay, you can stop making fun of me any time, now."

"I am dead-serious flirting with you, Hazel."

I looked up to see Kade gazing intensely into my eyes, totally exasperated with me.

"What do I have to do to get your attention, witch?"

A million replies whooshed through my brain. Like, *how can I possibly pay attention to your hotness while Britt's still on the run from slayers?* And *when Marie's like a walking* Medium *article about the victim-to-abuser playbook, and Carnivora's clearly up to no good?*

And then I thought back to the way Elliot's romantic gaze lingered on that Beige Witch Leia, and why shouldn't *I* have a little fun in my life? Hex Elliot. He wasn't the only man in town worth flirting with.

That annoying lock of auburn hair that kept falling over Kade's eye did it again. And this time I couldn't resist. I reached out, gripped his soft hair between my thumb and forefinger, and smoothed it behind his multi-pierced ear.

At my touch, his consternation melted away. His skin smelled warm and woodsy, and I wondered if he'd slept in the woods last night as a bobcat. With his mouth opened slightly and his eyes half-closed, I could picture him as that cat. Stalking his prey, a natural carnivore, yet still with human awareness lingering in his mind. How had I never seen what a complex being Kade was? More importantly, how had I never before gotten this close to his hypnotic, forest-scented body?

Now that my hand was in his deliciously-scented hair, my other hand felt totally left out of the fun. Experimentally, I ran both hands at once through his thick, auburn hair, short everywhere but the front. As if in a trance, I gently tugged at the short hair on his nape, lightly scratching the back of his neck and making him shiver.

He grabbed my face in his hands and kissed me, and I kissed him back.

"We're going to hang out," he said between kisses. "Outside of work." Kiss. "And if this blows up later." Kiss. "We'll never be able to look." Kiss. "Each other in the eye again. We'll die of awkwardness."

"Sounds like a problem for future us." I felt breathless. And more than willing to burden future Hazel for more of this. Britt had Graham; Elliot apparently had Leia. *Ugh*. Hex it, why shouldn't I throw caution to the wind?

Kade was hotness itself. This man I was kissing had biceps, and triceps, and probably other … 'ceps. He dressed like he knew what decade this was. He made me coffee. Had Elliot ever made me a mocha once? He probably didn't even own sugar.

"Where are we going on this date thing … this hangout?" He could have said the moon or the backseat of his truck. In that moment, I would have been down.

"How about getting a drink tonight?"

I stared. "Go out on a Monday?"

Monday night was for cozy tea and grimoire drills, and my new microwavable slanket. It was just like Tuesday and Wednesday nights that way. Also Thursdays.

"There's a great live band over at the Barrel on Mondays," Kade explained. "They play classic blues stuff. And there's dancing."

"The *Drunken* Barrel?" My voice didn't hide my disappointment. It's not like I thought I was too good for our local watering hole. I just didn't want to run into Britt.

Or Max, for that matter.

Oh no, how was Max going to feel about me dating her twin?

Was I supposed to say something—so she heard it from me first? It was too early for an announcement, but too late to ask permission.

Maybe this was a bad plan.

"Please let me introduce you to blues dancing," Kade whispered in my ear. "I'll do all the work leading. You'll just melt into the music. I never got to slow dance with you in high school and it's one of my major regrets in life. Plus, the berry puree margaritas are half off."

"Oh my God, yes. Just yes. Let's do this. Unless…" I hesitated. "We're not going to run into Max there, are we?"

"Huh?" Kade squinted like he couldn't figure out why I was bringing up his sister. Awareness was not among his stellar attributes. "She has her TTRPG group tonight at Gunar's Games."

Relief flooded through me. Whatever price I paid for this vacation from sanity, it would be worth it. Like herbs needed both sunlight and crappy soil, I desperately needed to cut loose for a night—to drink margaritas, dance with a hot man. And make out like there was no tomorrow.

"So, can I pick you up at seven?" Kade asked.

"That's perfect. Now back to your cash register," I admonished. "And take this monstrosity with you!" I pointed to the coffee cup.

"Yes, boss." He smirked. "But hang on, one more thing."

He kissed me again.

Still in a daze after work, I floated through the front door into my living room.

Britt and Graham were lounging on my sofa back-to-back, their legs and feet up resting on opposite sides of my couch, each reading from their own tablet. She'd changed into leggings and an oversized plaid shirt that had to be Graham's. A half-eaten bag of BBQ chips rested on the coffee table between them. I refrained from pointing out how totally *married* they looked, because I needed a favor.

"Help me," I said to Britt. "I have a date and I don't know what to wear, how to do my hair, or *anything*."

"Yesss!" Britt rubbed her hands together like a tiny evil genius. "Finally, I have a valid excuse to take you for a mall makeover."

"Mall makeover?" I glared at her. Two of my least favorite concepts, why would she put them together like that? My mind flashed back to senior year when Britt and her fellow mean girls tormented me and Max with the threat of a *forced* makeover, to make us less weird and dorky.

"Hazel, I know what you're thinking." Britt sighed. "Yes, I was a horse's butt in high school. But this is different. I'm not trying to change you who you are, I'm trying to do fun girlie stuff with you. And live vicariously," she added with a shrug. "As an undead person whose looks can never change, no matter what I do."

Aw. I'd never thought of it that way. "It's just, we don't have much time before Kade gets here."

"Your date is Kade?" Britt squeaked, staring at me. "Max's hot brother?"

"Maybe?" I hadn't wanted to tell her, but as I thought about it, she had no room to judge.

"Wow, I thought *I* was in trouble, dating her ex." She let out a whistle. "Her twin's worse. Those two are so protective about each other."

"And I've penciled in feeling guilty for tomorrow," I said. "Today, I'm not thinking about consequences."

"Got you. Okay, then let's pare down to the essentials." She held up three fingers. "Highlights, brow shaping, mani/pedi—girl, your toes need love. As your roomie, I see what goes on under those witch boots."

"My date's in an hour."

"Lip gloss. Can't go wrong with a little black dress and lip gloss." Poor Britt looked so deflated I went from wanting to smack her to wanting to hug her.

"Britt?" I asked. "Would you, um, put my hair up in a messy bun? The fringed donut kind? They're harder than they look."

She smiled. "Sure."

When Kade picked me up in his gleaming truck that smelled like lime air freshener (and not deer carcass), he was wearing faded jeans that hugged his smokin' hot body and a grey Henley over a black band shirt.

It was obvious that after running home to shower and dress, he'd stopped at Bubbie's Bubbles, the local carwash. A thoughtful gesture, but somehow it made everything too real. Who bothered with car washes? Not the bad-boy shifter of my high school fantasies.

A man on a date who wanted to impress her, that's who.

I also wasn't prepared for the awkwardness when we met each other's eyes as two people who'd impulsively made out in a food service kitchen. Kade's open, boyish face looked expectant, like he couldn't believe we were actually on a date.

Honestly, neither could I.

"You look amazing," he said softly.

"I do, don't I?" At his amused look, I conceded, "You *always* look amazing."

He grinned and glanced at his feet, looking oddly shy for Kade. "Didn't think you were paying attention."

I laughed as I buckled my seatbelt. "*Please*, how could I not notice my co-worker's hot like the Fourth of July?"

The shyness intensified. "I … just I didn't think you saw me as boyfriend material."

Well, shoot. I swallowed. He'd hit the nail on the head. My reservations about Kade as a boyfriend went beyond his checkered past. It was hard to picture him taking the lead in any situation, or sticking to a budget. Remembering to buy milk or eat vegetables. What kind of dad would he make, someday?

But I didn't want to have a big talk about the possible distant future, not tonight. I wanted to be crushing his lips with mine.

"Kade?" I owed it to him to make sure we were on the same page. "I don't know if we're a match. I'm better with cookies than crystal balls. But I know I like you and I like kissing you. Can we start there?"

His features relaxed. "Yeah, I'd really like to start there."

He rested his strong hand on my knee, and we drove down Filbert Street toward downtown.

Two heavenly strawberry margaritas later, my doubts about his ability to take the lead melted away on the dance floor. Blues dancing was absurdly sensual and the perfect antidote to stress. Kade was a crystal-clear lead, his touch signaling my next move with just the right amount of pressure. I wasn't a graceful dancer by any stretch, but he made me look downright *decent*.

It didn't entirely feel like a date, because I wasn't nervous. I felt like I was just hanging out with a good friend who happened to be kissworthy.

And I'd never had so much fun dancing.

Only thing was, every time the door swung open, my pulse sped up, thinking it might be Max.

"Why do you keep looking up at the door?" he asked me after I'd signaled I wanted a break. I'd sat down at the table nearest to the dance floor, and Kade had flagged the waiter over.

"I'm not looking at the door," I lied.

"Yeah you are." His expression softened. "Carnivora likes to drink beers here after ten. You're nervous about seeing them, aren't you?"

I seized on that excuse. "Yes, I am very nervous about running into scary gang members." It wasn't technically a lie.

"Well, don't worry, I would never let those idiots harm a hair on your head," he whispered in my ear. "But don't look now."

Terror flooded me. "Is Max here?!"

"No ... it's Carnivora." He gave me a weird look. "Like, almost all of them."

A dozen shifters strutted in and settled down at a long table in the back. Torrin, I couldn't help but notice, wasn't among them.

Scruffy the waiter, who'd been dragging his feet in a languid roundabout journey toward our table, instead rushed to bump fists with his brothers. He headed back to the bar to pour their pints, muttering, "Thanks for your patience," as he brushed by me.

"He's so *zealous* about the whole thing," I said. "Like, he genuinely hates me for being friends with Britt."

Kade nodded. "Scruffy was obsessed with Carnivora, like more of a fanboy than an initiate. His not being much of a fighter made him a tough sell, though."

"At least he's a barrel of fun," I said. "Why *did* he want to join?"

"For political reasons. He read *All Glory to Nature* by Silvan T. Lykos. Anti-vampire propaganda," he added. "He used to follow the gang around with a notebook recording what they said. Anything mildly interesting that happened, he said it was the harbinger of a revolution. He was so annoying they made him be their errand boy for years before they finally let him in."

Political, anti-vampire. That got my attention. "Do you think it would be worth interviewing him to learn more about the gang?"

An odd look crossed Kade's face. "I don't know. Maybe not a good idea."

"Why, you think he wouldn't talk to a traitor like me?"

"Nah, he'll talk your ear off, but I mean, what's the point? It's not like Torrin trusts him with sensitive info."

"Does he not like Scruffy?" The two did seem to butt heads.

"I get the impression Torrin's barely aware of Scruffy." Kade leaned in. "Why do you think Max wouldn't be happy to see us together?"

My eyes nearly bugged out of my head. *Damn it*, why did he have to suddenly get a clue? He really was just like Max.

"Because she's my best friend?" I said. "And you're her brother?"

And because she nearly murdered me in high school because she mistakenly believed I was another Ashlee Stone, a mean cheerleader who pretended to be Max's friend while scheming to get close to her hot brother. A touchy subject all around, as Ashlee was dead now and Kade was a suspect in her murder till we found the real killer.

"She loves you, and she loves me," he reminded me. "Us being together would be a dream come true for her."

Again, he was talking like there was an Us. Instead of two idiots who gave in to temptation and made out in the back kitchen of a bakery, one of them wearing a hairnet the whole time.

"Besides," Kade added, "she's always wanting me to date someone non-screwed-up and respectable for once."

I wrinkled my nose. "Is that how you see me, respectable?"

"And hot!" he said quickly. "Which, if you think about it, is a rare combo. Unicorn rare."

I laughed. "Nice save."

Scruffy finally showed up at our table, looking surly as usual instead of happy and convivial like when he was chewing the fat with his boys.

"More margaritas, the opiate of the people?"

"Yes, please," Kade said, ignoring the dig. "And we'll split the nacho plate."

"And," I added, hoping this wasn't my dumbest idea all day. "We have some questions about Ree and Orion."

Scruffy scowled. "What do you want to know?"

"Everything?" I gazed up at him with my best helpless damsel expression. "I heard you're an expert on all things Carnivora. The historian of the revolution."

Kade was right. Scruffy's principled dislike of me paled next to his love of hearing his own voice. He went and poured himself a pint, then settled into the chair across from me.

"They were high school sweethearts," he began in the tone of an eccentric historian being interviewed for a Ken Burns documentary. "Then Torrin talked his brother into joining Carnivora."

"And … then they were like Bonnie and Clyde?" I guessed.

"More like Romeo and Juliet."

"Star-crossed lovers?" I blinked, wondering if I'd understood him right. "But they were both shifters, what was the problem?"

"Hello?" said Scruffy. "This is Carnivora we're talking about. She's an alpaca. A fluffy freakin' llama, for crying out loud! She chews cud."

"Seriously?" It was the dumbest reason for rejecting her that I could think of. Surely Torrin and all the rest had eaten a few salads in their lives? If not, I didn't even want to imagine what their arteries must look like.

"But I thought family connections meant everything to shifters," I said.

Orion was Torrin's brother and she'd been his girlfriend since forever.

"Witch, these people are hardcore. They almost wouldn't take *me*. Can you imagine?"

I really could. Scruffy looked maybe thirteen and could not have won a street fight against my old lady customers Helen and Margaret. I feigned surprise though. "Wow."

"Right? And I'm a dog." Scruffy unfolded his arms and took a slug of his beer. "Dog, bone. It's classic. What could *be* more carnivorous?"

"Sorry," I said, "but aren't dogs sort of omnivores?"

"I am SO sick of hearing that. We strongly prefer meat!" Scruffy growled uncannily like a small terrier and launched into what sounded like a well-worn rant. "Sharp teeth are called canines, ever notice that? Sure, I'll scarf down a supreme pizza *because it's there*. You wouldn't let a glass of rosé go to waste, does that make you a wine-atarian?"

I held up my hands in surrender. "Didn't mean to hit a nerve."

"I just don't get why it's so controversial." He was getting twitchy.

"So back to Carina," I prompted.

"She didn't belong," he said simply. "Orion reluctantly dumped her under pressure. Last I heard, she was enrolled at the community college, majoring in film and video, trying to 'find herself.'"

Poor Carina, I thought. She'd found Gerard instead.

"Was Orion really killed by vampires, like Torrin says?" I asked.

Scruffy scratched his namesake beard. "Orion was talking about getting back with Ree, and then he disappeared. Torrin thinks it was vampires, but who knows. Orion was a wreck without her. And Torrin's been a wreck ever since Orion disappeared. Have you noticed he's not even here to show the flag? He pulls a fade half the time lately."

The words could have been compassionate, showing concern for a comrade in the grips of grief. But Scruffy's tone gave away his contempt for his leader.

"So, what's your problem with Torrin?" I asked.

"He's a disappointment." He spat out words like a furious typewriter, each keystroke punctuated with venom. "He *talks.*

About how vampires. Are an abomination. But does he take action? Sometimes I think his hate is performative."

It felt like a mischievous ice cube took a detour up my spine. "By action, I assume you mean…?"

"Hunting them down and killing them."

I made the mistake of looking into Scruffy's eyes just then and saw a revolutionary in his own mind. A self-important, would-be killer. The table swam in front of me as I pondered the odds that Scruffy here was the kingpin of the Vampire Hunter Society all along. What if it was right under our noses? Like Keyser Soze turning out to be the meek, mild-mannered accountant.

Or … more likely … was Scruffy the one who was all talk?

He sure did like to talk.

"I used to dream about being part of something as glorious as Carnivora, back when I was a pup." He propped his feet up on the chair next to mine, giving me a view of his pristine hipster sneakers, and closed his eyes to reminisce. "That was in the golden age of Hugin," he said. "A legendary thief who stole only from vampires. Booster and Viper were still alive, Nova and Wildfire hadn't gone to prison. All the great criminals of Blue Moon Bay were active in those happy days."

"Okay, enough about the stupid past," Kade spoke up, proving he was listening. He'd looked pretty bored while Scruffy went on and on but now he was squirming. "No one wants to talk about ancient history."

Of course. The last thing he wanted to discuss on a date was the past. When Kade himself ran with Carnivora.

As if reading my mind, Scruffy hooked a thumb toward Kade. "This guy was something else, back in the day. They called him Ghost Wing. He could find his way into locked buildings that seemed airtight. How'd you do that, bro?"

"Yeah, how?" I asked.

"See?" Scruffy said to Kade. "*She's* interested." He turned back to me. "Hugin should have been my leader. But it's just my luck, his own clan punished him for breaking the rules of their society. They hired a Red Witch who ritually pulled the magic right out of his being."

My breath caught. Red Magic was taboo, and from this cruel story I could see why. "She took away his shifter magic? So he no longer had super senses and had to stay in human form forever?"

Scruffy shook his officious head. "The Great Hugin might as well be dead now, which is why we have Torrin the green-haired wonder. He can barely plan a simple heist, so the gang's turned into a social club. Story of this dog's life," he whined. "I show up just as the Golden Age is petering out and turning into the crap age."

It was all I could do not to mime playing the tiniest violin for him.

To my great relief, Scruffy stood to serve a table on the opposite side of the room after warning me not to side with vampires anymore because, "As the group's memory and soul, I will not forget."

"I thought he would never shut it." Kade kneaded his face dramatically. "I thought we'd both croak of old age at this table, listening to that little creep moan."

I winced. "Sorry I called him over. He was creepy and whiny, but ... I did learn some things."

"Yeah, like what?"

Why did Kade suddenly sound suspicious?

"Like that Carina would have been in a vulnerable state of mind when she agreed to let Gerard turn her," I said. "And that Orion loved her, even though Carnivora forced them apart."

Did Kade look relieved? His brow unfurrowed. "So, what does that tell you?"

"That if Orion wanted her back, he might have gone to Gerard's house and confronted him."

Kade rubbed his chin thoughtfully. "You think Gerard's the vampire who killed Orion?"

"Maybe? No one seems to know what happened to Orion. There's a big piece missing to the story that I think only Carina can fill in. Tomorrow, when I interview the other newbloods, I need to get my hands on something of Carina's and get Gran to help me do a memory spell."

"Okay. Let me know if I can help in any way." Then, his voice turned sultry again. "In the meantime, wanna dance?"

The live band had packed it up, but a dozen tipsy, fun-loving souls were still out on the dance floor, grooving to the deep house booming from the Barrel's speakers.

"No, I better get some rest." I stood and untangled my purse from the back of the chair. "I'm afraid tomorrow's going to be exhausting."

"Say no more." Kade fished his keys from his pocket. "I'll take you home, Boss."

I smiled at him calling me boss.

"This has been an *amazing* vacation from reality." I could have cringed the moment the words were out of my mouth.

Kade stared at me. "Okay," he said finally. "I can start off as your 'vacation from reality.' Challenge accepted."

The entire ride home, his hand on my thigh, I wondered what just happened. Did I really issue a challenge? I didn't mean to.

Sure, I was open to dating Kade, seeing how things unfolded ... but I kept coming back to that thing he'd called me earlier: *respectable*. I wanted to be his fun fantasy like he was mine. *Respectable* was a Roth IRA and five servings of dark green veg. Not very swoony stuff.

I kissed him on the lips before I climbed out of his truck to head into my house. But it wasn't the lingering kisses we'd shared earlier. Something had cooled.

Setting down my purse, coat, scarf, gloves, and hat inside, where Graham and Britt were cuddled up asleep on the couch, I told myself it was just because I was tired. But as I brushed my teeth, my brain was spinning, replaying all the things Scruffy said about Carniovra's ill-fated lovers, Carina and Orion. Spinning on the missing random money, and Amethyst's heavy bag of late-night tacos. How many people were those meant to feed? I spun on Yolanda's enchanted fairy tale princess-like week of sleep. Jacinta's pancakes frying on a griddle that didn't smell like magic. The long march to the spruce trees where I could have sworn the sound of crunching leaves weren't coming from Elliot's group. Was Torrin deliberately trying to slow us down?

And why was Leia popping up everywhere?

I was *this* close to solving the case but there were so many jagged pieces that didn't quite fit. It was driving me insane.

Yet I was so tantalizingly close, I could taste it … almost.

The strange thing was, when I imagined myself cracking open the whole smorgasbord of a mystery, the first thing I wanted to do was rush to the police station and throw in Elliot's stupid, gorgeous face what an amazing sleuth I was.

It was very annoying that this thought kept popping up in my head.

And if I were honest, my recurring thoughts about Elliot were another reason I didn't feel like kissing Kade.

I'd tried to get over Elliot, and it hadn't worked.

Now I had a new problem to add to the growing list.

If Kade really liked me, then Max *was* going to kill me. Not for kissing him, but for breaking his heart.

CHAPTER TWENTY

THIS TIME WHEN the Mini pulled up to Marie's black iron gate, someone inside buzzed us through before Britt could even roll down her window to mess with the intercom.

Graham opted to stay in the car for security.

As Britt and I walked over to the house, Bronwen waved to us excitedly from the upstairs window. Two seconds later, thanks to vampire speed, she was throwing the front door open with a triumphant squeal.

"I can't believe you two are here!" She shook her pink head of hair in wonder. "My napkin note worked."

"Girl, that note was *brilliant*," Britt said. "Not to mention brave."

Bronwen ducked her head shyly, as if it was the first time she'd heard such compliments about herself. Sadness washed over me as teenage Hazel peered out of my eyes for a moment. I knew what it felt like to be starving for a kind word.

"You'd better come in." Bronwen seemed to catch herself and glanced around worriedly, as if Marie might be watching. "We don't have much time till she's home from church."

The newblood led us into the house and down the hall, her long hair swaying behind her, freed from its usual tight bun. She wore a feathered boho mesh top over a curve hugging slip-dress and moved through the house with slinky grace. Without Marie hovering over her, Bronwen was a different person. A bubbly free spirit.

Was there a reason she had to keep living here, even after Gerard's death? Was it loyalty to Marie, or fear of being out there on her own?

A second teenager was waiting on a giant beanbag in the TV room. With her slouchy blue button down and rectangular glasses, she too was gorgeous, in a "future high-powered lawyer" sort of way. Coily bangs framed a stunningly symmetrical oval face with high cheekbones.

"Hey, I'm Landra." The teenage girl held up a vial of blood. "Mind if I eat lunch while we talk? We just got a new shipment from HemoLife."

Britt smiled tightly. "Go for it, babe."

I averted my eyes while Landra chugged. It was healthy blood from well-paid donors, but it still squicked my stomach.

"Sounds like Gerard didn't get the chance to teach you three how to hunt discreetly?" Britt ventured. "You know, before he … got gooed." She mimed staking herself in the heart.

"*He* didn't teach us stuff," Bronwen said flatly. "He was as useless alive as he is dead."

Ouch. As a Green Witch, I couldn't think of a worse thing to have said about me.

"Is it true those Vampire Hunters are the ones who killed him?" Landra adjusted her glasses, frowning in confusion, and looked at me. "Vampires sleep deep, and Bron and I didn't hear any commotion from downstairs. Marie broke the news to us the next morning. She was crying so hard, it took a while to get out the words. That Gerard was dead. Staked, in his own kitchen."

"And then you made mimosas?" Britt asked cheerfully. "I would have."

Landra raised her eyebrows.

"Gerard's my sire too," Britt added. "Ask me anything."

The newbloods looked at each other, their eyes as wide as saucers.

"Okay, how'd *you* get out of here?" Landra put the cap back on her empty vial of blood product.

"Ten years ago, I walked out that door." Britt pointed down the hall. "You can, too."

"And be target practice for the hunters?" Bronwen shivered. "No thanks."

Landra folded her arms and glared at Britt. "Face it, things were easier ten years ago. It's bad out there. We have nowhere else to go. So don't try to sell it to Bron and me like we have some great option somewhere."

The honesty in her anger tore me up. It spoke to what Gran had been trying to get me to see all along. Most kids weren't choosing between me and some perfect mentor. Too often, it was a choice between nothing … and something awful.

Britt leaned in and glared right back at Landra. "You realize, by your own logic, the Vampire Hunters can get you in here, too?" There was a fire in Britt's dark brown eyes, a glint of mean girl energy from high school. Now she was using it for good.

"You two want your last night on the planet to be this?" Britt gestured around the TV room with its equal-but-odd mix of dorm lounge and Medieval Museum energy. "Popping HemoLife and dusting Marie's antique armoires?"

"Marie promised to keep us safe," Bronwen protested, as if she were trying to convince herself. "She's getting the house warded for us! Abandoning ship would *destroy* her. We're her family now."

"Carina didn't see it that way." Landra reached for a fluffy couch blanket and wrapped herself up like a burrito, looking pensive. "Hope she's okay, all alone out there."

"What makes you so sure she ran away?" I asked Bronwen. "Instead of staying with her parents, like Marie said."

"She didn't take any of her stuff," Bronwen said.

"And Carina's parents are shifters," Landra added. "They wouldn't accept a vampire daughter."

I nodded. "That tracks. But why would Marie lie about it?"

All three vampires groaned and started talking at once.

"Eh, she's always trying to sugarcoat things," Landra said.

"Marie's *obsessed* with protecting us," Bronwen added.

"Or saving her husband's reputation," Britt added, "even after his death. Going home to your parents? Sounds respectable. Runaway newblood? That's a scandal. Marie can't stand any whiff of disgrace to the household."

"Well, that's hilarious," I blurted out, "given Gerard was on a performance improvement plan all these years!"

I was suddenly painfully aware of all three vampires staring at me, giving me no choice but to look at the ceiling. They hadn't known. Hadn't even suspected. Britt was savvy enough to grasp the concept of "unregistered newblood," but not that her maker had been sanctioned for creating them.

"Performance improvement plan?" Britt's petite features twisted in confusion. "You mean his job was at risk?"

"Not exactly…" *More like his unlife,* I thought. Spilling secrets I'd overheard at a council meeting might make the elders angry, and that terrified me. But it felt wrong not to tell Gerard's childer the truth about him.

So, I told them. Everything.

"Whoa, Gerard was slated for execution?" Landra couldn't believe it.

"We're unregistered?" Bronwen sounded worried. "What's that mean?"

"Nothing good," Britt said.

"So, to recap." Landra's voice was bitter. "He charms us with compulsion, turns us into vampires, then gets staked. Carina vanishes. We get a death threat from the Vampire Hunters. And now we learn Gerard left us high and dry, in every way there is."

"Um," I said. "You mean *Gerard* got a death threat from the hunters, not you. Right?"

"Trust me, I *think* I remember having my unlife threatened," Landra snapped. "That letter came weeks after his death. Why do you think Marie's so freaked out? If we die, she's out of lifeblood."

Britt and I exchanged grim looks. When Marie had showed us that letter, she'd been very clear that it had been sent to Gerard. That she'd agonized over whether to take it to the council. And after his death she deeply regretted not doing so. These errors of fact couldn't be accidental. Why would she make this story up?

There was one possible benign explanation: she was trying to protect the newbloods. To draw suspicion to the hunters instead of to Carina.

Even so, evidence was piling up that Marie was a skilled, habitual liar. Her word couldn't be trusted.

And that made me even more worried for Carina's safety. The safety of *all three* girls.

"Can we check out Carina's bedroom?" I asked. "I might be able to enchant one of her possessions with a memory spell and get some idea of what her last memories in the house were."

Bronwen nodded, and upstairs we went.

The upstairs floor was a glossy, honey wood and the room at the end of the hall had a white shag rug straight out of Pottery Barn Teen.

"She was sharing a room with me." Bronwen gestured to the frilly twin bed nearer to the door. Its duvet, a crushed rose velvet, matched the bed on the other side of the room. Meaning it wasn't Carina's own style, but something Marie had likely bought it for a generic newbloods' room. Creepy thought. How many girls had slept here, over how many years?

At least the nightstand looked personalized to Bronwen, holding a mason jar of dandelions, a Kindle, and a pair of sparkly purple hair combs.

Bronwen slid open the mirrored closet door. "I packed up her clothes and stuff," she said, reaching for a large cardboard box on the top shelf. "I kept thinking all these things were important enough for her to bring to a new life. Maybe she'll come back for them?"

If she hasn't been murdered, hung in the air unsaid.

While I pored through the box's contents, Bronwen went about folding her laundry and putting it away. I took it as her graceful way to give me a little space, but still keep tabs on me.

Carina had left behind jeans and T-shirts, socks and underwear, a cute little black dress and a cream cropped leather jacket. Sneakers and manga. Airpods. An antique watch, still ticking. A silk scarf similar to Marie's … a love-bombing gift from Gerard, maybe? A framed photo of two baby alpacas gazing up at their mother.

Right. Carina was an alpaca shifter. Was that a photo of her family, in animal form?

A carved wooden jewelry box was stuffed with handwritten notes: *love you forever and ever, O.*

More photos, and a ring with a tiny, sparkly fleck.

This was the motherlode of personal effects. I tried not to choke up. Wherever Carina was, she'd fled without her most prized possessions. I wished there was a way to give them back to her.

At the bottom of the box was a lumbar pillow with an

embroidered case that read *You are home.* A double meaning? Must have had sentimental value, because the pillow felt lumpy and misshapen.

Unless ... *why* was the pillow so lumpy? Surreptitiously, I felt around until I had unzipped the case as quietly as I could. Instead of one of those white inserts, I found a stuffed animal. And not just any stuffie—a cuddly meerkat.

Torrin was a meerkat, so his brother must have been one, too. Had Orion given her this, a playful token from one shifter to another? Even after they split, she'd kept his memory close. Even gone to the trouble of hiding it from Gerard and Marie.

I rezipped the little pillow. "May I borrow this?" I asked Bronwen, who glanced up eagerly. "I'll bring it back, promise."

She nodded. "Whatever you think will help her."

When we came back down the stairs, Britt and Landra were arguing in the living room.

"I can't *not* work, okay, Miss Ten Years Ago?" Landra sounded defensive. "Or the lights will get turned off around here. And my parents sure aren't going to support me; they think I'm in some weird drug scene."

"So, get a part time job and student loans." Britt was no more fazed by Landra's attitude than Landra was intimidated by Britt's. The two of them were, in a strange way, sounding more like cousins or bickering old friends than people who just met.

"Dropping out is for losers," Britt added flatly. "Ask me how I know."

"Wait ... you're quitting school, too, Landra?" I asked.

Just like Bronwen. They were giving up on college to support Marie, because they felt she was the only one offering them safety. What a mess.

Landra's perfect face looked tired. "You think I'm happy about this?" she said. "I love school. Love my classes. Even the new prof who took over from Gerard is fantastic. Teaches video editing techniques, taught us about special effects. But there has to be money coming in, or there will be no HemaLife. So … I'm starting a full time job next week., Bookkeeping for a law firm."

"She's got mad accounting skills," Bronwen bragged, but the look in her eyes was one of compassion. "We're both gonna get our degrees someday … plenty of time now, right?"

Resignation dulled Landra's voice into a monotone. "At least I can work from home."

Britt pulled out her phone and held it out to Landra. "Text yourself."

"What?" Landra narrowed her eyes. "Why?"

"Because I need your contact info. You too," she said to Bronwen. "I'm going to work out a plan to get you both into non-dysfunctional housing for next semester. In the meantime, reach out if you need anything. Or you just want to talk. It would…" Britt stopped and shrugged, like she wasn't sure she should say this out loud. "It would mean a lot to me to be able to help you."

Landra hesitated, then snatched Britt's phone. Her texting thumbs were a blur.

"Now get out of here," Landra said, handing the phone back. "Before the Queen of Passive Aggression gets home from church."

It was still the lunch rush when Britt dropped me off in front of the bakery, and there was a line out the door.

Kade's eyes twinkled as he nodded at me from behind the counter, where he was serving paninis and gourmet hand pies to one hungry customer after another.

I headed straight to the back—and was surprised to see Gran's old-fashioned purse resting on the counter. The woman herself sat on a high-backed stool sipping fragrant lavender tea, gazing into the middle distance.

I gasped. "Crap, was I supposed to take you to your doctor's appointment today?"

Gran looked up and smiled serenely. "Oh, no, Hazel dear, that's what I dropped in to say. I've canceled that appointment. Got better things to do with my time."

"Um, are you sure?" *Where is this coming from?*

"I thought it over," she said in a calm and reasonable tone. "And what's the point of seeing a magiopath? I know what's wrong with me. Age!" Gran chuckled. "Nothing can fix it, because it ain't broken."

"Gran, I know you don't like doctors but—"

"I gotta suck it up, buttercup," she interrupted, pushing away her mug. "And be grateful for what magical ability I still have. Rather than sitting at home watching soaps while my magic dwindles, I should be mentoring you."

I forgot whatever argument was about to come out of my mouth. It had been so long, so *very* long, since she'd helped me learn a new spell. It would save me time, energy, and frustration.

"Well, now that you mention it," I said slowly. "I could use your support casting a memory spell."

"What, right now?" Gran gulped. "With that line stretching out the door? You want to start a panini panic?"

"Kade's got it." Funny how fast I'd gone from not trusting him with the till to low-key avoiding him. I feared our relationship had peaked somewhere between the first kiss and the middle of our only date, and it was, as we'd anticipated, super awkward.

"Besides," I added, "it's kind of urgent. I need to help this newblood who ran away the night her sire got staked and—"

"All right, all right." Gran waved her hand in front of me. "Enough about the nocturnal neck-nibblers. I'll help you with the dang spell. Now, what's your memory anchor?"

"It's a stuffie. From the boy she loved." I opened my messenger bag and retrieved the lumpy pillow, then pulled out the meerkat stuffie.

"Get a copper bowl," Gran commanded. "Rub it with a lemon balm tincture to clear past energies. Then fill it with the dried white rose petals we charged under the harvest moon. I'll get the seeds and herbs ready."

A few minutes later, I was deep in a magical trance. Birds sang honeyed harmonies directly to my ears while neon dandelions bloomed en masse across the kitchen floor. Side by side at the counter, Gran and I chanted together:

"With this token left behind,
Your tragic loss I gain.
Inside my mind alights
Another soul's remembered pain."

Instantly, the counter faded away.

I was lying on the floor in a dimly lit room. Above me, two figures were yelling, fighting. Men. An older one and a younger one. I felt revulsion, terror, despair—and … love.

Then both men were gone. The dim room was gone.

I was back in the bakery kitchen.

Granny Sage was slumped over her bar stool, face down on the counter. Her mug was knocked over, spilling herbal tea everywhere.

Gran had fainted in the middle of the spell.

CHAPTER TWENTY-ONE

THE MAGIOPATH'S OFFICE was an hour's drive up the coast in Pacific City, a peaceful beach town with golden dunes, dramatic cliffsides, and a beach-front pub that was ideal for hosting weddings on the sand—that is, if brides didn't mind a chance of fog and drizzle. Even in July.

On this freezing December afternoon, though, the beach was deserted except for a lone jogger.

Gran had been so quiet all through the drive, I'd flipped on the '80s station, hoping some upbeat tunes would make things feel less dire. Weird that I never noticed it before, but it turns out the lyrics to most '80s songs are *depressing as hex.*

Following my phone's directions, I steered us away from the stark empty beach to an unbusy street on the edge of downtown. I parked in front of a sagging old inn that at some point got converted into business suites. The witch doctor shared the second floor with a weight loss hypnotherapist and some guy hawking blue-green algae smoothies. *Not sketchy at all.*

But I didn't have time to question the witch doctor's reputability: guiding Gran up those stairs, in her current state, was a process. I had to steady her from one side while Gran clutched the railing on the other.

On the top landing, I pretended not to notice that my normally energetic Gran was severely out of breath. As I rapped on the locked office door, I was fighting back tears.

A woman Gran's age, with a bright silver mane and a spring in her step, opened the door, startling me. I don't know what I'd been expecting her to wear—scrubs? A white coat?—but the cone-shaped hat and black rag dress was kicking it *really* old school. Like the Middle Ages.

"Hail, fellow crone." She greeted Gran with ritually opened hands held out in front of her. "No matter how ails thee, thou art welcome."

"Welmet," Gran replied softly, and they said at the same time, "Blessed be."

Okay, were they going to talk like Shakespeare the whole time? This would be worse than avoiding Kade all day.

The magiopath nodded to me. "Hey, nice to meet you, I'm Susan."

"Oh thank God!"

I *may* have said that out loud.

"That you're here!" I added quickly. "I'm Hazel, Sage's granddaughter."

"Hazel, I know who you are." Susan seemed stunned that I would introduce myself. "Your bakery's reputation precedes you. Not that I'm much of a dessert person." It was a sentiment I sometimes encountered, but Susan was the first to speak it with neither judgment nor apology. "More of a lentil gal myself. I make a mean red lentil loaf with date ketchup."

Gran, despite her weakness, managed a snort of derision. "On second thought, getting healthy doesn't sound worth it."

"Ah, there she is!" Susan's face lip up in a smile. "You're exactly who I thought you'd be. Now let's see what we can do to help you get back to feeling your best."

Susan ushered us through the lobby and into a parlor—not an exam room—with comfy armchairs that didn't look the slightest bit medical. Her clear glasses and bold geometric earrings looked reassuringly modern, as did the tablet she pulled out of the front pocket of her rag-dress.

"So, what seems to be the issue for you today, Sage?" she asked. "I notice your aura's looking a little muted."

I listened as Gran explained to Susan how her magic had gotten more and more difficult to access in the course of normal spellwork. None of it was news to me, but that didn't make it any easier to hear.

"Hmm." Susan's electronic pencil glided over her tablet. "When did this start?"

"A month or so ago," Gran said. "But it's probably just aging, right doc?"

The doctor's eyes were sharp behind her glasses. "If you believed it was normal aging, would you have come all the way over here?"

"Guess not," Gran admitted.

"Did you teleport?" Susan asked.

"No ... my granddaughter wanted to drive me." Gran avoided her eyes. "We're making an afternoon of it. Probably get some pie on the way back—"

"Gran, you're leaving something out!" I blurted. "I just asked her to help me with a complex memory spell, and she fainted in the middle of it. She's been feeling groggy and weak ever since. I don't know if she *can* teleport."

I was half-expecting Gran to toss me an annoyed look, but her eyes just looked frightened. "So, if it's not aging," Gran said, "what is it?"

"I don't know yet." Susan's voice was gentle. "Is it okay if I ask you some more questions?"

Gran barked a laugh—"I s'pose that's why I'm here."—but she sounded like she was no longer sure she wanted to find out the truth.

Susan didn't just ask *some* questions, she asked *all* of them. Which spells were feeling harder? How quickly were the changes progressing? Were her other senses affected? She asked about Gran's eating, sleeping, hydration, and bathroom habits, as well as vitamin intake. When was the last time she danced under the full moon? Had she ever been aware of eye floaters or indistinct, smoky shapes at the edge of her vision? She even asked therapy-type questions, like how did it feel to be moving toward retirement after such a long, illustrious magical career?

All in all, she asked more questions than Dr. Nguyen, my GP, had ever asked me in five years of seeing her. I was trying to decide if Susan was a total quack or Nguyen was a lackadaisical lump when Susan looked up from her tablet grimly.

"In my medical opinion," she said, "the most likely cause of your symptoms is a deliberate magical attack. Sage, I believe you've been the victim of Grey Magic."

I gasped. "You mean someone did this to her *on purpose?*"

Gran scrunched her brow. "Who'd want to harm *me?*"

"It likely wouldn't be personal," Susan said. "Most Grey Magic victims are targeted for financial reasons. Has there been a lot of Grey Magical activity near you lately?"

"No," Gran started, just as I said, *"Yes."*

I turned to Gran. "It could have been that corporate café that was competing with us, Java Kitty. The whole place ran on Grey Magic. I could smell it coming off their Automagic espresso machines."

"It what?" Gran's eyes widened. "How could I have missed that?"

"Are you the sole legal proprietor of Sage's Bakery?" Susan asked. "If they were aiming to sink a competitor, attacking you would be written into their business plan. Beginning with the subtlest of strikes and slowly turning up the onslaught till you were incapacitated."

I snapped my fingers. "Didn't your symptoms start right around the time Java Kitty opened?"

"Well, I'll be hexed, they did indeed." Gran frowned as if thinking back. "The first symptoms *were* very mild. So mild I wrote it off as rust."

"As if a diamond like you could ever rust," Susan chided her.

"Well, *now* you're talking sense, sister," Gran said with a small smile, but it faded fast. "There's still one thing I don't understand. That tedious café closed down weeks ago. Why am I still getting worse, not better?"

Susan cleared her throat. "Because you haven't treated it, Sage. It's a magical wound and it needs to heal."

"What's your prescription?" Gran sounded suspicious. "Not lentils, I hope."

"Rest," Susan said simply. "Complete magical rest should halt the condition from progressing and in time, we hope, reverse it."

My eyes stung with unshed tears. "So, reversing it is possible?"

"At this stage, yes, but you have to take rest *seriously*, Sage. Your aura needs time to heal. Several weeks at minimum. Complete magical rest means no spellcasting," Susan clarified, in case there was any doubt. "Can you comply with that? Doctor's orders."

"Gran, please, you have to," I begged.

Gran crossed her arms over her dress. "So, I gotta sit still and die of boredom, then?"

"Isn't it worth a few boring weeks to get your full powers back?" I reached for her hand and squeezed it.

Gran sighed and squeezed my hand back. "You're right, Hazel dear. Thank you for being the grownup in the room," she said with genuine feeling. "And thank *you*, Susan, for all your help. It's a huge relief to know what's going on with me … and that it's treatable."

Susan bowed. "Go thy way, hale be thou. Cometh back in ain moon cycle."

Honestly though, she could have just said "month."

Gran and I stopped for pie at Pacific City Creamery on the way home. Gran insisted it was her treat.

"Date ketchup, what in Hecate's realm is date ketchup?" were the last words she'd grumbled to Susan, who laughed with delight as if she was being ribbed by the goddess of magic herself.

But sitting in the diner booth across from me, Gran admitted, "She's very good, Susan. It won't be fun following her prescription, but I don't want to see what the next stage of this looks like."

"I don't either." We clinked coffee mugs.

The waitress arrived then, balancing my cherry pie and Gran's strawberry rhubarb on a tray, and we dug in.

"Hazel, dear?" Gran ventured. "Why didn't you tell me before? About that Java Kitty café being riddled with Grey Magic. That must have been a real cauldron of trouble to stir."

"It was, but…" I floundered. "Guess I wanted to handle it myself?"

Her opal eyes saw through to my soul, as always. "You didn't want to burden me with that magical mess. Didn't think I was up to it, and you made a wise call." She patted my hand. "I owe you an apology, Hazel. I've been giving you guff about not understanding your duties as a witch, but I was the one who didn't understand how much you had on your plate."

"Aw, Gran…" Warm tears stung my eyes. "Thank you for saying that."

"Still am confounded as a toad in a hat, though," she went on, "as to why you're so interested in helping *vampires*."

I laughed despite the sentimental lump in my throat. Gran was still Gran.

"Don't you worry." She reached for a spoon and dug into her pie. "I'm going to do what that doctor tells me, and then I'll be right as rain. Ready to lead my heir straight to the next level of magic, because now I know she's ready in her heart."

I let the tears fall, unembarrassed. No cherry pie was as sweet as Gran's understanding.

The moment was ruined by a cranky voice behind me. Carping and familiar.

"Excuse me," it boomed. "*Why* don't these napkins have napkin holders? What is the world coming to?"

I turned to see the cashier, a smiling young man, tilt his head in bewilderment at the customer bullying him.

A red-faced older man with a face I'd been seeing in my nightmares.

"Holy hex." It was definitely him. The kidnapper. I scrambled to set my phone camera to video. "Gran, hold the phone up so you're filming that guy—but don't make it obvious. I'm going to go talk to him."

Gran squinted across the room. "What guy?"

"The rude customer up front," I said impatiently, waving the phone at her. "I'm ninety-nine percent sure that's Yolanda's kidnapper."

"Can't be, he's dead." Gran still hadn't taken the phone from my hand. "Not undead but dead dead. The Vampire Hunters got him."

"Apparently not!"

While we were arguing, the old man had started to walk out. I couldn't just let him get away. Never mind that I was a mere Green Witch, alone, without shifter backup. Leaving Gran at our booth with my phone, I raced outside onto the beach to catch up with him.

I was planning to sneak up behind him and put him in an Analysis Paralysis hold, a defensive spell that rendered the subject unable to decide on his next move, but he was moving slower than I'd expect from a vampire and I ended up knocking him down instead. He must have been surprised because he went down like a ton of bricks, cursing a blue streak.

"Stop, kidnapper!" I said and prayed I could recite the incantation despite my body's trembling:

> *"In the face of your might, so fierce and so grand*
> *I cast this enchantment to level the land.*
> *Hesitation engulfs you, a wavering veil,*
> *To muffle your mind so that I might prevail.*
> *Decision eludes you, struggle you shall—"*

"Ow, my shin!" His horrible voice knocked me right out of my trance. "Are you on drugs, young woman? Or merely under the influence of bad slam poetry? Never mind, I'm suing you either way!"

Slam poetry? I faltered. Did he not realize I was casting?

I needed to finish the spell before he could get to his feet, but all I could do was stare at the bloody bruise forming on the old man's shin. Why wasn't it healing instantly? Vampires didn't get bruises.

Humans got bruises.

Did I knock over the wrong jerk? *But that face.* That voice from the videos. It was unmistakably him ... unless he had a more evil twin?

"Idiot, look how you made me drop my doggy bag," he lectured, pointing to the Styrofoam container splayed open on its side several feet away. A pair of seagulls were fighting over the pancakes strewn on the sand. "For shame!"

"I'm so sorry, sir." I helped the old guy up. The least I could do, having just assaulted a senior. No way was this elder strong enough to have carted off Yolanda. "I didn't mean to crash into you, I was just … practicing my poetry like you said."

"Is it something in the sea air?" he taunted me. "That makes all you Coasties dumb as driftwood? Boy, I can't wait to get back to Barstow."

"I'm sure Barstow can't wait either," I muttered, and hoped Gran had gotten at least a few snaps for me to forward to Elliot.

But if rude guy from Barstow was just a tourist … then whose jellied remains had the Vampire Hunters proudly presented to us in the forest?

And, even more baffling, who really kidnapped Yolanda?

The moon glowed a little too brightly over Marie's backyard as Britt's shovel worked the loose soil like a sewing machine needle through fabric.

Max and I stood by her side, under the weeping willow tree where Marie claimed she'd buried Gerard.

At least, I *assumed* Max was nearby. It was hard to be sure, since I'd glamoured her invisible while Britt was parking the Mini a block away from Marie's. As for myself, I opted for good old Invisimints, since glamouring took more magical energy.

I was conserving mine for the memory spell I would now have to cast alone.

Thunk.

Britt's shovel hit something harder than dirt.

"Here we go," Max muttered. She *was* nearby. I was glad I'd gone to the trouble to do a glamour spell instead of handing *her* an Invisimint, or she'd have just blown it by speaking.

No judgment. Took me years to stop doing that.

"Let's see if you're really in there, you jerk," Britt said, dropping her shovel.

She leaned into the hole, which was little more than a foot deep—had it been dug hastily?

My heart was leaping out of my chest when she pulled out a designer shoebox, tore the box open, and peered in.

I steeled myself for brownish greenish goo—but there was none.

"Holy hell," Britt said and I gaped along with her.

Gerard wasn't in there. The box held nothing inside but a skewer, like you'd use to roast marshmallows at a bonfire.

Part of me I wanted to believe its dark stains were innocent char, but even I wasn't that naïve. Not anymore.

"That looks like our murder weapon." I flashed visible on purpose and held out my hand to Britt. "Here, I'll hold onto it for now." Elliot would want that skewer and that shirt for forensics. "When you're done backfilling, hand me the shovel. Then you two hop the fence. I'll pass you both items and squeeze through the bushes like before."

Britt backfilled the hole in mere seconds. She patted down the dirt by stomping on it, which must have been therapeutic despite Gerard's remains not technically being there.

I timed popping my second mint for the exact moment she handed me the shovel, which disappeared along with me and the shoebox.

When Invisimints were good, they were very good.

"Ooh," Britt said, "that's really clever, Hazel."

"Yeah, slick move," Max agreed.

"Thanks, guys," I said, and promptly turned visible.

So did the shovel.

And the box.

So much for having mastered Invisimints.

"Hazel! What are you doing?" Britt hissed.

"Ugh. Sorry, I can't resist a compliment," I said, and popped my third mint—the last one I had on me—just as Marie's kitchen light blazed on, illuminating the back deck.

Britt blurred into a run toward the side yard, easily vaulting the eight-foot fence. Max was slower, but not by much. Making as little noise as possible, I snuck to the very back of the yard up where Marie's pink flower bushes butted up against a neighbor's roses.

The sliding glass patio door opened and Marie stood on the deck in a long white nightgown, a baseball bat in her hand.

"Who's there?" she called, sounding frightened. "You stay away from my house, evil Vampire Hunters!"

I stood as still as a rabbit while she stalked the yard, brandishing the bat and muttering under her breath in what might have been Middle French.

"Stay away from my girls!" she growled at the whistling wind. "They are all I have left. Mark my words, I will do whatever it takes to protect his line."

With a banshee wail, she raised the metal bat over her head and smacked it hard against the hot tub lid. The lid cracked.

Several minutes after she'd gone back inside, I was still frozen in prey animal mode. Max and Britt tried to coax me into giving them the shovel and box, but their voice sounded far away to me, as though filtered through pea soup fog. Eventually they had no choice but to jump back over the fence, boost the items themselves, and threaten to pick me up with their super strength and "help" me over the fence, at which point I rallied.

Tossing and turning in my loft bed that night, I dreamed that Amethyst and Yolanda were Gerard's latest newbloods, locked in a stifling pink bedroom in his house in Sunset. If they dared open a window, the Vampire Hunters shot arrows at their hearts.

When I woke up sweating, I tried to soothe myself with the knowledge that Gerard was dead and gone.

But after all I'd seen today, no knowledge seemed certain anymore.

CHAPTER TWENTY-TWO

I SPENT ALL OF Wednesday, my day off, reading about memory spells.

At sunset, I ground seeds in my pestle and gathered herbs to brew in my stovetop cauldron. After some thought, I'd decided to do things a bit differently from how Gran showed me yesterday. Having a mentor to guide you was great, but the benefit of doing something alone was you got to do it exactly how you wanted.

By the time Max rang the doorbell, I had been chanting for half an hour and was in a semi-trance.

Barely looking their way, I motioned for my friends to join me around the table. Graham sat on the couch reading, staying out of our way and keeping Max from guessing what was becoming more and more undeniable: that he and Britt were a couple.

I pulled the meerkat stuffie from my carpetbag. "Carina."

The bowl of herbs and ground up seeds glowed a deep green at the sound of her name. The shiny glowing mass jumped from the bowl, pouring itself down to the floor like magic Jell-O. It stretched and spread into an ethereal green grass that blanketed my living room. Giant stems formed next, flowering into daisies and dandelions. A mint green butterfly landed on Britt's shoulder and she stared in amazement.

My vision tunneled and a familiar dizziness took over as I began the spell. *"With this token left behind—"*

A crunch interrupted my trance. At the smell of buttered popcorn, I looked up at Max, who was holding a large bag. "You brought popcorn to view someone's tragic memory?"

"*You* said it would be like a movie," she said, defensive.

"Where'd you even buy that?" Britt frowned as her butterfly disintegrated into pale green pixels.

"Downtown theater, concessions are still open." Max held out the bag generously to Britt and me. "Want?"

Ignoring her, I squeezed the stuffie and chanted in earnest this time:

"With this token left behind,
Your tragic loss I gain.
Inside my mind alights
Another soul's remembered pain ."

Instantly, the dining table faded. I was in a dark kitchen, lying on cold tile. Marie's kitchen, where we'd munched almond cookies and sipped tea.

The young man had just been knocked to his knees on the tile. The older figure swooped down on him, moving so fast his body blurred.

Gerard.

He would prevail, kill the young man. The only reason he hadn't yet was that *I* was fighting too. Not the real me, but Carina. In memory-mode, I felt *almost* like I was her.

Desperate hope flared in my chest as I pounced on Gerard's back, giving Orion time to scramble to his feet. I'd do anything to save the boy I loved. He'd dared to enter a vampire's den to find me and bring me home.

Never mind that I'd become the thing our families hated most. Love was love.

Brave was brave.

Both were ribboned with darkness, though. Hopelessness. Even two against one, how could we win against the old vampire? He'd been growing turnips since before US history books began.

He might be trifling, pathetic, a loser among vampirekind. But weak he wasn't. My body thudded with pain when Gerard hurled me across the room.

We had no chance and it never stopped us from fighting. I didn't even have to meet Orion's determined dark eyes to know his heart: he wasn't going to run. He would fight to the death.

But it wouldn't be long now.

Waves of sadness rippled through my chest as a reel of Orion memories hit Carina. Sweet memories of holding hands at school. Hot memories of dancing at a beach rave. Goofy memories of running through woods and meadows as an alpaca and a meerkat.

I forced myself to my feet again, but Gerard pushed me again hard, throwing me at the far wall. Terror swamped me as Gerard advanced on Orion, spun him around. I winced at the snap of a neck being broken.

Orion collapsed in a lifeless heap on the kitchen floor and Gerard turned on me, sobbing over my boyfriend's body.

"So, this is how you repay my gift of eternity?" he snarled. "I elevated you from your animal status. I alone saw your potential. And this is the thanks I get? If you beg my forgiveness, I may spare you."

I kept sobbing and did not attempt to defend myself, but neither did I cower. It was clear that in that moment that I—that

Carina—would rather face the true death than bargain with this monster.

So that was how she died, I thought in a panic.

Then with a sickening squish, a stake pierced Gerard's barrel chest from behind. The film and video professor swore in French and looked utterly annoyed, then clutched his heart and fell, convulsing and dissolving into a greenish brown hunk of sludge. *Ew.*

"Oh God!" Britt cried out in shock. "I can't believe this."

"I know, right?" Max commiserated, pushing away her popcorn. "I so didn't want to see that while I'm eating. Anyone want the rest?"

I forced myself to take a step back from the mind-meld with Carina. "Max, you're missing the point of this memory," I snapped. "Look who's holding the stake."

It was Marie, a stoical look in her eyes.

"Thank you," Carina breathed. "But if you'd done that *earlier,* Orion would still be—"

"You owe me your life, child." Stepping over Orion's body, Marie stalked over to Carina. "A debt you can never repay. But you may start by making a small cut in your wrist with the fangs he gave you."

"What?"

"I need to feed, girl," Marie hissed. "Hold out your wrist."

"Oh!" Until that moment, Carina hadn't known Marie drank blood from Gerard. She hadn't really had much time to consider Marie's situation at all. She'd been in a daze ever since Gerard brought her here. Truthfully, she had been since Orion's gang started pressuring him to dump her. Now she was thinking clearly, though. More clearly than she'd ever thought.

"Of course," she told Marie.

After greedily drinking from her wrist, Marie looked up with a victorious expression, as if she'd gotten away with more than just murder.

"Now both of the men who worshipped you for your beauty

are dead," she jeered. "Only I am left to protect you. To teach you the ways of vampirism. You never should have been turned. But if you want to survive, I am your everything now."

Yep. No surprises. It was coldly satisfying to have Marie spell out every prejudice and envy Carina had guessed from the first. All in all, a nice little speech, but she couldn't stay focused on it. She was too busy noticing that Orion's pulse was still beating. Weakly. His breaths so shallow they could not be seen. But with her new vampire senses, she could hear his body humming with life. She wanted him to keep living.

"Of course, uh, yes, ma'am," she stuttered, eager to placate the valet and get her the hell out of the room. "What should I tell the other girls?"

Marie would want to control the message, after all.

"I will speak to them myself," Marie hissed. "Go dig a hole to bury the boy's body, since it is your fault he came here. Bury Gerard with him. *Don't* forget the stake. And the clothes he left behind."

She wanted Carina's fingerprints everywhere.

And how was anyone supposed to bury a lump of sludgy jelly?

Carina wiped away her tears and focused on the only task that mattered. Gently, she slipped her hands under Orion and picked him up like a sleeping child.

In the backyard she bit her wrist and brought it to his lips.

"Come on, baby," she murmured, "I know you're in there."

He didn't stir. She smacked him, across the face. Hit his mouth. He groaned.

"Drink it, babe. I won't promise you eternity like that fool promised me. We'll be hunted down by your gang family. But if all we get is one more day together..." She swallowed, hard. "Then we can go dancing, go to the beach one more time ... come on, *drink!*"

She forced his mouth open. It might just have been animal

instinct, but she felt a tug of pressure as he sucked the blood from her wrist, gurgled, and fell back into unconsciousness. All she had was hope, but hope was enough for now.

She marched back to the kitchen. Wrapped the gory stake—it was just a skewer, really—in Gerard's white shirt. Her gaze fell, disdainful, on the sludgy remains. Marie kept a shoebox on the counter, packed with mail for girls who didn't live here anymore. Carina emptied the shoebox, tossing all the mail in recycling, and donned dish gloves. It was a mercifully brief transfer from floor to box, though Carina couldn't help gagging at the *jigglier* parts of the operation.

There was a shovel in the garden shed. With vampire super speed, Carina became a blur digging a hole under the willow tree. She hurled the box into it and backfilled the hole.

Sinking to her knees, she threw her arms around Orion's limp body and began to sob from sheer exhaustion and stress.

But her vampire senses picked up subtle vibrations running through his body. He was changing … or he was dying. It would take about a day to know for sure.

Either way, it was time to go. She stood and slung Orion over her shoulder like a sack of potatoes. No need to treat him like a fragile package now; he was either a dead man, or no mere jostle could ever harm him.

Her soul sang with gratitude to whatever powers had led them to be together again, racing away from her old prison. The two of them were one blur in the night.

CHAPTER TWENTY-THREE

THE PENDENT LIGHTS flickered over my kitchen island, and the garden of neon astral blooms around us faded to nothingness. Britt, Max, and I gaped at each other across the butcher block countertop.

"What did I just see?" Max asked.

"That memory spell must have been a doozy," Graham said mildly from the living room couch where he was watching a basketball game on TV. "Y'all doing okay over there?"

A thumbs up was the only response I could muster. My muscles felt melty, a wrung-out feeling I associated with wielding magic a step beyond my skill level. But I also felt emotionally wiped.

Carina's memory was *complicated.*

"So did Orion die in the end, or not?" Max wondered aloud.

"We don't know, this memory's from a month ago," Britt reminded her. "They could both be dead now. Or…" She forced a smile, showing her fangs. "They could be newbloods together, living the dream."

Graham whistled softly. "More like a nightmare."

Britt's brows knitted with annoyance. "Wow, you're usually better at reading the room," she said. "It's not a time for vampire jokes."

"I'm being serious, ba—Britt."

I cringed. He'd almost called her babe. Their obvious couple vibe was out of hand.

Luckily Max still didn't seem to notice.

"Getting turned sucks for us shifters," she said to Britt with trademark Max bluntness. "It makes the shift extremely painful. Some people can't even turn into their normal animal, they can only turn into bats. Then there's the social stigma, family denouncing one as a turncoat. If Torrin found out his brother wasn't just *killed* by a vampire, but *was* a vampire, he'd stake him."

I shuddered, then a thought occurred. "Wait … how'd Torrin find out about his brother's death at all?"

Graham scratched his chin. "Maybe Orion was telling people he was going to confront Gerard?" he said. "And the gang figured they both died in the fight?"

I shook my head. "If everyone knew Orion fought with Gerard that night," I said, "then how could the Vampire Hunters claim credit for the kill and have it stick?"

No one had an answer, and it was going to bug me till I did, like a pebble in the bottom of my sneaker. Was someone slipping info to Torrin? Other than us, who out there knew the whole story? Marie and Carina both seemed unlikely informants for the gang leader, though Carina was at least plausible.

"I just can't believe Marie was the one who staked Gerard." Britt shook her head, tears in her eyes. "I guess she'd finally had enough."

"Yeah, but why now?" Max glanced down at her cold popcorn but couldn't bring herself to dig in. "He treated her like garbage for centuries."

I thought of how the newbloods were grudgingly accepting Marie as their mom figure. Their mentor.

"Yes, but he always took care of her, too," I said. "From the time Marie was a young girl, Gerard was her ticket to survival. And what could be more powerful than that?"

"Principles?" Graham offered from the couch. "Love?"

"For *you*," Britt said. "Marie's not that evolved. I can't see her putting anything ahead of survival."

"That's it!" I pounded the counter with my palms. "That's why she killed him. Gerard stopped being an asset to her when he defied the elder council because—"

"He put b*oth* their lives in danger," Britt finished, her words tumbling over each other in excitement. "Since she can only feed from vampires of his line, she must have thought the girls were a better bet."

"Which is why she's so desperate to protect them from threats," I added. "She's practically sitting on them like a mother hen."

Max's head was whipping back and forth between me and Britt like a cat driven insane by a laser toy. "Gerard defied the elder council?"

Graham whistled again. "*Moron.*"

"Probably shouldn't have shared that detail." My blood ran cold as I imagined myself forced to defend my blabbermouth to Flavia, Sheryl, and Friar Tuck—who would probably not be offering wine. "Sorry, would you two mind terribly if Britt poofs away that memory with her compulsion gaze?"

"You want to let a vampire mess with our minds." Graham's tone was icy, and it felt like our relationship had suddenly regressed back to day one.

"It's just *Britt*." I gestured in her direction, feeling petulant.

Britt snorted. "Hazel! I'm not your genie in a bottle."

"Even if she were, compulsion doesn't work on shifters," Max reminded me.

"Oh, broomsticks!" I let out a frustrated sigh. "But the elder council's so scary."

"Believe me, I've noticed." Britt zoomed to my side to pat my arm with her cool hand. "Which is why your secret's safe with me."

"Me too." Max nodded somberly. "Lips sealed."

Graham pantomimed zipping his together.

I rolled my eyes. "All right, fine."

Hex it all, I had no alternative but to trust my friends.

"And speaking of Britt's undead overlords…" Max narrowed her eyes. "Doesn't Gerard's murder fall under their jurisdiction?"

I stared at her. "Are you saying we should turn Marie in to the council? What if they execute her?"

The three of them looked unruffled at the prospect.

"Well…" Britt threw out her hands, shrugging. "She's had a good run?"

"It's not for us to decide," Max added. "This is a vampire matter."

Graham pointed to Max as if to amplify her point. "Let the undead bury the undead."

I squirmed. "But we don't know that's what's going to happen." I turned to Britt, hopeful. "It's not like the elders are gonna miss Gerard. They had him on a kill list. Won't they be grateful she took a task off their plate?"

"Yeah, but they'd still put her to death," Britt said airily. "To make an example. They'd just do a nice champagne toast in her honor afterwards. And then sit down to an eleven-hour game of Twilight Imperium."

Harsh … and decadent.

I shook my head. "You guys, I don't think I can do this," I said. "Marie's terrible, but I'm a Green Witch—and we're all about life magic. I can't send her off to certain doom."

Britt locked eyes with Max. "Well, we don't know for *sure* what they'll do," she said and raised her eyebrows at Max.

"No one can predict the future ... yet," Max conceded, sounding reluctant.

"So, there's a chance they'd let her off with a warning?" I said eagerly. "Or maybe a ticket that says she has to take a class online and pay a fee?"

Britt groaned.

"You're making this really hard, Hazel," Max said.

"Okay, okay." I reached for my cell phone. "I'm never going to be okay with vampire justice, but it's the law of her kind. I'm calling Elliot."

In the week since Farm to Beachhouse, I'd given myself more than one stern talking-to.

Just because I'd crushed on a man forever didn't mean I was entitled to him. Elliot was free to date anyone he wanted. Including a Beige Witch.

It was high time I stopped pining and flirting and began treating him as a business associate. Maybe someday a friend, when it didn't hurt so much.

None of these sober thoughts slowed my heart's drumming, though, while his tall frame filled the center of my living room. Dressed in faded jeans and a blue T-shirt, Elliot scribbled notes on his tablet computer as we caught him up quickly on the memory spell, the skewer, and all of Marie's lies. I tried not to notice that he had bags under his eyes. Too many dates with Leia this week?

I was also trying not to take it personally that he'd rejected my overstuffed couch and squishy armchair in favor of the hardwood floor. "Sure I can't offer you a cushion?" I asked.

"I'm comfortable." Elliot didn't take his eyes off his notes, squinting in concentration. "In the memory sequence you all watched, the shoebox Carina buried contained Gerard's vampiric remains, correct?"

We all nodded from our various comfy perches in my living room.

"But when you three dug it up last night," Elliot went on, "in your crazy cloak and dagger operation—seriously unsafe and ill advised, by the way—"

"Get to the point, bro!" Max cut in from my velvet chaise, which she was hanging off in a show of exaggerated impatience.

"—the remains were gone," Elliot finished.

Crap, he was right.

Elliot looked at each of us in turn. "So, who moved Gerard, any theories?"

"Well, the Vampire Hunters had motive," I said. "They needed *some* remains as proof they'd slayed the kidnapper. And they had to plant that proof themselves because there was no vampire kidnapper to slay. That rude tourist is just some Ordinal. He had nothing to do with kidnapping Yolanda."

"So, who *did* kidnap her, Hazel?" Elliot did that thing where he bored into my eyes and for a dazzled moment I couldn't tell if he was stumped or had a theory he wanted me to corroborate. A few moments later, he showed his hand. "Was she kidnapped at all, or was it just a hoax?"

I blinked. "Both. Because it was *the Vampire Hunters*!" It was the only thing that made sense. "We know there's a witch working with them, the invisible witch who crashed into me running out of the forest. We know Yolanda was under a sleep spell the whole time. What if they nabbed her, then led us to her so they could be heroes for slaying her fictional captor?"

Graham's jaw dropped. "You're saying Yolanda's entire kidnaping was a Vampire Hunter hoax?"

"For the money and the notoriety," Elliot confirmed. It kind of annoyed me that he wasn't shocked, because it meant he'd gotten there before I did. How had he beat me to the punch? "Was Yolanda in on the take?" he wondered aloud.

"No," I said quickly. "The sleep spell suggests Yolanda was kidnapped by people she knew and would be able to recognize and tell on."

"Or," Elliot said dryly, "that she wanted a fig leaf of deniability. In case the others all got caught."

I shook my head. Yolanda was such a sweet kid, there was no way she'd deceive and worry the whole community for cash. "No, my gut says she's not capable of something like that."

"You never know what people are capable of," Max said. "Even people you know and trust."

Everyone but Elliot winced.

"Okay, but what about all those videos of the vampire kidnapper?" Britt said. "Are you saying they're deepfakes?"

"Exactly," I said. "And who could pull off a combination of special effects and glamours?" I snapped my fingers. "A film student with a Beige Witch mentor."

"Amethyst!" Britt and Max said together.

I turned to Elliot and as casually as I could, and said, "Next time you see Leia, ask her if she taught her mentee complex glamours."

I was proud of myself for bringing it up without maximum bitterness, but my words came out a bit strained nonetheless and it led to an awkward silence.

Elliot swallowed, his face hard to read. Finally he said, "Sounds like you really want it to be Amethyst, and not Yolanda."

I glared at him for dodging the Leia thing. "Amethyst has

been acting suspiciously this whole time," I retorted. "She *has* to be one of the Vampire Hunters."

"Though that is pretty weird," Max said, "she's the furthest thing from anti-vampire."

"Well, it's not like they're actually harming real vampires," Graham pointed out. "They've claimed two kills so far. Turns out the first one was killed by his own wife. The second one didn't exist." He laughed with more frustration than joy. "To think I've upended my life for weeks, Britt was driven from her home, and Hazel's given up hers because of these jokers. As far as we know, they've never committed a single violent act."

"Gosh, you're right," I said. "Everyone's so scared of the hunters but they're all talk."

"Actually," Max said, "they're mostly just writing."

"So, what *are* they after," Britt said, "if not killing us vampires?"

"Street cred?" Graham said, just as Elliot suggested, "Ransom money?"

"Maybe they don't all want the same thing," I said. "We know Amethyst isn't acting alone. There's at least that one young guy involved too." We'd heard his voice. "Plus, Amethyst would need help from someone who knew where Gerard was buried."

"That would be Marie and the newbloods," Max said.

"And Orion," Britt said, "if he survived as a vampire."

"It's got to be Carina," I said. "Amethyst and Yolanda even mentioned at the pancake breakfast that they had a vampire friend."

Britt let out a dry laugh. "So Carina, a vampire, is one of the hunters?"

"Well, don't forget she's still a shifter too," Max said. "And you know how we feel about you nasty bloodsuckers."

"Oh, go cough up a hairball," Britt replied cheerfully.

"But do today's teenagers still carry the old enmity?" Elliot wondered. "Outside of Carnivora, it seems like they're all hanging out. Shifters, vampires, witches."

"Wild idea," Graham said, leaning forward. "What if *all* the supernatural kids you know are in on this Vampire Hunter thing? Just for kicks, or to get attention. I don't know."

"If it's literally everyone, I'm retiring." Elliot rose to his feet, only to lean against my wall with his knees bent at a ninety-degree angle, as if holding himself in an invisible chair with the strength of his quadriceps alone. "I don't have the energy for a bright new generation of creative criminals."

"My God, why do you hate my furniture?" I blurted out before I realized it was a form of flirting.

"I don't *hate* it." Elliot's lips curved up in a smirk that seemed as flirty as ever. "It just doesn't support an upright posture."

"Yes, by design." Why couldn't I stop myself? *Girlfriend, he has a girlfriend.* "Most people like slouching. You're the weirdo."

"So I've been told, many times." His lips twitched up again, then he was back to business. "So, on the issue of Marie, I agree with you all. It's a matter for the vampire council. There's a protocol for this, but it's a ton of paperwork. I'll warn you that it can take a week or more to wind through their bureaucracy. And they probably won't ask for my assistance in the arrest or even update me on the case. We're handing it off, into a black hole."

Britt groaned. "Sounds like them."

Elliot turned to me. "Hazel, your word will mean more than anyone else's in this room. I need you to write a statement as a witness once removed, that's the term used in co-memory testimony."

I censored myself from saying that I loved it when he got all technical.

"Of course." A thought poked me in the shoulder. "Wait,

Marie's house is getting warded tomorrow morning, is that going to be a problem? Could she hide from the council in there?"

His eyebrows went up. "Maybe for a little while. But the elders are insanely powerful."

Max spoke up. "Two seconds of eye contact with a newblood and they'd have an invitation to enter the house. Under compulsion, the girls would probably even help arrest Marie."

"Well, that doesn't sound traumatic for anyone," Britt said, looking distressed. "Maybe I should text Landra and Bronwen, give them a heads up…?"

"I can't let you do that." Elliot's voice wasn't loud but it left zero room for dispute. "It could easy tip off Marie. If she decides to vanish, she might talk them into going along. Now they're accessories to her evading justice."

I shifted in my seat, knowing I would have to share something vulnerable. "I was going to go and try to talk the warding witch out of doing the gig. Sister to sister."

"No, not a good idea, your interference could spook Marie," Elliot said, and it was the first time in a while I'd begrudged him his authority.

"Warding could harm this witch's magic," I said.

"And that's unfortunate, but she signed up for the gig." Elliot seemed to notice me bristle, and his voice grew milder. "Yeah, I'm making you mad, I know. I have to, sometimes." He sounded regretful though not apologetic, and his self-awareness was a little soothing. "Look, it's imperative that Marie doesn't see this coming. For the next week, we don't want her to change her routine, much less flee."

"I get it," I said shortly.

But all I could think of was Gran's weakened magic, how much suffering it caused her. It wasn't fair that this other witch should have to sacrifice her powers for a little cash infusion.

Britt folded her arms. "I don't want the newbloods caught in the crossfire."

Elliot nodded. "Agreed. I'll recommend to the council that they arrest Marie on a Tuesday, on her way home from confession."

"Well," Max said, "at least now we know what she's been confessing to."

Everyone laughed, though it wasn't all that funny. It had been a long, draining night ... and it wasn't quite over.

When I walked Elliot to the front door, he wasted no time locking me into his gaze.

"Hazel, Leia's not my girlfriend," he said firmly. "That was not a date. I haven't been on a date in two years. To be honest, I can't be bothered to. Most people aren't that interesting. Present company excluded obviously."

"Uhmmm...?" So much to unpack, and unfortunately my brain had just been replaced by a pack of marshmallows. "What? But I thought ... Leia said—"

"It was a consultation-thing," he said impatiently, as if his meeting with Leia was too uninteresting to recall. "Her idea. To discuss redecorating the police station."

"Oh!" Well, that made sense; it *was* pretty 1950s in there. "She's very good at marketing herself. I mean, her decorating business." I could afford to be generous now.

It was still sinking in: *Elliot wasn't with Leia.* I tried not to smile like an idiot but the corners of my mouth kept turning up.

"Try to get some sleep, witch." Elliot touched my arm. Electric. "Now that I know you're down with dodgy spy missions," he added, a wicked gleam in his eye, "I want your help with tailing Amethyst. We're going with your theory. Tomorrow night, we're going to uncover the Vampire Hunters' HQ."

CHAPTER TWENTY-FOUR

I'D REALLY MEANT my promise to Elliot last night.

I was *not* going to go talk the warding witch out of her gig. But Mother and Gran agreeing was as rare as St. Elmo's Fire, so if they *both* said warding spells harmed witches, I couldn't exactly stand there and do nothing.

"Nice truck, Hazel!" boomed a tinny voice from the intercom as I rolled up to Marie's front gate at ten a.m. in Graham's elk hunting horror-mobile. "But where's my sorority sister?"

"Oh, it's just me today." I smiled at Landra's bespectacled image, lit up on the video screen. "I was hoping to lend a hand with the warding spell, I mean, if you don't—"

The buzzer interrupted me before I could launch into my spiel, and the metal gate pushed open.

"We appreciate you," Landra said with feeling. "Tell Britt if she doesn't get her butt out here to visit soon, I'll bite her ... okay?"

"Can do!"

I parked in the driveway and strolled through the front yard, pleased with how smoothly my plan was going so far. Wintersweet and burning incense scented the cool morning air and made me cough. I could hear mumbled chanting before I saw her, standing proudly in warrior pose between two pink camelia bushes. A tall witch with cinnamon red, bobbed hair.

Welp. I'd rolled and gotten snake eyes.

Jacinta looked up from her mumbled chanting. "Hazel?" She tugged on her hair self-consciously, and a high-pitched, nervous laugh escaped her. "What are you doing here?"

"I came over to be your magical support," I said with forced brightness. "If you want assistance, that is."

I'd spent many sleepless hours the last night researching my options and I'd come up with several concrete ways to help: cast a shower of magical protection to shield the witch's aura, conjure a curative balm post-spell to speed her magical healing, or—and this one freaked me out, no lie—I could roll up my sleeves and assist with the warding. I was no expert, obviously, but I could take directions well. And take a little of the damage myself.

I don't know what I'd been expecting, but Jacinta's narrowed eyes and confused chuckle were not it.

"What are you wearing?" she asked.

"Just ... warding clothes?" With a sinking heart, I looked down at my jeans and ancient Sage's Bakery T-shirt.

Everyone kept talking about how warding was such a dirty job, so I'd naturally put on grubbies. But now I was noticing Jacinta wore a hunter green pencil skirt, flowy peasant top, and chunky heels. Her statement necklace sported a jade pendant.

As if on cue, her fingers flew to her pendant. "I always wear this on my gigs." She straightened to a dignified posture. "It reminds me I'm still a Green Witch."

I blinked, wondering why she'd need reminding. Even if warding spells weakened her a bit, what else would Jacinta *be* but a Green Witch?

"I mean, yeah, you're the chapter president," I said dumbly.

Awkwardness clung in the air. That was when I realized I had no idea how warding spells worked—none of my grimoires even alluded to them. In my effort to be helpful, I'd wandered out of my depth. Self-doubt engulfed me like a tidal wave. *What was I thinking?*

To my utter shock, Jacinta reached out and hugged me. Her plumeria perfume enveloped me, peachy and flowery. "Come on, Hazel, let's go inside ... while we still can."

I feigned a laugh at her bad joke, and followed as she jogged up the porch steps with visibly renewed energy.

Marie's front door was unlocked. In the quiet house, everything looked immaculate, including the kitchen floor. After Carina's memory, being in here made my stomach queasy. I kept imagining the spotless tile stained with blood. And goo.

All clutter was on the kitchen tabletop, which Jacinta had set up as her makeshift spell station. Dozens of clear vials and test tubes with brightly colored liquids were strewn around a large, industrial-looking steel mixing bowl. A plasticky, chemical smell pervaded the room.

"So, where are your herbs?" I asked, confused.

"Oh, Hazel, don't play down your generosity with silly jokes." Jacinta shook her head at me, and her eyes filled with tears. "It's really quite touching, the way you're showing up for me ... to think I ever doubted your commitment to the Blue Moon Bay Green Witch Association."

"It's not a big deal," I said, embarrassed. "Any witch could've ... wait, you *doubted* me?"

Jacinta shrugged. "You always seemed reluctant to participate. I wondered if you lacked the pluck and mettle befitting a proper Green Witch."

"Ouch!?" But kind of fair, too. Not long ago, I was even afraid to enter this house.

Okay, I was *still* terrified of this house. Who could blame me?

"But now, I get you." Jacinta winked conspiratorially. "You're not a witch of small gestures. You've got more community spirit in your pinky finger than any witch in Blue Moon history."

That was a bit much. I was about to beg her to tone down her gratitude—before I died of blushing—when a vacuum cleaner blasted on in the next room.

Bronwen walked by the open doorway, brandishing a steam wand. As usual, she looked like an alt fashion model in a sheer black minidress over neon green joggers and white tank advertising the Drunken Barrel's annual battle of the bands. Her hair was in a bandana.

"Oh, hi Hazel!" she yelled, and turned off the vacuum. "Don't mind me, I have to go over this room again. My lines weren't neat enough the first time."

"Oof." I winced. "Marie must be in a mood. Where is she, by the way?"

"Hiding in her room until the spell's over." Bronwen leaned toward me and spoke quietly. "No offense, but witch magic creeps her out."

"Ah, too bad, I was hoping to say hello." Lies. I was giddy with relief that Marie wasn't around for tedious small talk.

Having agreed to rat her out to the vampire elders, I didn't want to have to look her in the eye. And not just for vague, weaselly reasons; I had a rotten poker face. It was hard enough chatting with Bronwen here, when I wanted to scream, *"It was Marie, in the kitchen, with the skewer… and she is so busted!"*

"Hey Bronwen, you're a hard worker," I said instead. "You ever thought about getting a barista job? Or a bakery job?"

She puffed out her lower lip and blew at her pink bangs. "I would, but Marie doesn't want me to limit myself to 'lit major clichés.'" Her deep brown eyes bored into me, conveying silent horror a la Jim from *The Office*.

I instinctively averted my eyes from her vampire gaze.

When Bronwen moved on to vacuum the parlor, I turned to Jacinta. "Did she seem okay to you?" I asked. "I'm a little concerned…"

Jacinta shrugged vaguely. "I have a teenager at home, they're never okay."

She'd been busily re-arranging her vials the whole time I'd been talking to Bronwen. Almost as if she hadn't wanted to be anywhere near her.

"It just seems like she's cooking and cleaning all the time," I said, more to myself than to Jacinta. It chilled me that Marie was turning someone into her unpaid servant, just like Gerard had done to her so long ago. "And Landra's working fulltime."

"She keeps 'em busy." Jacinta shrugged again. "I'm sure it's good for their personal development." She pursed her lips. "Better than having them run wild, anyway."

I knew at once what she meant. She didn't give a fig about the girls' personal development. She just wanted them far, far away from her precious Yolanda. Jacinta had valid reasons to be on edge—after all, she believed her daughter had been kidnapped by a vampire.

But that didn't give her license to be a bigot for the rest of her life, did it?

"Ready to get this over with?" Jacinta asked, gesturing to the brightly colored vials and tubes of Hecate knows what.

"Oh! Sure." My pulse was racing, but I calmed myself with a deep exhale. "Here, let me do one thing first. A supporting spell."

I reached into my belt bag and held up a tincture of lavender and savory herbs. Dabbing a drop onto each wrist, I half-closed my eyes till I could see green astral dandelions bloom along the wall. I recited the incantation I'd learned last night:

"Enveloped in emerald, a deluge divine;
guarding your aura, protection is thine."

A shower of shimmering dots surrounded Jacinta, and she

startled as she sipped coffee from a big silver thermos. The dots created a soft green glow around her from head to toe.

"Aw, thank you!" Her shoulders relaxed and she closed her eyes for a moment, as if receiving a spa treatment. "You really are amazing, Hazel. Now shall we get to the main event?"

"Let's do it."

But Jacinta didn't do anything.

We stood there staring at each other in the murderer's kitchen.

"Hazel," Jacinta said softly at last. "What the sweet syrupy hex are you waiting for?"

Light dawned. "Oh ... you thought *I* was going to...?"

"You said you were my 'magical support.'" She moved her head in small circles, blinking over and over as if this repetitive motion could rewind us to a moment that made more sense. "What was I supposed to think?"

"*Not* that I'd do the whole spell for you!" I couldn't believe this witch. This was my worst nightmare: I offer to help, and my help is pathetically inadequate. "I don't mean to disappoint you," I added, as calmly as I could. "But I think you heard what you wanted to hear back there."

To my surprise, Jacinta's confusion deflated like a balloon. A heavy sadness poured off her. "I wanted to think that someone would show up and take care of me for once. Feels like I've been taking care of everything and everyone for so long..."

I felt her sadness, her exhaustion, and suddenly I felt compassion for her. "I'm sorry I've kinda taken your leadership for granted all these years," I said." I never thought about how much you might be carrying."

Her face softened. "Ah well, that's what being young's about. You never see the glue that holds things together. Glue's boring, you only notice when it stops working. When things fall apart."

In one graceful motion, she rotated her arms and clapped, fingertips connecting with her opposite palm. Grey smoke poured from the space where her hands had touched. It smelled familiar: like burning grass.

Holy hex, did warding use Grey Magic? Is that why no one wanted to talk about it, why it was so taboo?

I stared in disbelief as the neon-bright vials and tubes flew up from the tabletop and collided with each other mid-flight. Glass shattered, but instead of landing on the floor, every shard traveled in a sparkling arc over our heads, clattering neatly into the steel bowl. Meanwhile, the liquid that had been in the vials swirled together in the air as if stirred in an unseen cauldron by an invisible spoon. Within moments, the liquid assumed the shape of a giant, grey padlock.

Jacinta's voice echoed strangely in my ears as she recited:

"Ward this place from ill intent,
Thieves and pirates intercept.
Its gems for thee alone are kept.
Ne'er unlock and ne'er relent."

Suddenly, I felt myself being lifted off the ground by a strong, cold wind. The grey smoke from before carried me aloft, three feet above the floor.

"What on earth is going on?" I shrieked as it swept me out of the kitchen and towards the front door. "Is this normal?"

"Absolutely!" Jacinta was right behind me, borne on the same smoky wind. "I had another client buy this package once for her beach house."

"What do you mean, this package?" We were hovering three feet above the front porch, zooming for the lawn.

"Super Ultimate Ward!" she explained as the grey wind slammed the door behind us. "Goes above and beyond to keep valuables protected. Marie's house is full of precious antiques, millions of dollars' worth of chaises and ottomans. It made sense for her. Hold on, second verse."

She held her hand up and continued:

"In shadows deep ye shall reside.
My essence sold, my soul denied.
Heed all ye sisters my sad plight.
Beware the spell that binds too tight."

The grey smoke dissipated into the cloudy sky, and I was unceremoniously dropped to the dirt. I landed in a deep crouch on the misty grass, thankful I'd worn sneakers. Jacinta, meanwhile, floated down like an emerald Mary Poppins, making me wonder how many times she'd had a chance to practice that move.

"Tell me to shut up if it's too personal," I began, dusting myself off, "but how many warding gigs *have* you done?"

Her kohl-lined eyes darted from left to right as though doing mental math. "Let's see," Jacinta said. "I've been shut out of Green Magic for seven moons so far. And I have eight to go, plus another three added to my total today … so. A lot!"

"Shut out?" I said. "You haven't been able to practice Green Magic since *last spring?* Who … sentenced you?"

She looked at me like I was stupid. "The magic."

"Oh!"

I knew as well as anyone that performing Grey Magic spells went against our Green Witch vows. But until this moment, I hadn't realized the penalty for breaking a vow was imposed automatically. My mind flashed back to Scruffy's tale of the gangster who'd had his shifter magic removed. Unlike shifter packs with their stern ritual punishments, or the vampire council with its paperwork and executions, witch justice was private and relatively gentle.

But there was also no hope of leniency. No one you could appeal to.

Suddenly I was triply grateful Jacinta hadn't ended up using my help. If my access to Green Magic was denied, how could I ever do my job at the bakery?

Come to think of it, how did Jacinta do *her* job?

My mouth fell open as the truth hit me.

"All those shifts Yolanda and Amethyst work," I said slowly. "They're so tired. They're the ones doing all the magic, aren't they?"

Because *she* couldn't.

Jacinta looked down at the clumps of heather growing beside the driveway. "I had debts to pay," she said. "I never meant to burden my daughter or kill her dreams."

"Hey!" I patted her arm. "Working at the magical family business isn't such a burden. I mean, that's my life with Granny Sage and I wouldn't trade it for anything."

She shook her head. "That's different—for one thing, your mentor's a legend. I haven't been able to teach my girl any magic for seven months and counting."

I blinked. "So, the mentoring program you forced on us…"

Jacinta's eyes shone with an emotion I couldn't read. "It was all for Yolanda's sake," she said. "I'm so afraid that she'll have no one to guide her into adulthood."

Damn, this witch had mad guilt trip game. Almost reminded me of my own mother.

"You know what? We'll figure something out." I hoped that didn't amount to a thirteen-hour-a-week commitment. Though if it did, I could probably deal. "How's Yolanda doing, anyway?"

Jacinta averted her gaze to the heathers again. "All right, I think, considering?"

"Is she talking to someone about what happened?" I pressed. "A therapist, anyone?"

She shook her head. "She's very resilient. I guess it helps that she remembers almost nothing. Basically slept through the whole thing."

A chill ran up my spine. "That is a blessing."

When I got home, Graham and Britt were out, probably enjoying a leisurely breakfast together at Purrfect Pancakes. I pounced on having the house to myself and took an extra-long shower, using up the last of my homemade rosemary and clary sage scrub. Cleansing herbs. As I breathed in the stringent herbal scents, Jacinta's words echoed in my head:

"I didn't mean to burden my daughter or kill her dreams."

And yet:

"He told me fall into a deep sleep."

That's what Yolanda had said, about the vampire kidnapper who wasn't.

And what *were* her dreams? What would Yolanda be doing if she weren't stuck bailing out her mom's restaurant?

In my green velvet kimono, I combed my long hair in front of the foggy bathroom mirror, and whispered a simple spell:

"Goodbye steam, bathtub gleam."

The mirror cleared and a fresh, grassy scent filled the bathroom. I let out a sigh of gratitude for my magic. That I had access to it anytime I wanted. It was not something I would be taking for granted again anytime soon.

I texted Kade to say I'd be at work in fifteen, then texted Elliot: Forget following Amethyst tonight, let's follow Yolanda. She was in on her own kidnapping from the start.

CHAPTER TWENTY-FIVE

E LLIOT SAT ACROSS from me in the bakery's corner booth, his hands resting on the table as I'd requested. His eyes were closed, but every muscle in his body looked tense.

He was waiting for me to put a spell on him.

Except for the energy crackling between us, the bakery was silent, its blue and white star-pattern floor swept and mopped to a high shine. Countertops sparkled, and you could see your reflection in the empty cold case.

Kade had lingered after closing while I finished the kitchen sink scrubbing spell, then asked if I wanted to join him for drinks at the Barrel. I owed it to the cat shifter to get real with him that we probably weren't going to be a thing. But that talk wasn't in me tonight, so I reached for the world's most tired excuse: working late.

Handily, it was also true.

We were mere hours, maybe even *minutes*, from getting proof that would unmask the Vampire Hunters.

And, if I was right, put Yolanda's kidnapping case to bed, too.

"*Astral essence, shimmering veil,*" I began, stirring my bright green bowl of fairywand and candyleaf, along with other boiled herbs that together smelled sweet and spicy. "*Conceal these forms, their presence pale…*"

I paused my stirring. Elliot's facial muscles had tensed up in anticipation, as if he were about to receive a painful shot. "What, are you scared of my magic?" I teased.

"No." His eyes flew open and he looked annoyed. "Get on with it."

"But you look so nervous, aww…"

Was I taking him saying he found me more interesting than most as a license to flirt? Yes, I was.

"I'm about to let a witch turn me invisible," he growled. "Wouldn't you be nervous?"

I shrugged. "Not really, cause I could just"—I snapped my fingers—"go visible again anytime?"

"Yeah, I asked the wrong person," he conceded.

"Ooh, idea!" I reached into my purse and pulled out my trusty silver tin. "There's a simpler way to do this. It's not as foolproof as a glamour, but it'll give you more control."

He narrowed his eyes. "What are those, breath mints?"

"Not just *any* breath mints," I said "You just eat one and go invisible. The catch is, it only lasts until you speak. Which can make for awkward times." It felt strangely intimate to be sharing one of my oldest spells with him.

"Gran gave me my first pack when I was sixteen," I added, warmed by the memory. "Told me not to get into too much trouble."

He cracked a smile. "But you did anyway? Being a teenager…"

"Me?" I laughed. "Elliot, you were there. I wasn't that kind of teenager."

His look of surprise made me wonder what kind of secret life he'd imagined I'd led. Or had he forgotten about my gaggle of citizenship awards? My high school nickname, Goody Two-shoes?

No, outside of one or two magical shenanigans with Max, I'd been a model youth. No wonder I'd assumed Yolanda was innocent. She was quiet, well-behaved, polite. She reminded me of me.

"I mostly used these mints to hide from bullies," I admitted. "And my family, but same thing."

What was left of his smile faded. "I didn't know that. About your family."

"Yeah. Well. Anyway…" I felt flustered, though I'd brought it on myself. "Here."

I placed the tin in his hand—then pulled back. Shifter skin ran hot, but Elliot's palms were icy cold. He wasn't just a *little* nervous. Given all the dangers he faced, supernatural or not, in his line of work, why would sitting still for a glamour throw him? He'd been okay with the cone of silence thing. Then again, that spell was much less … personal. Was it the lack of control?

"Would it feel more comfortable," I ventured, "if you could change yourself back anytime? What do you think?"

"That I hate witch magic," he said hotly. My surprise and hurt must have shown, because he added quickly, "It's not you. I had a bad experience once. Long time ago."

"Got it." Opening up like that, even in a small way, was big for Elliot. It made me determined to be helpful. To ease his anxiety. "Well, which option do you hate less, mints or glamours? I can make a list of pros and cons, if you want."

He shook his head. "You're the expert, you decide." He didn't say it straight out but I heard the subtext: Make up your mind before I change mine.

And he trusted me enough to put the choice in my hands.

"Glamour," I said. "Mints, now that I think about it, have a learning curve. Turns out it's pretty much impossible not to talk."

"For you," he muttered with a ghost of a smirk.

Seconds later, I made Elliot's smirk disappear along with the rest of him when I dipped my fingers in the fragrant herbal mix and brushed his open hands with mine.

Suddenly both our seats looked empty.

"That's it?" said Elliot's disembodied voice. He let out a breath.

What were you expecting? "That's it," I said. "How do you like being invisible?"

"Oh, I could get used to this level of stealth." He was halfway back to his cocky self already. "The applications are endless. I'm assuming there's a cone of silence built in too, right? So no one can hear our invisible selves?"

I blinked. "Actually, I never thought of combining those spells."

"How could you not? It's a no-brainer."

The real answer was, they were both heavy lifts in terms of magical energy. Also, I'd just done that tough memory spell by myself last night ... would I even have enough juice to hold our glamours *and* keep up a cone of silence?

Still, it was a smart idea. Such a smart idea I couldn't help but be annoyed that the shifter had thought of it instead of me.

"Let's do it," I said, and a rush of exhilaration swept through me. Maybe I was finally pulling out of my magical rut.

Undetectable by sound or sight, we reached the alley behind Purrfect Pancakes right at six p.m.—their closing time—and caught our first lucky break. Amethyst was taking out the day's trash to the dumpster and had left the back door open.

We slipped through it and into the spacious restaurant kitchen where Yolanda was deftly boxing up what looked like the day's final to-go order. Eighties music belted from the sound system. Singing along half-heartedly to Madonna's "Who's That Girl," she stuffed two eco-tainers full of club sandwiches, spooned out mac and cheese sides, and stacked all four containers into a white paper bag.

Jacinta stood by the sink, a look of quiet contemplation on her face as she washed the dishes by hand. She didn't have to do it—the girls could have sparkled up the kitchen in a jiffy with Green Magic.

But Purrfect Pancakes was Jacinta's other baby. I could only imagine that her pride demanded that she contribute to the running of it somehow. Any way she could.

If I were being honest, I'd have felt the same in her place.

She swiftly worked her way through the stack, till a soapy plate slithered from her wet hand. I cringed at the oncoming crash.

Jacinta cried out, *"Magic wake, stop the break!"*

The bone-white dish nosedived anyway, smashing into pieces.

A gust of burning grass wafted through the room.

Elliot couldn't smell it of course, but I could, and it was all I could do to keep from coughing. I put my invisible hands over my mouth just as Yolanda started coughing.

Jacinta whirled around, shame in her eyes. "I'll open the windows."

"It's okay, mama." Yolanda squeezed her mother's shoulder, then snapped her fingers. A broom and dustpan sailed over from the supply closet to clean up the shards. "I was about to go up to my room to study, anyway."

"Yeah, right," I said aloud to Elliot, reveling in the cone of silence . "What do you want to bet she's meeting with the other Vampire Hunters?"

"Half a million dollars?" Elliot said drily. He sounded like he was sitting on the counter, mere feet from Jacinta. Bold for someone who'd never been invisible. He was adapting fast.

Jacinta's eyes traveled to the to-go bag. "That's your study snack? Wish I had your teenage metabolism."

Yolanda wrinkled her cute nose. "Whatever, mama, you look amazing."

"If I had to guess," I said to Elliot, "the second she gets upstairs into their apartment, she'll run down the fire escape to go meet the other Hunters."

"We'll be right behind her," he assured me.

"Hon, before you go?" Jacinta hesitated. "I heard about a young witch uptown, a crisis counselor. Lorelei says she's quite good."

Elliot said what I was thinking. "Poor Jacinta, she really doesn't know."

Yolanda's face was all sweet innocence. "Mama, I told you, I don't remember a thing. I was very lucky."

Jacinta's frustrated expression softened. "*We* were lucky, dear heart," she said, and gently kissed her daughter's forehead.

"Glad their closeness isn't a hoax." It felt awkward, snooping on a sweet family moment.

"No, there's clearly a lot of love there." The discomfort in Elliot's voice mirrored my own.

It wasn't just love, I realized. This mother and daughter were a *team*, even more than me and Gran. And just like us, they tried to show up strong for each other, even when they felt weak. To sweep imperfection and infirmity under the rug … or in this case, into the craft closet.

Yolanda's sky-high regard for her mom had survived the revelation of her mistakes. But a craft addiction and a lapse in magic were small potatoes. If Yolanda really was the mastermind of her own hoax kidnapping, I sure didn't want to be there when Jacinta found out.

I was thankful when Amethyst walked back in, bundled to the teeth. Her adorable purple knitted hat and the matching fluffy scarf wrapped around her neck were almost certainly Jacinta's handiwork. *Well, it has to go somewhere.*

"I just had a brilliant idea!" She threw out her arms dramatically, and I caught a whiff of perfume with cocoa notes. Like the invisible Vampire Hunter who'd crashed into me in the forest. "Now that Yo's home, we should host an event for the Green Witch community," she went on. "To show our gratitude for all their help!"

"Great idea, Am!" Yolanda's instant enthusiasm made me suspect this was all pre-rehearsed. "We could offer breakfast-for-dinner and maybe invite some cool speakers. To raise awareness about bias against vampires … and shifters and other beings."

"Well, well, well, isn't *that* interesting?" I said to Elliot.

"It's possible they feel bad for having stirred up hate," he said, sounding thoughtful. "Maybe they came up with a crazy scheme to get money to pay off Jacinta's debts but didn't think about the big picture. Who does, at eighteen?"

"Discrimination?" Jacinta made a lemon face. "Wouldn't it make more sense to host a fundraiser gala for victims of vampire attacks? We could dedicate the evening to the heroes who rescued you."

Amethyst and Yolanda looked at each other with concern.

"Wow, they're really trying to backtrack." I felt oddly sorry for the girls. "But it's gotten bigger than them."

"It always was," Elliot said quietly. "They just didn't know they were playing with fire. I hope to God no one gets burned."

"Jacinta, um, why don't we table the idea for now?" Amethyst said, pulling her mini backpack off its hook on the coat rack. "I have the feeling once you attend our DEI Night, you might have a new perspective."

Jacinta looked peeved but she said primly, "Of course, dear, we can revisit my plan when you're ready."

Jacinta looked like she wanted to say more, but Amethyst was packing up and Yolanda had turned to head upstairs with her giant bag of food.

We followed Yolanda and caught another stroke of good luck. When she unlocked the door to the apartment she shared with her mom, a tiny white kitten bolted through it and charged down the hall.

"Oh, Sugar!" she yelled out, exasperated.

It took me a moment to figure out it was the cat's name.

While she corralled Sugar, Elliot and I slipped through the open door into the apartment.

I gasped.

It wasn't quite as bad as TV's *Hoarders*, but there was a strong warehouse vibe. Cardboard boxes lined the living room walls, Crafters' Cove shopping bags took up seating on the couch. A stack of boxes blocked the TV.

With Sugar purring in her arms, Yolanda strode right past it all as if she didn't notice how off things were. Maybe she didn't, anymore.

We trailed after her down the hall into a small bedroom that nonetheless felt spacious because it was kept so neat and tidy. The twin bed was made, the floor bare and swept. Framed posters from famous witch movies adorned the accent wall. A photo of her and Jacinta and Amethyst, grinning in aprons and chefs hats, was perched on the nightstand next to a doorstop of a grimoire.

With a parting scritch, Yolanda deposited Sugar on her crisp white bedspread, and marched back to the living room. Seemingly unaware of Elliot and me bumping into each other as we scrambled to follow.

Yolanda snatched up the to-go bag of food.

"Fire escape time," I said. "I vote we wait till she's all the way down the steps before we follow suit."

But instead of opening the fire escape door to sneak out, Yo whispered something under her breath and snapped her fingers.

In a blink, she was gone.

"Wait, did she go invisible too?" Elliot had rarely sounded so perplexed. "Think she detected us, somehow?"

"No, she just…" It was hard for me to say it. "She teleported."

He swore with admiration. "Green Witches can do that?"

"Some of us." I pushed down the feelings of inadequacy that were older than my Invisimint habit. "Well. Someone's been studying hard."

Elliot's boots clanged down the hall, away from me. He returned holding Yolanda's grimoire in his invisible hands, and it appeared to be floating in midair. Its blue leather cover looked well-worn. Numerous pages were marked with scraps of pastel-hued sticky notes. He cracked it open and the page it turned to was a chapter heading. *Snore Through the Apocalypse*: *Heavy Duty Sleep Spells.*

"Can you do a memory spell on this book?" he asked, urgently. "Or use magic to trace her location?"

"No time, and no." I shook my head, even though he couldn't see it. "We're just going to have to catch up with Amethyst!"

His invisible hand pushed open the steel fire escape door and I followed him out onto the rickety metal platform.

At the sound of his tactical boots echoing down the stairs ahead of me, I felt a twinge in my temples. Was it nerves? Magical fatigue?

Don't look down, I told myself.

But I had to look down, or I might miss the next step and trip. And fall.

And die because I was out of spell fuel.

"Is it a heights thing?" Elliot was already halfway down, from the sound of it. "I can carry you. Just say the word."

"No, no, I got this!"

Pride was so annoying sometimes. He hadn't sounded judgy at

all and it would have felt *amazing* to be carried in his arms ... but I had to be all, "I got this." Self eye roll.

The fire escape stairs dropped into the alley behind Purrfect Pancakes, right by the dumpsters. We jogged around to Ocean Street just in time to see Amethyst storm out the front door in her regal purple knits. Her backpack like a gold mini shell behind her.

"Thank goodness she's so brightly colored," I said. "Easy to track."

I spoke too soon. Amethyst was booking it down the block, heading toward the bustling downtown nightlife core of bistros, bars, and lounges. This close to the holidays, Thursday night foot traffic was insane.

"I don't want to lose each other in that crowd," I began. "So I'll veer left, till we get to the statue. Then I'll go around it ... no ... *you* go around it–"

"Or we just hold hands and stick together." Elliot sounded like he was gearing up for pushback.

"Yes, yes, yes, brilliant!" I said.

I was expecting our unseen limbs to comically flail around in their search for each other. Swimming through the air. Brushing one another's invisible forms most awkwardly.

Instead, they found each other like two magnets.

Shifter heat coursed through his skin as his big hand pressed mine firmly.

Oh my sweet gingerbread, *I was holding hands with Elliot James.*

Not like I had time to savor it, though. To keep up with Amethyst, we were walking at a quick clip, and Elliot's legs were roughly twice as long as mine—okay, not really. But it sure felt like it.

Maybe because all the magic I kept juggling was exhausting me?

My temples felt that strain again, and for a split second Elliot's black boot flashed visible. Panic washed over me, then resignation.

I was about to let Elliot know our glamours were living on borrowed time when a teal arch door in the next building burst open up with a squeal.

The leader of Carnivora strutted out of the Howling Hogshead, alone.

"Hmm, Torrin's leaving the bar awfully early," Elliot observed.

"Maybe he's heading to the same place as Ameth…" I blinked. "Where'd she go?"

Suddenly everyone in the throng seemed to be wearing dark-colored coats and hats. Amethyst's purple knits were nowhere to be seen.

"Shoot," Elliot said, "I lost my bead on her, too."

I groaned and smacked my own forehead. "*Lost in the Crowd*, it's a beginner level spell. She must have glamoured herself to blend in, because…" I stopped as the truth hit me. "Because she didn't want Torrin or anyone spotting her."

"Does that mean Torrin's *not* one the Vampire Hunters after all?" Elliot said, and I could almost see his forehead wrinkle. "But if he's not in on it, then—"

"Why's he acting sus?" I finished. "Wish I knew."

As if to prove the point, Torrin was currently skulking toward a dark alley.

"Can you do a counter-spell to see through Amethyst's glamour?" Elliot asked hopefully.

I sighed. "Even if I knew a spell for that, I wouldn't have the energy to hold up *our* glamours," I confessed. "We can't spy on either of them. We're toast."

"Nope." Elliot didn't miss a beat. "I have an idea, come with me."

CHAPTER TWENTY-SIX

TIRED, HEADACHY, AND more than a bit demoralized, I let Elliot's hand guide me toward the bronze statue of Percival Moonbeam, one of our eccentric town founders.

Elliot let go of my hand. His boots thudded on the statue's two-foot-tall marble base, then he reached out to help me climb up beside him.

As soon as we were away from the bustle of the sidewalk, he said, "Okay, you can drop the glamours now."

"But, what about Torrin?"

"Just take one of your mints and follow him," Elliot said like it was obvious. "*Without* me."

My jaw about hit my collarbone. "*That's* your big idea, abandoning me?"

"No, Hazel, you're ditching *me*," he said calmly. "I'd only be deadweight. You're stealthy, you've got years of experience with this magic. Besides, I'll make sure you're safe."

"Yeah right, how are you going to do *that?*" My head felt like a spinning top from trying to guess his plan, but there was no time to chat.

When it came down to it, I trusted him. That would have to do.

I popped a mint in my mouth, exhaled deeply, and released all my spells. My glamour. His glamour. The cone of silence.

Instantly, my legs felt lighter.

My temples stopped throbbing.

It was the most profound relief I'd known since yeeting my stiletto heels into a ditch after Bea's six-hour lawn wedding.

Elliot's form flashed visible—then he seemed to melt away, leaving a pile of clothes strewn across the marble statue base. I scanned around frantically, my heart pounding in my ears.

Look up.

The thought whispered itself, almost as if I'd heard Elliot's voice in my mind.

I glanced up. On top of Founder Moonbeam's stovepipe hat, a majestic crow stretched his wings. He was closer in size to a raven, with unnaturally shiny black feathers.

I froze. I'd never seen Elliot's crow before.

Until this moment, I realized, a part of me had been considering a far-fetched theory: that *he* could have been "Hugin," the legendary thief of Carnivora. Who, for his crimes, had his magic wrung from his soul by a Red Witch ten years ago.

But no, Elliot's shifter magic was intact. To my immense relief.

I popped a mint and dove into the alley. My plan was to stay twenty-five feet behind Torrin and keep quiet while he cased local businesses and smashed windows to grab cash boxes. Whatever was on bro's agenda. But Torrin wasn't doing crimes in the alley, he was just using it for transportation—and moving fast.

I was already two blocks behind Torrin's dark form and had to jog to keep him in my sight. Elliot's crow flew from rooftop to rooftop, from ledge to ledge, always between us. It felt good knowing he was looking out for me.

Even if he couldn't actually see me.

The alley ran north to south right along Ocean Street for miles, and Torrin showed no signs of slowing. Was he just out for a moonlight stroll? Needing a break from his boys? I was totally confused.

Torrin reached the north end of the alley and dashed to the right, through the parking lot of New Life Church. As I followed, Elliot's crow swooped onto the church spire.

We weren't even technically downtown anymore, but Torrin kept up his eastward march. Away from Ocean Street, crossing onto Sandview Street and then Meadow Lane where the road was poorly lit and less traveled.

In fact, there was really only one thing on this road until you reached farmland: Peaceful Bay Gardens, the town cemetery.

Is that where Torrin was headed? What kind of horrible crime was he planning to commit in a graveyard?

Determined to know, I power walked after him. The gleaming gold cemetery gates were closed, but with his shifter agility Torrin hopped over, not even skimming the art deco finials.

The gate was a no-go for me, of course, and the fence around it was twelve feet high. Its curvy, intricate designs were too small for my feet to gain purchase, unless…

Reluctantly, I slipped off my bulky sneakers and dropped them into a bush. Hooking my socked feet into the fence's metal curlicues and flourishes, I began to climb.

The metal was cold. Midway up, I hit a dicey part. I dug deep for elementary school monkey bars memories and grabbed the next rail up with both hands so I could shimmy my foot up to the next foothold.

Going over the spiky top rail was no picnic either, but I bit my lip to keep from cursing out loud. I lowered myself down, feeling like a freakin' Olympic athlete.

Torrin was stalking across the manicured grass but stopped at a grave marker that looked new and well-tended, decorated with wildflowers of every color. From the pocket of his leather jacket, he took out a smooth rock and placed it on the gravestone. I saw many other rocks had been placed there.

Wincing as cold, wet grass drenched my socks, I crept closer till I could read the name of the deceased. *Orion Mongusta*, of course.

Nineteen years old.

Torrin's eyes were dry but his thick eyebrows drooped with grief.

So Torrin had feelings? Okay, I hadn't wanted to know that. It was easier to think of him as the square-faced crook who'd delighted in ransacking my bakery.

Was his grief for Orion? For what had driven him to hate vampires? Had I been overthinking the bakery break-in, the posturing, the name-calling, abandoning his vampire charges in the forest that night? All along, maybe it was the simplest of motives. The most understandable. Vengeance for a loved one lost.

Elliot's crow perched on the back of a granite memorial bench, but Torrin's moment suddenly seemed too personal. Weren't we just intruding on a man's grief for his brother?

Then I heard a rustling, and a pale figure appeared behind one of the tombstones.

It was a teenage boy with a familiar face, beige and square and similar to Torrin's, yet somehow more innocent.

A face I'd seen in his beloved's memory.

Unexpected tears of gratitude welled up in my eyes. So, Carina's blood *had* worked its magic on that desperate night.

"Dude." Orion smirked at his brother. "Took you long enough."

"Yeah, well, I had to get another pint with the guys." Torrin sounded weary of it all. "Jasper and that stupid little dog were giving me crap again about never being around. Anyway, screw it … I'm here now." Without another word, Torrin pulled his jacket collar away from his shoulder.

Orion dove for his flesh like he was starving. He came up fangs dripping blood.

I blinked. Did I just see the leader of the shifter gang let a vampire feed from him? I would have pinched myself, if I weren't afraid I'd squeak and blow my cover.

"Thank you." Orion wiped his face, then licked his hand for good measure.

Torrin grunted. "Don't want to talk about it."

Course he didn't. What would happen if his gang mates saw what I just did? I had a feeling that would be the end of both brothers—and this time there would be no flowers or rocks to honor their memories.

From his troubled expression, Orion seemed to be thinking along the same lines. "Bro, did you ever think maybe the whole problem here is none of us talk? We just growl and attack."

"Great. A fanged philosopher, just what the world needs." Torrin growled, but he sounded amused.

So, he was a little high from the bite. Even shifters weren't immune to that side effect, I noted.

Suddenly, Torrin sniffed the air and seemed to focus. "What's that minty smell?"

I stood as still I could on my frozen feet, willing the wind to change.

"Flowers, maybe? Who cares, man?" Orion seemed annoyed. "You should be glad it smells like mint around here, given the other options. You're just trying to change the subject and you're not even going to ask me how she's doing, are you?"

Torrin shrugged. "You'll tell me anyway."

Orion did. "She's really scared, we both are. That money was supposed to buy us cred or get us safely to L.A. Now we're stuck here, with nothing."

Nothing? I begged to differ. Unless L.A. was even more expensive than people said, a quarter mil was not too shabby. Even factoring in the split with their co-conspirators, Yolanda and Amethyst.

"I don't get it, we followed the plan to the letter." Orion shook his head like he couldn't see the edges of the puzzle. "Unless … you don't think those witches double-crossed us?"

Was he implying Yolanda and Amethyst nabbed the ransom money from the gym locker and kept it for themselves?

"Green Witches?" Torrin snorted at the idea. "Naw, they live by a code. It's ancient or something."

He sounded strangely … respectful.

Orion's tone turned bitter. "Maybe Ree and I are just doomed no matter what we do."

"What'd you expect?" Torrin said. "Once the old man turned her, it was game over."

"None of this would have happened if you all had accepted her in the first place!" Orion shouted.

"Carnivora has standards. The code of carnivores means something."

"No, it doesn't. Not anymore." Orion met Torrin's glare, and his own eyes sparkled with a revolutionary's charisma. "Who cares what she shifts into? Who cares if I drink beer or blood? Just random body stuff, isn't it? Like being tall or short, it's not that important. All that matters is love, and I love her."

"Yeah, well, that's great, Romeo. Because now you're all each other has left." Torrin looked disgusted. "You gave it all up for some llama chick."

"*Alpaca, damn it!*" Orion corrected him.

"Thought it wasn't important," Torrin snarked, and playfully shoved his brother.

But Orion was so solid now that the shove didn't move him a

centimeter. Torrin gaped, and Orion laughed, displaying new fangs. Eventually Torrin laughed too.

"Shoot, maybe we don't need to go to L.A.," Orion said, clapping his brother on the back. "If *you* can accept me, then why not the rest of 'em?" He grinned. "You and me together could always talk 'em into anything, right?"

"No. No, no, no, you gotta wake up." Torrin's voice was harsh but his eyes gave away his fear. "Let go of that delusion. They will stake you on sight."

"Not when we took credit for two kills. We proved which side we're on." Orion was high on hope, his magnetism suddenly flaring bright again. Infectious. I could see why he'd been a promising member of Carnivora before the vampire thing derailed him. "Anyone could see we're not loyal to the elder council, we're loyal to our shifter kin."

"You could barbecue that whole council and it wouldn't matter to our kin." Torrin's face was as bleak as his humor. "You're dead, Ry. At least to Carnivora."

Orion looked up sadly at his brother. "Am I dead to you?"

It was a straight-forward question and I had to give the baby vamp props for daring to ask when clearly the answer meant everything to him.

Torrin shrugged and glanced up, then down again. "Nah, you dumb meercat. I'm still here."

Orion threw himself at his brother in a hug-attack that looked like it would have caused injury to an Ordinal.

Then he turned in the direction of the cemetery entrance, became a blur of vampiric superspeed, and vanished over the gate.

☾

"All these supernatural brats are impossible to follow," I complained half an hour later, back at the bakery. "They teleport. They self-glamour. They blur with superspeed. It's beyond rude."

I shook my head in disgust, and stirred more sugar into the tea I was guzzling at the kitchen counter.

"These kids are exhausting, for real." Elliot, back in human form, stood next to me, downing black coffee like water.

We were getting testy as the night wore on and the caffeine probably wasn't helping much. I'd stopped to retrieve his clothes from the statue downtown and marveled at how no one had stolen his wallet. Classic Blue Moon Bay.

"At least we learned something about big brother Torrin," Elliot said, and added, "He's an accessory," just as I said, "He has a heart."

I sighed. "Okay … so we failed to follow the real hunters. But what if we don't *need* to follow them?"

"What do you mean?" Elliot eagerly reached for his third soft pretzel. He was so hungry after shifting that he'd consented to eat a baked good: a red-letter day.

Or night, really.

"If they're all going to the same place," I said, "then we just need to guess where."

"Right." He rubbed his stubbly chin. "If I were a young Green Witch, where would I take my newly-turned friends to hide out?"

"Never mind, it'll be the last place we'd ever guess," I said. "Since we don't think like criminal geniuses."

Elliot's mouth twitched in amusement. "Oh, come on, they're just college kids. We were them ten years ago—with better hairstyles."

I snapped my fingers. "Oh my gosh, that's it!"

"The hair thing?" He tilted his face.

"No, the college thing," I said. "I think I know exactly where their hideout is!"

While we sped toward campus in the police car, I told him,

"Remember when Max and I were searching all over town for that dirty floor that matched the one in the video? We ran into Amethyst double parked outside the library. She had a ton of food. I think she was delivering it to the group. But instead, she hopped in her car and left."

"Because seeing you so close to the hideout spooked her," Elliot said, nodding, as he pulled into the south campus parking lot. "She must have texted the others to clear out."

I closed my eyes, trying to picture the scene in my mind. "Carina and Orion panicked," I guessed. "They grabbed sleeping Yolanda and blurred off into the woods with her. Then they dashed off a final video and planted Gerard's remains as evidence they'd staked the kidnapper. They went invisible to watch us 'rescue' Yolanda. But when it was all over, Carina and Orion went right back to their hiding spot—in the college library basement."

Elliot parked in front of the library and glanced toward me, looking proud. "I don't know if you're right or wrong. But you've got great instincts."

I beamed.

Rather than messing with invisibility, Elliot simply asked the librarian to unlock the service elevator so he could check something downstairs.

Being a cop must be its own kind of magic, because they did what he said without asking any questions.

In the elevator car, I rested against the back wall as we sank down a level and a half. Elliot and I exchanged expectant looks. It had been a long night, and we were approaching the moment of truth.

"Either way this goes," he said, "be proud of your instincts."

I nodded, though anxiety and exhaustion were dueling for control, and pride was far from what I felt.

The doors parted. Right away, I could smell coffee, dust, and truffle mac and cheese.

In the far corner of the basement, a white bookshelf on its side formed a makeshift dinner table. Sitting slumped on the floor around it were four teenagers:

Amethyst.

Orion.

Yolanda.

And a pretty girl with bouncy curls and golden-brown skin. Carina.

They looked up at us in disbelief.

"Oh thank God!" Amethyst pounded her coffee cup on the table. "Sorry fam, this went off the rails. I've been dying to turn myself in."

Yolanda groaned pitifully. "You keep saying that, but you're not the one my mom's gonna kill."

Just when I thought apprehending them was going to be easy, a pair of blurs charged me and Elliot. Before I knew it, we were flat on our butts on the cold, dirty floor.

"Ow!" I rubbed my hip.

"Hey, nice move," Elliot said to Orion, who'd just knocked him down. He made no attempt to fight back.

Carina stood over me, her bee-stung lips frowning in confusion. "Okay, um, what do we do with them? I don't want to harm a human…"

"And I don't want to harm a shifter, Deputy James," said Orion, staring down at Elliot. "But I can't let you deliver us to our true deaths."

"Noted, and cool clubhouse," Elliot said, still unfazed. "No one's true dying here, but there will be consequences. No way around that."

Carina and Orion didn't look reassured.

Yolanda gave another pathetic moan. "Does this mean you're taking us to jail?"

"Worse." Elliot's voice was stern but not devoid of sympathy. "I'm taking you home to your mother."

He got back on his feet, and no one even tried to stop him.

"Listen, Yolanda, I'm not going to book you for an Ordinal charge when almost everything about your crime was supernatural. Green Witches have a fair justice system. I leave you in their capable hands to decide your punishment."

"What, punishment?" Amethyst's eyes were saucers. "Is that necessary? If I could just explain—"

"Not how it works," Elliot cut her off. "Trust me. But you'll be okay."

"You Green Witches are *lucky*," Carina said bitterly. "At least you have a community that cares. What about us, Deputy, you going to leave us here to rot?"

"Guess that's what he means by consequences," Orion said darkly. "Now that we're turned, we're his enemies."

"You think I care about your damn fangs?" Elliot snapped, surprising me a bit after his whole "it's a war" speech. "I have a problem with vampires who control the world," he added, stealing a glance at me. "Who take things away from me and mine. Who use us. Exploit us. *Kill* us. Until you're doing that, I recognize you … as kin."

Carina and Orion hung on his every word. With their wide eyes fixed on his face, both looked suddenly younger. Elliot was a highly-ranked and visible member of the town shifter community, and he was offering them belonging. They drank it in.

"Normally," Elliot went on, musing aloud, "I'd turn you in to our brothers and sisters. But they haven't demonstrated much regard for your safety. The elder council's not rooting for your continued existence, either. Marie's a non-starter. So, who can I, in good conscience, release you to?"

"No one," Carina blurted out.

Orion nodded at the floor.

"Do you see why we had to help them?" Yolanda asked. "No one else would!"

"Yeah, but. You could have gone about it differently." I wasn't about to cede the high ground to teenaged criminals. "You had a whole community to reach out to at any time. Just saying."

"Who was going to help with this? Leia?" Amethyst scoffed, wrinkling her button nose. "All we ever talk about is lip liner and kale. And you were all like, 'I'm too busy to be your mentor. I have to run my amazing, successful business. And solve mysteries. And be friends with everyone in town.'"

I groaned at her mincing imitation of me. How come this clueless first-gen witchlet always seemed to have my number?

"Oh, for the love of cupcakes, I will mentor you both," I growled. "I'll mentor you till you're magically exhausted and you're sick of me and I'm even sicker of you."

"Really, Hazel?" Yolanda's small smile was like a sunbreak on an overcast winter day.

I shrugged, then nodded. "Yep."

I was immediately gratified when Amethyst hissed, "Yessss! Real mentor five," and they clapped each other's hand hard.

"Okay, here's what I can do for Carina and Orion," Elliot said, turning everyone's attention back to the vampire couple. "I'm willing to put you up in a safehouse for up to three weeks. But you'll have to stay hidden and take direction from other vampires to learn survival skills."

"Like what?" Carina sounded genuinely curious.

(I was too.)

"At a minimum, you need to learn how to hunt safely," Elliot said grimly. "And how to stay out of the crosshairs of shifter gangs." After a moment's hesitation, he added, "Your line has strong powers of compulsion. It's up to you if you want to be taught how to use them."

"Powers?!" Orion looked like he'd just been told he won the state lottery. "Uh, yes please?"

Elliot nodded. "After newblood bootcamp, I'll provide you with uncompromised identification, and enough cash to seed your new unlife in L.A. till you can land jobs. After that, it's on you."

"That's exactly what they wanted, how's that a consequence?" Amethyst sounded incredulous.

So was I, but for different reasons.

I could see Elliot being generous enough to dig into his own pocket to fund their escape—even though a deputy sheriff couldn't possibly make that much money. But offering to make the couple fake IDs? That was *illegal.*

Except, what else could a vampire *do* but get a fake ID?

"They have no choice," I said, more to myself than to Amethyst. I remembered Torrin's warning to Orion in the graveyard. "They don't really want to leave town. They did all this because of how much they wanted to stay and be accepted by their families. Leaving town is the best offer they're going to get, but trust me. They don't want it."

"No, we don't." With a sad smile, Carina reached for Orion's pale hand.

A long look passed between them.

"But we'll take it," Orion said at last, to Elliot. "Thank you."

After Elliot left with Carina and Orion, I had Amethyst sign up online to reserve one of the library's bigger quiet study rooms. As soon as we three witches shuffled into it, Yolanda conjured a cone of silence.

"There's going to be a lot of yelling," she said. "Trust me."

When Jacinta stormed in ten minutes later, she didn't waste

a moment proving her daughter right. Since she couldn't currently teleport, she must have been speeding like a bat out of hell.

"Yolanda Wisteria Hyacinth," Jacinta accused, hands on hips. "How *dare* you frighten the heck out of me like that? I have six new grey hairs because of your lie. Six!"

"Mama—"

"Don't 'Mama' me, young lady. You lied to the whole town. Committed fraud to get your hands on that ransom money … why on earth would you do such a thing?"

"Because…" Yolanda burst into tears. "Because I don't want to run the diner with you! I want to study film and eventually make movies and TV shows about witches—Green Witches like us. I want to share our story with the world."

Jacinta recoiled in shock. "Well, you could have done me the courtesy of telling me," she said. "Instead of running this cockamamie caper."

Yolanda shook her head and sobbed. "I was too scared to disappoint you. You need my magic here and I thought…" She sniffed loudly. "I thought if I paid off your debts, then you could get your own magic back. And then I wouldn't be letting you down as much when I left."

"Letting me down?" Jacinta's brows knitted. "Honey, I'm the one who's let *you* down, with my … well … my crafting problem. I've made you worried. Trapped. And worse, I've made you ashamed of me."

Yolanda threw her arms around her mother. "Mama, stop it. I could never be ashamed of you. I love you more than a field of irises!"

"I love *you* more than an acre of heliotrope!"

"It's a whole Hyacinth thing," Amethyst said under her breath while the two of them hugged and cried. "They started saying it to each other when Yo was little. Weird and embarrassing, but whatever."

I shrugged. "Kinda jealous. Wish somebody loved me that much."

Amethyst snickered, then her eyes darted left and back. "Me too."

With a gasp, Jacinta pulled back from the hug. "Wait, did you put a sleep spell on yourself so you could deny any wrongdoing if you were caught? That's diabolical!"

Yolanda nodded, looking guilty. "You always told me a witch's reputation is everything."

Jacinta gave a short laugh. "Well, I meant a witch's *integrity*. And there's little integrity in ransoming yourself, even to pay your mother's debts."

"It wasn't *just* for that," Yolanda admitted. "I also needed to help my vampire friends. They were in danger of being hunted down by shifters."

Jacinta did that over-blinking thing she'd done back at Marie's, as if the repeated motion could erase her confusing reality like an Etch-A-Sketch. "But, dear heart, this scheme just made that worse. Your actions fanned the hatred against vampires. Why, even *I* fell for it," she added the second part in an overly emphatic tone, as if to say that an evolved witch like her was hard to fool.

"I know." Yolanda stared at the wall dismally. "We messed up bad."

"There's got to be a way we can fix this," Amethyst said. "I just can't think of it."

"Luckily, you don't have to have all the answers yourselves," I said, gently. "We have an entire community with very strong opinions who'll want to weigh in."

"In fact, they should be arriving any second," Jacinta said somberly. "I called an emergency meeting of the Green Witch Regional Council for Restorative Justice."

"Wait, what?" Yolanda's head jerked up in panic, as if she'd heard the buzzing of angry bees.

"We're so screwed," was the last thing I heard Amethyst mutter before the study room began to fill with teleporting Green Witches.

They were dressed in everything from athleisure wear to pajamas and robes.

Most sported white or silver hair—though one was hot pink.

And every elder witch in the group wore a deeply serious expression.

I wanted to tell the girls that it was going to be okay, but I wasn't sure that was true and I didn't want to lie to my new mentees.

From now on, I wanted them to be able to trust me.

CHAPTER TWENTY-SEVEN

"I CAN'T BELIEVE I let them talk me into this," Max said with a sheepish look as she, Britt, and I walked across the well-lit parking lot of the Blue Moon Bay Aquarium. "A DEI speaker? What am I supposed to say?"

"You could always just take questions," I said. "I'm sure everyone will have lots—for you *and* Britt."

Amethyst and Yolanda had traded a month of free pancakes to the facilities director to host their first supernatural diversity event at the aquarium tonight. It was to feature a sleepover in the ocean roundabout room, where all the local young Green Witches could snooze in their sleeping bags surrounded by lazily swimming fish. There would be bottomless smoothies, games, and all-night snacks … that was the draw. The price was the three hours of educational programming beforehand, which everyone in the Green Witch community was invited to attend. And from the full parking lot, this hastily-planned shindig was the talk of the town.

Or, more likely, Amethyst and Yolanda's crimes were the talk of the town and everyone was curious to hear them confess in front of a crowd.

Last night's emergency meeting of the Council for Restorative Justice had gone decently, overall. Amethyst and Yolanda were lectured ad nauseum about the harm they'd done. They broke down in tears early in the process and kept crying most of the way through. They promised to share their burdens and troubles with the community next time, rather than spin a web of deception that made everything worse. Along with heartfelt apologies, the girls suggested their own atonement which the council unanimously approved: a year's worth of service to the magical community at large, under the direction of the council and their mentor, *gulp*, me. After sentencing themselves to twenty hours a week of volunteering, their panic faded into relief. When I finally went home, hitching a ride with Jacinta, the girls were still in the library building a spreadsheet.

"I don't want to answer a bunch of ignorant questions from witches," Britt said, zipping up her cherry red, vegan-leather jacket. "No matter what I say about the vampire condition, all they're going to be thinking is, 'blood, blood, she drinks blood.' They'll cover their wrists with their sleeves and pull up their turtlenecks."

"Guaranteed they'll ask me to shift in front of them," Max commiserated. "So they can laugh at the weirdo. It'll be just like high school but supernatural."

"Oof, I'll go first and try to warm them up," Britt said. "I know how much you hate public speaking."

"Thanks, Brittany," Max said, and they fist bumped.

I pulled on the heavy chrome-and-glass door to the main entrance. The walls inside were patterned with shiny blue fish. As our footfalls echoed on the aquarium lobby's heated floor, I reflected that Max and Britt were getting along awfully well tonight. Maybe it was because for the first time in weeks, Graham wasn't with us. Earlier today, after presenting me with a dove-grey, upholstered, Scandinavian-style futon as a thanks for letting him stay over, he'd jumped in his truck and headed back to Portland. Britt said things weren't over between them, that she had plans to visit over the winter holidays. But she'd still seemed wistful as she packed her own things to return to her apartment.

Rather than a cashier, Jacinta greeted us from behind a table, dressed in a green blazer that perfectly matched her jade pendant. "Welcome!" She smiled, clearly in her element. "You can go straight through to the fish roundabout. Follow the arrows."

From her polished demeanor, you would never guess anything of the chaos in her life. It struck me that if Yolanda struggled to reach out for help with her problems, she'd learned that habit at home. But I didn't blame Jacinta, not entirely. How could I, when I'd spent a decade rolling my eyes at her PowerPoints without ever offering to take a turn at leadership myself?

The sound of laughter and applause grew louder as we approached the fish roundabout. The door was open, and as we walked up the spiral ramp, thick acrylic walls revealed the captivating cylindrical tank with fish of all shapes and sizes swimming around it. Artificial reefs and rock formations were lit from within with gold and aqua.

At the top of the roundabout, a blue carpeted circle of floor was packed with young witches, their snacks, and their sleeping bags. A willowy, long-haired woman was talking animatedly about dryad culture, and a back row of chairs had been thoughtfully set up for older or disabled witches.

I was astonished to see Gran in one of those chairs, listening to the dryad with such rapt attention she didn't notice us walk in.

Britt peered through the crowd. "Do you see Landra anywhere?" she whispered to me. "She's not responding to texts. I was hoping she and Bronwen would show up."

I shook my head, hoping all was well at Marie's. The spooky memory of being carried out of the house on a grey wind would not be leaving me soon.

The dryad finished her speech to thunderous applause, and then it was Britt's turn onstage.

Yolanda's warm introduction began, "It's my pleasure to present to you local waitress and former Blood Moon High cheerleader—shoot. I meant *Blue* Moon." She face-palmed. "Why did I say blood?"

"Must be my red jacket," Britt quipped with a smile, and the audience smiled back. I'd forgotten how good Britt was with crowds.

But she'd no sooner picked up the microphone from Yolanda when a young witch called out without raising her hand. "What's it like drinking actual blood?"

Without missing a beat, Britt pointed to the girl's energy drink. "What's it like drinking that Pissed Off Wolverine?"

The witch shrugged. "Tastes kinda gross."

"Exactly," Britt said. "You just drink it for the boost, right?"

The girl nodded.

"Same deal," Britt said.

Another witch held up her hand. "What happens to you if you go out in direct sunlight?"

"Oh my gosh, I'm glad you asked! It sucks. I am very sensitive to the sun."

The witch leaned in eagerly. "Do you burst into flames and stuff?"

Britt laughed. "Not literally, but sometimes a sunny day gives me a headache."

"That's it, an occasional headache?" The witch looked disgusted. "I get *tons* of headaches."

"We're just like you," Britt bantered. "Only with super speed and super strength, and the whole eternal youth thing. But please don't hate me. Because I can also gorge on wine and chocolate with no bad effects."

By the end of that Q&A session, I gathered that most of the girls in the room wanted to be vampires. Britt had charmed them, even if she hadn't persuaded them that she faced any challenges whatsoever.

"Your turn," she told Max, after taking a bow to thundering applause. She stole a seat in the front row and was immediately hounded for selfies.

Max bounded to her feet. "All right, just like with her. Ask me anything."

"Can you shift for us, right here right now?" a witch yelled, not missing a beat.

Max spoke slowly and carefully into the mic. "No."

After a minute's sullen silence, someone from the audience asked half-heartedly, "So like, what kind of were-animal are you, anyway?"

"Don't say 'were,'" Max snapped at her. "Makes you sound ignorant."

"Fine, what animal do you shift into, I guess?"

"That's personal."

"Is she going to answer *anything?*" one witch asked.

"It's probably something boring," another guessed. "Like a hamster. Or a goldfish."

"It's not those," Max growled. "Next question."

"My brother said the full moon makes shifters want to kill," said a witch whose hands were cupped around a bowl of popcorn.

"Urban legend," I scoffed before Max could.

"I should have known." The girl sounded disappointed. "I mean, he also said when shifters go back to human, they're butt naked."

The whole room giggled uncontrollably.

"That," Max said with great dignity, "is true."

No one had the guts to ask a follow up.

"All right, this is *atrocious.*" Amethyst was on her feet, striding to the front, treating the whole room to her furrowed brow. "I apologize on behalf of this group for the lack of respect being shown to our speaker. Let's get some thoughtful questions going here, fam!" She clapped and a few others joined her, including me.

A witch who looked about thirteen stood and also raised her hand, for maximum earnestness. "Do shifters and vampires hate each other, for real?"

Max and Britt just cackled together.

"Yeah, pretty much," Max said.

Britt nodded. "Absolutely."

Yolanda looked aghast. "*That's* the message you two want to send?"

"Oh whatever, you two, I'm calling b.s.," I protested, marching to the "stage" area. "I know it started off with the ancient hatred and the threats and all. But admit it, you two like each other now. You're best friends."

"We're associates," Britt said. "We solve crimes together. We don't, like, *hang*."

"That monster over there is correct."

They grinned at each other. Britt even hopped back up on stage and put her arm around Max, who forgot to shake her off for several seconds.

"Fine, okay, so we're kinda friends," Max said. "So, I'm the one shifter who doesn't hate every vampire."

"Well, you and Graham too," I said, then realized I'd said too much when Britt's glare sliced into me.

Max looked from me to Britt and back. "Okay, what's going on there?"

"Nothing." Britt's eyes were daggers. "Graham and I … we … don't hate each other anymore, okay?"

"You unbelievable, human-shaped leech," Max seethed.

"Hate speech!" Amethyst yelled.

Max ignored her. "I offered you protection and you betrayed me in the lamest way. My *ex?*"

"It's not like she planned it!" I said, possibly thinking of a different illicit couple. In a bakery kitchen, with a hairnet. "Circumstances forced them to interact a lot."

"No one forced their lips to interact," Max said icily.

The baby witches were all turning to their friends with open-mouthed expressions of shock and glee. Their faces seemed to be saying, These *are the speakers we're supposed to learn from?*

I knew I should be shutting it down. Airing our dirty laundry in front of a literal audience was not the plan. But I. Was so. Sleep. Deprived.

Hex it, I was diving in.

"Max, I'm not saying what Britt did was okay," I said. "But … well … she's been under a lot of stress."

Britt coughed "*Hypocrite,*" at me.

Crap. My heartbeat sped up. "Um, Max? I kinda have to tell you something."

The audience *oohed.*

"Okay, the plot thickens." Amethyst cracked her knuckles.

"Not a good time, Hazel," Max snapped, her prizewinning obliviousness endearing her to me even as I wanted to run from the room. "I get to be angry about this. Here Britt goes on and on about the girl code and she's the one who broke—"

"It's about Kade."

Max groaned. "Whatever my genius brother did this time, save it for when it's relevant."

The witches laughed like they were watching a comedy.

"*Oh.* It is relevant. I'm an idiot." Max sank to the floor. "Both my best friends just stabbed me in the back."

Yolanda spoke up. "Hey, don't you think your response is a little sexist? I mean, why are you putting all the blame on the women instead of the men they were involved with, your brother and your ex?"

"You ask why I'm mad at the women?" Max barked a short laugh. "I already know men suck. It's not news."

Yolanda frowned. "Wow. Not the kind of sexist I was expecting, but still not great."

"It's not like you own those two men," another witch spoke up. "They have rights. They can date whoever they want."

"And Blue Moon Bay's not exactly New York City," another added. "You're going to run into the same people and the same families."

Max spoke into the mic. "That's fair, but Hazel and Britt should have communicated better. They blindsided me. That's not good friendship."

"It's true." I hung my head. "I'm sorry."

"I just don't see how my thing was that bad?" Britt folded her arms and shrugged, defiant. "You briefly dated the guy and broke up with him because you're essentially gay. Is that fair?"

Max considered it a moment. "More or less."

"So yeah," Britt went on, "I should have checked with you to begin with. I'm sorry. But I didn't because it was the middle of a crisis. My unlife was at risk." She frowned. "At least we *thought* my unlife was at risk. Turns out it was all just a hoax, by these two lovely witches." She nodded to Yolanda and Amethyst.

Am's eyes nearly bugged out of her head. "We're not your all-purpose scapegoats!" she yelled from her seat. "You can't blame us for your drama!"

"Well, okay, but … devil's advocate," Max spoke again into the mic. She relished that thing. I was concerned she'd try to take it home. "Whose fault is it that Britt was freeloading on Hazel's couch and needed a bodyguard?"

"And having long-term guests was stressful to *me*!" I put in. "In fact, the first thing I connected with Kade on was my sudden roommate stress."

"Oh please, *I* sent you into Kade's arms?" Britt gave me an *Are You Serious* glare. "You've had a crush on the bad boy since I first met you."

"How did you know that?" I had no idea Britt paid any attention to the crushes that losers like me had back in those days.

"She has *eyes*," Max said. "You always wanted Kade but you never had the guts to admit it to yourself. Much less bring it up with me."

"Well," Amethyst said, "can you blame her if this is how you react?"

Max looked like she wanted to rip Am's head off, then slumped her shoulders. "No, you're right." She sighed. "Kade's my twin, but sometimes I treat him like a baby brother. I need to stop doing that. Hazel's amazing, he'd be lucky to land her as a girlfriend. And eventually, wife."

"Whoa," I said. "Slow down. It's only been one date—"

"Shoot, I would be so lucky to have Hazel as not only my best friend but also my sister-in-law." Max's eyes were shining with the prospect of welcoming me into her family.

"Um, Max, whoa," I cut in. "I'm not marrying Kade."

"Well, no not after one date. You can't know yet, I'm just giving you my bless—"

"Max?" Hexes, this was harder than admitting I'd kissed him. "I *do* know. After one date. We're not … we're not right for each other."

"Oh, crap." Max's jaw dropped. *"You witch, you hurt my little baby brother!"*

"No, you're hurting him by infantilizing an adult man," spoke up a witch with a confident voice. "And you don't get to say 'you witch.'"

"Yes she does, Hazel's literally a witch." Britt clearly had no more figs to give.

"Yeah, and so are you," Max piled on, pointing out the audience member aggressively. "So are *all* of you. I'm in a room full of witchy witches. And fish!"

She dropped the mic.

Absolutely no one applauded us when we stepped off the stage.

"So ... that went pretty well," I said, when the three of us were safely through the door out of the fish roundabout. "By which I mean, *we're* okay." Silence. "We are okay, aren't we?"

"I'm not," Max said glumly. "That *was* just like high school, all bullies and sheeple. How do you get everyone you meet to connect with you, Britt?" The question caught me by surprise. "Teach me your ways."

"Actually, I had to work really hard tonight," Britt said. "Tough room. I'm going to need a debrief sesh at the Barrel, with margaritas. And nachos."

"I'm going to need a whole bucket of wings," Max said. "Hazel, you're buying for making us go to this."

"Genius idea," Britt said brightly and turned to me. "I want the good tequila."

"Glad we've all made up then," I said, rolling my eyes.

On the way out, we ran into Gran standing by the penguin exhibit taking pictures of the goofy birds. I prayed she'd walked out after the dryad and missed our star turn.

"Hazel dear! It's good to see you three." She hugged us with one parka-clad arm, the other holding her phone. "I just heard the most amazing speeches. All talking about how much stronger we'd be as a magical community if we all banded together. Instead of emphasizing our differences and using stereotypes as a crutch."

My mind reeled. "Wait. You listened to some DEI speakers, and it changed your views?"

She nodded. "How could it not? We're stronger together, Hazel. It turns out, we witches are only one piece of the puzzle."

I'd only been trying to tell her that *forever*. But as Britt and

Max took turns high fiving Gran I wondered: had I not been the right messenger?

If I was honest, I'd never *fully* believed she–or anyone–could break through eighty plus years of prejudices.

Yet astonishingly, I was seeing it now.

Even now, while on magical rest, Gran was still mentoring me. Showing me by example that a Green Witch never stops learning and growing.

During the five-minute drive to the bar downtown, our conversation meandered from subject to harmless subject. Max mentioned an attractive woman she'd been seeing around town, and Britt urged her to talk to the woman and find out if she was a supernatural—or interested in women, for that matter. Britt said she was considering taking night classes at the college and Max clapped her on the shoulder supportively. They both listened with obvious interest as I described how cool and sort of intimate it felt to put a spell on Elliot the night before.

While I wouldn't have chosen to air everything in public like that, it felt good not to have any secrets. Without saying a word, I think all three of us agreed that we needed a break from the intensity of the last few weeks.

Then we got to the Barrel.

The moment we walked inside, Britt tensed. Max and I followed her gaze to the big oak table in the corner, where half a dozen Carnivora members had gathered to shoot the breeze, but they were all standing menacingly. Growls and snarls filled the air. Scruffy stood over them, balancing two platters with chicken wings, but he clearly wasn't just serving food. His face was contorted with rage and hatred.

Standing just five feet beyond the table were Carina and Orion.

CHAPTER TWENTY-EIGHT

BRITT, MAX, AND I ducked into a tall booth where we could eavesdrop on the shifter gang but they couldn't see us.

"What are you doing, baby vamps?" Britt muttered under her breath. "You're supposed to be in a safe house."

"Hey, I'm back," Orion said unnecessarily, and turned his charismatic charm on his former gang brothers. "I know you missed me. All the rocks and flowers meant a lot."

Carnivora booed and hissed.

I hid my face behind my long brown hair and peeked out just in time to see Jasper spit on the floor.

"My friend is dead," he said. "You're just his walking corpse."

"Not walking for long," another shifter said, and was met with ominous laughter.

Carina shrank, her face miserable. Clearly, this hadn't been her idea, but she was standing by her man. Her only family left.

"Hear me out, brothers and sisters." Orion's green eyes focused on the crowd one by one, quieting them. Compulsion didn't work on shifters; it was all his charisma. If he hadn't been turned, he'd have made a good leader. "Give us one chance. We'll prove to you we're still Carnivora."

Torrin had on his coolest, most opaque game face. Whether or not they'd run this stunt by him, he was caught in a double bind.

If he spoke up against them as a cover, he'd be signing their death warrants. If he spoke up in their defense, he'd be signing his own.

"There's something in it for you," Orion added, "I promise."

Scruffy set down his double order of wings and pointed to Carina. "That hoofed creature was never one of us. And *you*," he told Orion, "it's 'Carnivora till I die.' And you're dead."

"Look beyond the surface," Carina pleaded. "We're the same people as before. We still hate vampires."

It made me sad to think she meant it. That she hated herself.

"We staked our own progenitor, Gerard," Orion put in.

Lies. These kids hadn't killed anyone. But Orion sold the lies. His eyes burned with determination. He craved acceptance.

"Thanks, I guess?" an elder Carnivora member said. "For removing that other monster from the planet. But I can't help but notice that you're *also* monsters. You said it yourself, Gerard *made* you."

"Gerard's bloodline isn't what we're loyal to," Carina insisted. "We're shifters to the bone."

Another round of hisses.

"You won't have bones after we're through with you," Jasper taunted.

I could hardly believe they were doing this in front of Ordinals. These shifters were the most indiscreet supernaturals I'd ever met. I stole a glance at the tables around us, half-expecting to see phones out calling 911. To my surprise, most customers carried on talking and drinking as before. A few looked over with annoyance. None looked scared.

A white-haired man dipped his onion ring in ranch dressing and smugly explained to the young woman across from him, "Drugs, Olivia. It's all a code for drugs."

"I *know* that, Grandpa." She straightened her posture, indignantly. "And no, I'm not doing them."

Orion's smile was starting to look more desperate than compelling. He dragged a money clip from the pocket of his jeans and blurted out, "We stole twenty thousand dollars from Gerard's bloated coffers."

Max, Britt, and I exchanged a look. The lie was obvious to us. I knew more about the state of Gerard's finances than I wanted to. His coffers were as empty as his coffin. Where'd they find that money?

But cash—whatever its provenance—was sacred here. The hissing and threats ceased for a moment. All eyes turned to Orion.

"It's all for you, our shifter family," he announced firmly. "And it's just the beginning. Ree and I, we know where to get more. See, we can pretend to be on their side. Unlock those rich vampire homes so we can fleece the bloodsuckers."

"We could use the money." Torrin's voice was painstakingly casual. "And two loyal fighters, of course."

Impassive silence followed his speech. Terrifying silence. Max put her hands on top of her head and screwed up her face like she was bracing for impact. From Britt's wistful eyes, I knew she was daring to hope.

Then Scruffy burst out laughing. "Loyal fighters? They're undead monsters. They're everything we hate."

Jasper banged on the table. "Torrin's lost his edge because one of them's his brother. He can't be trusted anymore."

"Where've you been all these nights, Torrin?" another shifter member added. "Not with Carnivora."

"He's been scheming with vampires!" said a third.

A sheen of sweat coated Torrin's face but he was still trying to sound calm. "If you all feel so strongly about it, I'll step down."

"It's too late for that," Scruffy said. "You're *out*, Torrin. You're as dead to us as they are."

"*Dead to us*," the others responded in one voice.

All the Carnivora members leaned forward and sniffed the air. I've never witnessed such a thing in my life, but it was obviously some kind of ritual. It filled my guts with foreboding.

"Outside," Jasper said to Torrin. A command.

Torrin was done calling shots.

The brothers' eyes met, defeat in both their gazes. Even outnumbered like this, the vampires could use their superspeed to flee. But would they leave Torrin behind?

Torrin's whole life was Carnivora. Would he even want a life without his crew?

Remembering the little I knew about gangs, I whispered to Max and Britt, "If he doesn't get out of here, are they like going to beat him half to death?"

"If he's lucky," Max whispered, "it'll only be half."

Adrenaline coursed through me as Carnivora marched Torrin and the newbloods toward the Barrel's swinging doors. Luckily, they were too busy with their vengeful rage to notice other customers.

"Britt, can you pull up the car?" I passed her my tin of mints. "If you take one with your hand on the steering wheel, the whole car goes invis."

Britt snatched up the tin and blurred out of there.

"What are *we* going to do?" Max asked as the last of the grim procession headed out.

"Distract them." I grabbed her hand and squeezed it. "*With a cloak of disguise, you'll blend and sway. You'll be the one who got away.*"

In a flash, Max's long red hair turned mermaid teal, her symmetrical features transformed into Amethyst's cute, round ones.

"Seriously, you made me Amethyst?" Max scowled down at her purple knit mittens.

"Go out there and school everyone fearlessly," I said, "like she would."

I glamoured myself invisible and ran into the parking lot. I expected to find Carnivora members savagely attacking Torrin while attempting to fight off the newbloods, but no.

They were taking a smoke break before the proceedings.

Jasper handed Torrin a cigar and Scruffy lit it for him. On closer examination, this too seemed like a creepy ritual. His last smoke?

Not if I could help it.

"Jasper!" Max yelled, and everyone turned to look at "Amethyst." "I thought you quit cigarettes."

"I thought you never wanted to talk to me again," he sputtered.

"Oh, I don't," Max said flatly, rolling with it. "Your hatred for vampires makes you about as attractive to me as a Wendigo."

The distraction was working. Drama was hard to look away from, even when you had a former gang leader to beat up. But Orion and Carina were giving fake Amethyst odd looks. Funny how her friends knew it wasn't the real her but her ex-boyfriend didn't have a clue.

Ten feet away, car exhaust that seemed to come out of nowhere seeped into the night air. I hoped I was the only one who noticed.

"Wendigo is an acceptable insult," Max went on, as I knew she could forever. "It disparages no supernatural groups, only a demonic creature that feeds on hate. Conversely, terms like animal, hag, or bloodsucker are objectionable … offensive … and … *harmful*…"

While she was sallying forth, I tiptoed over to Torrin, figuring the newbloods' super hearing would transmit my whisper. "An invisible car just pulled up. You three get ready to run in."

I approached the car and felt around for a door handle. I had just opened the left backseat when a heavy weight slammed into me. Torrin, Carina and Orion were suddenly in a heap beside me in the backseat.

The newbloods hadn't taken any chances; they'd used their superstrength and speed to grab Orion's brother without waiting around for his consent.

Max-as-Amethyst hurled herself in after them and we peeled out of the Barrel parking lot with a screech while every Carnivora member stared.

It was like a clown car. But invisible. All you could see were the backseat passengers sardined together.

Several gang members ran after us, but gave up after a block or so, during which we thankfully didn't get into a crash.

"Okay, who's sitting on my lap?" Torrin said irritably.

I felt myself blushing. "That would be me, Hazel."

"Hazel!" Orion and Carina said my name with more admiration than most people do.

"Thank you," Carina added. "All of you, whoever you are."

I released Max's glamour just as Britt spoke up. "You're welcome."

The car turned visible.

"Anyone mind if I climb into the front?" Max said.

"I would mind if you *didn't*," Torrin said. "Not that anyone listens to me anymore."

Orion and Carina exchanged a look.

"We weren't going to let you get killed," Orion said, as if he weren't the one who forced the issue. "And we still have the money. Elliot bought us a car along with the fake IDs."

"He what?" I spat. How could Elliot be capable of such grand gestures—was he independently wealthy?

"And you turned around and sold it?" Britt said. "Now how are you going to leave town?"

"I ain't gonna let them run me out of town." Torrin looked disgusted. "I will fight them tooth and claw."

"I can't believe I'm saying this," I began, "but I'd rather you kept your teeth and claws."

"Ugh, I'm surrounded by pacifists." Torrin attempted to appeal to his brother. "Bro, the Bay's always been our home."

"Places aren't home, people are." Orion put his arm around Carina. "You're my home, Ree. I go where you go."

Carina held out her hand to Torrin.

"You already made your choice back there," she told him. "Might as well embrace it."

Groaning, Torrin reached out to touch Carina's hand and at the last second turned it into a fist bump. "I go where you two idiots go. Till we're caught and killed."

"Where am I taking you?" Britt said. "The airport? Bus station?"

"I don't care," Orion said.

"Whatever's closer," Torrin said, as a sharp turn bounced me in his lap. "This car ride's kinda intense."

"I just texted Landra," Carina said. "Asked her to drop off my stuff in the driveway." She shuddered. "I don't want to go back inside Marie's house for a second, but I'm not leaving without my family photos and my meerkat stuffie."

"Okay, I'll head to Sunset." Britt sounded relieved. "I'm glad Landra's responding to texts, even if it means she's ghosting me."

"Oh, um, she hasn't replied yet." Carina shrugged. "But I'm sure she will." A minute later, she added, "I'll try Bronwen, too."

Neither girl had replied by the time we reached Marie's front gate.

"I have a bad feeling about this," I said as Britt rolled down her window.

"Well, don't jinx it Hazel!" Max hissed.

Britt pushed the intercom button, but no one picked up.

"I don't get it," she said. "Why is no one home?"

"Do you think the council might have ... made its move?" Max made a cut-throat gesture.

Carina gasped. "What would the elder vampire council want with Bronwen and Landra? They're totally innocent."

"They are," Britt said grimly. "The council, not so much. I'm getting worried. I'm going to hop the fence and see what's up." She opened the door and got out of the car, vanishing over the gate a moment later.

"Me too!" Carina joined her before anyone could protest. Orion followed, quick as lightning.

"Man, it feels lazy to sit in the car," Max said. "But they're so much faster. If something's going on, they'll just tell us and we'll join them then. Am I over justifying my choice to sit in the car?"

Torrin crossed his arms. "I ain't going inside a vampire den. Gotta draw the line somewhere."

In the distance I heard a bloodcurdling scream. Then Orion and Britt were back, their expressions twisted in fear.

"Where's Carina?" I demanded, my pulse pounding.

"An upstairs window was open," Orion was so upset he could barely get the words out. "Ree climbed up the balcony and went in, but then she was like ... trapped. Stuck."

"She was screaming for help." Britt's voice shook. "I tried to go through the window after her, but it's like there was a magnetic forcefield blocking my way."

"Oh no," I said. "Jacinta's ward."

"What ward?" Orion demanded.

I had to clue the shifters into what was happening. "Gerard's valet Marie had the house enchanted, to keep thieves from hauling off her valuables and to keep the girls safe. That's what she kept saying. And I fell for it. I believed she had good intentions."

"What are you saying, Hazel?" Max said.

I turned to Britt. "Remember how Bronwen was always cooking and cleaning? And Landra quit school to work from home, because Marie needed an income. And then the crux of the issue: she needs their blood to live. They can't move out or she'd die."

Britt gasped. "The ward isn't to keep people out, it's to keep them in!"

"And now Marie's got Carina trapped in there," Orion said, and then he cursed.

Torrin looked thoughtful. "Do wards work on animals? Do they keep them out, too?"

"No…" I saw where he was going with this. "But the moment you shifted back into human form, you'd be tossed out."

"Hmm, don't the girls still have to drink blood?" Max said. "How can they do that if they're trapped?"

"They only drink vials of Sanguinity and HemoLife," I said. "Britt, do you ever drink that stuff?"

Britt nodded. "When I'm tired or peopled-out."

I filed away the stunning news that Britt ever got peopled-out. "Where do you buy it?"

"Online. Gets delivered by FedEx, it's real discreet."

"So glamour your car to look like FedEx," Max said, "and glamour Britt to look like a driver."

Britt snapped her fingers. "Then I can force her to invite me in with compulsion."

I shook my head. "Even if you could, it won't help get the girls out. Not if the point is to keep them in."

"Then we break the ward," Orion said.

I stared at him, horrified. He didn't seem to get that he was asking for the impossible.

"Wards are complex magic," I said. "I was here when this ward was cast and I couldn't even begin to sense where the seam is. That's the weak spot; the only place you could theoretically break through. It would take, like, dozens of skilled witches working together to find the seam. And it wouldn't be anywhere near a door or window."

"So, get that many witches over here!" Torrin snapped at me. "And we'll figure it out as one big gang."

"It's a good idea," Max said, and Britt nodded.

I threw up my hands. "All right. I don't know if we have that much juice even working as a group. But it's worth a try."

We relocated further up the street so Marie couldn't see us.

Jacinta was the first witch I called—and she turned out to be the only witch I *had* to call. Even though she had no access to her Green Witch powers at the moment, she contacted every other witch and had the clout to demand they show up. Even if they were still having fun at the aquarium event.

All in all, two dozen witches reported for duty, including Gran, who arrived in her beat-up car since she was still on magical rest. I made her promise not to get carried away and use magic, and she assured me she was only here to lead the chant. She also brought a variety of baked goods and lemonade.

Amethyst glamoured Britt to look like a FedEx Driver, and Yolanda glamoured the Mini into a van. Torrin shifted to meerkat form before Lorelei glamoured him invisible, too.

Marie opened the gate for the "FedEx guy." When she opened the door, the invisible meerkat charged in after the van.

A text from Britt two minutes later: Okay, used compulsion to lock Marie in a closet guarded by an aggressive and adorable meerkat

I texted back: How are the newbloods doing?

Britt: Hopeful, now that we're all together

The gate buzzed open, and we witches, Max, and Orion stormed through.

On the back deck next to the hot tub, Gran herded all of us

Green Witches into a circle and led us through several verses of an incantation that would locate a ward's hidden weakness.

Right away we got a sense of it, along the back wall of the house.

"I'm visualizing it in the kitchen," Lorelei announced excitedly.

"Or maybe the room above the kitchen?" said another witch, frowning.

"Hmm," Gran said. "It's going to be a toughie."

We hit the refrain again, chanting loud and strong: *"Seams frail, I shall rend. Rescue, my intent to send!"*

But no matter how many verses we chanted, we couldn't get any closer than "the kitchen or maybe above the kitchen." And since we were looking for a spot with a circumference of one foot, that wasn't good enough.

Jacinta had set up a tea and coffee station out of the back of her car. I couldn't imagine how she must feel, knowing what her ward had done.

"Jacinta," I whispered to her as I poured my tea, "don't *you* know where the seam is?"

She shook her head. "Grey Magic spells don't even trust their caster."

"Figures."

"I just feel terrible that I can't join the chant," she confessed. "It's obvious you need more strength than the circle has to give."

That was a grim thought.

I held up my paper cup. "Bet caffeine will help."

But I didn't believe it.

A roar of pure frustration from the backyard startled me alert, then I heard a series of sickening thuds and a crack. I ran over to see Orion kicking the siding of the house with his steel toe boots. Like all vampires, he was strong. But if he kept indiscriminately pounding away at the house, he'd run out of energy and go into torpor, and that was worse than doing nothing.

"Save your strength," Max pleaded with him. "Wait till the witches nail the location spell, then you and Britt can take the place apart from both sides. Precision strike."

"I'm tired of waiting." Orion kicked again, and a tile of siding fell off the house. "I love her." Another kick. Another tile. "I need to free her." Another kick. Another tile. "I need to destroy this evil house."

"I'm just worried you'll destroy yourself first!" Max said.

"Ah, hexes," Gran said, a new gleam in her eye. "Next verse, ladies."

This time when we chanted, it felt different. We'd been on the verge of exhaustion, and Jacinta was right—without her, we didn't have quite enough power. Till now.

This time we were juiced up to turbo.

I could feel the seam like an empty ache. Could locate it in my mind's eye with perfect clarity.

I wasn't dumb; I knew Gran had used her magic even though she wasn't supposed to. But in the heat of the moment, I couldn't hold it against her.

We all started excitedly barking instructions:

"To the left, Orion!"

"Little higher!"

I texted Britt: **The seam is in the kitchen about four feet high, and six feet to the left of the screen door.**

Immediately I heard sharp banging from inside the house. The newbloods must have given Britt a crowbar, and she was going for it like it was her own personal therapy. Orion and Britt's efforts grew more frenetic until I could see Britt through the hole they'd made in the wall.

Landra forced her way through first, to wild applause from

all of us waiting outside. Then came Bronwen, crying with relief. Then Carina, who burst through the seam and straight into Orion's waiting arms. We'd freed the girls.

Britt caught my eye as she hugged Bronwen and Landra, and I knew how much this win meant to her personally.

"I think we can safely say this ward is broken," Gran said with a wink, and everyone whooped and hollered.

Now there was only one thing left to do.

We witches banged on the sliding glass door and when Britt opened it without any trouble, half of us pushed in.

"Time to confront Marie," I said. "And let Torrin get back to being human ... ish."

We followed Britt upstairs to the dorm-style bedroom where countless young women had stayed over the years. Britt threw open the closet door. A meerkat ran around the room excitedly, trilling and chirping.

"Are you here to kill me?" Marie said calmly. "Like the mob of savages you are?"

I was taken aback. "Oh, yikes, no."

She seemed to consider this. "Then you will not mind if I wander off."

"Also no." Britt stepped in front of her. "The witches are going to do a spell that restrains your movement to this neighborhood so the council will have an easy time finding you."

Marie rolled her blue eyes and cursed, I presume, in Middle French.

"So, the most annoying outcome, then," Marie complained. "To be captured alive as a dead woman walking!" She threw out her arms dramatically. "I curse you all. That you too may know the pain of being left like this, hanging between life and death."

Several of the witches gasped or grabbed for their protection amulets.

"Uh, I don't mean to be rude," I said, "but your curses aren't exactly meaningful given that you're not even a witch of any kind."

It felt good about shrugging her off, till Britt said in an oddly tight voice, "Hazel … outside…"

I immediately ran to the window and looked out into the backyard. The Green Witches who'd stayed outside were hovering around a prone figure.

My stomach dropped.

A short, white-haired figure whose limbs were splayed where she'd fallen on the grass and who, no matter what the others did, would not revive.

Coda

My parents and sisters were already at Gran's place when I arrived in the morning with Susan the magiopath. I was grateful Susan was wearing scrubs to make her house call. It seemed more official that way.

Dad opened the door, looking inappropriately calm for the situation. "What's with the long face, Slowby? Your Granny will be fine, it turns out. The doctors can't find anything wrong with her."

"I'm one of her doctors, actually," Susan said brightly.

My dad nodded at her scrubs. "Oh, how cool that you still make house calls!"

Dad put on his hat and bounded out into the snow like a big, dumb husky. He seemed to be discharging the stress of Gran's health crisis, now that she was "fine."

It must be nice to be so unaware.

Susan glanced around the cozy, cluttered living room that smelled like lavender sachets and vanilla. Gran's Christmas tree was lit up, her beloved brown tabbies Cardamom and Cinnamon napping on the fur-lined tree skirt where presents were already stacked. Cardi and Cinn weren't familiars. Just sweet little strays who'd been hanging around the bakery trashcan as kittens two years ago and gotten a lucky break when Gran scooped them up and claimed them. Gran was always giving, expecting nothing in return.

Nothing, but for the giver to pay it forward.

"Hazel, this can't be easy for you." Susan's hand on my shoulder interrupted my guilty thoughts.

I could hear Mother and my sisters arguing in Gran's room.

"Give me a minute with them first," I told Susan, and headed down the hall.

"This tray is so shabby chic," Cindra drawled, grabbing it from its perch on the side table.

"Right?" Bea grinned at our little sister. "Big twenty-twelve energy."

I shook my head at them from the doorway. "Are you already fighting over who gets Gran's stuff, right in front of her?"

"Oh my gosh, Hazel, don't be weird!" Cindra sounded offended. "You couldn't pay me to take that tray."

"We're expressing concern," Bea said in an "adults explaining things to kids" voice. "That it might be a real challenge to downsize should Gran need a nursing home. Because all her things are very…" Bea squinted, as if searching for a politic term.

"Gran?" Cindra supplied.

I half-hoped they would piss her off so much she'd wake up and kick them out into the snow.

Mother sighed. "It's the house I'm worried about. Her magic's still lingering all over it." She sniffed. "So earthy and grassy. How are we going to clean it up for sale?"

"We're not," Bea said flatly. "It would be an impossible task for anyone but me, and I'm busy chasing after two toddlers. We offer it up as is. Call it charming."

"Cozy and rustic," Cindra offered dryly. "A piece of Bay history. Someone's bound to snap it up."

"Some equity locust from Seattle, no doubt." Mother shuddered. "Can you imagine some techie newcomer taking over Sage's house?"

Four pairs of Greenwood women's eyes zeroed in on the bed. Surely if anything could wake Gran from her magical coma it would be the notion of bequeathing her beloved cottage to some "tourist," as she called Bay's newcomers. And their future children. And grandchildren.

Gran's chest moved up and down, but her face remained still. Gran lay in bed, needing a miracle.

At four-thirty the next morning, I bundled up in snow pants, snow boots, puffer coat, and an assortment of knitted goods I'd bought from Jacinta.

I drove Gran's beater car to the edge of Corvid Woods and began to walk. I climbed the old oak tree—a serious challenge in snow boots. I had to do a quick spell to make the trunk grippy like Velcro and stick the bottom of my boots. Then I waited.

Elliot once told me he liked to run, not jog. He wasn't kidding. He tore around the curve huffing and puffing, booking it at superhuman speed, grey shirt soaked, blue shorts showing off his powerful calves. The man was wearing shorts in the snow. *Shifters and their metabolisms.* It would be super annoying if I didn't also get to look at his hotness.

"Hey, *Hugin!*" I called out.

Elliot stopped in his tracks, literally, because the snow was deep enough he was making tracks. He looked up my dangling legs to the oak branch and all the way up to my face, where he met my eyes with a cool, calm expression. Calmly wiped sweat off his brow. But when he spoke, the deliberately slow tone told me I'd rattled him.

"Don't really go by that name these days … Goody Two-shoes."

Ouch. Well, that settled that; my high school crush *had* been aware of my embarrassing nickname.

"My mistake. *Deputy* Hugin." I jumped down from the tree, using just a little magic to cushion my fall. "Don't feed me a line about how it's all ancient history. I know you stole the ransom money from that gym locker. It came from a wealthy vampire, the kind that controls the world. Your favorite kind of mark. But you felt bad for Carina and Orion so you bought them a new car out of your stash."

Elliot breathed out heavily. "Well look at you." The corners of his mouth turned up ever-so-slightly. So *that's* what he looked like when he was equally amused and irritated. "You must think you're the Bay's answer to Sherlock Holmes."

I ignored him. "There's only one thing I can't figure out," I went on. "Your magic was forcibly removed by a Red Witch when you were eighteen. How'd you get it back?"

He leaned in, close enough to kiss me. "Maybe I stole it back."

Was he toying with me? Or being serious?

"I don't get it, Elliot, are you just a crooked cop?" I said. "You backed out of joining the gang so you could be a criminal with a badge, is that your deal?"

"There's a nose hair of a line between a helpful citizen and a goddamn nuisance."

"I am not trying to meddle in your nose hair, I mean your life!"

"Then what? Are you here to blackmail me?" The menacing bite in his words surprised me. "Because that would be very stupid on your part."

The accusation hurt. "You should know me better than that."

"You should know better than to confront a criminal on his home turf."

Was he right? Should I be scared of him? He *was* a criminal. But he was also a good guy. He was still irritable, irritating, hot, logical, justice-minded Elliot.

"Don't pre-threaten me," I said. "Stop trying to look ahead and guess and strategize and just listen to me for once."

His jaw relaxed. "Okay."

"I just need to know who you are. If I can trust you."

His dark brown eyes searched mine, open for a moment. "Why?"

"Because I need a favor," I said. "Something only you can do for me."

"Hazel…" His husky voice was a dangerous kaleidoscope of warning, anguish, and also tenderness. "I'll do whatever you need me to do."

I swallowed and said the words. "I need you to steal back my grandmother's magic."

Granny Sage needs a winter miracle. Could Elliot's secret be the key to saving her...or will it destroy his romance with Hazel?

CHECK OUT BOOK 3 NOW!

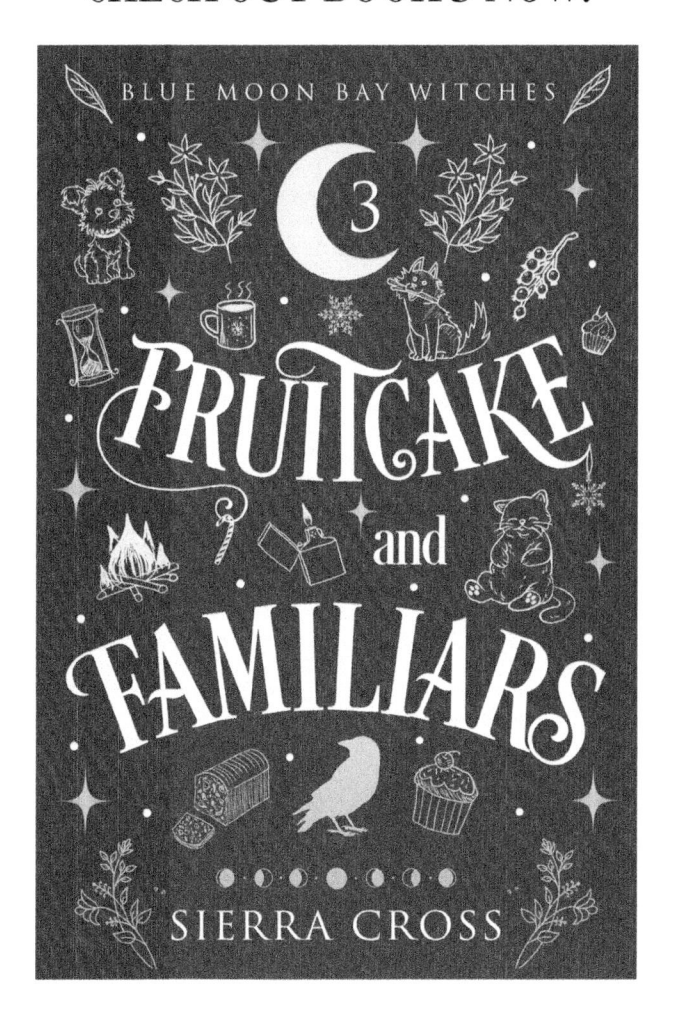

Printed in Great Britain
by Amazon